UNDER AUTHORITY

ENDORSEMENTS

Kimalee Finelli relates a true story though the genre of fiction that is neither fabricated nor imagined. Unlike many works of fiction, her story is well documented. She shares, in this memoir-like account, disturbing, tragic, and factual events that happened to a congregation and friends under the guise of Christianity. She writes to encourage others who find themselves in an abusive religious environment and to inspire them to seek the grace of God and the healing and forgiveness he offers. When God is misrepresented, when people endure a distressing relationship with a hell-on-earth organization that presents itself as a church, long term emotional consequences can result. *Under Authority* is a story of rescue, salvation, and healing—from a dark and desperate place.
—Greg Albrecht, President, Plain Truth Ministries

You will be captivated by this true story of how the writer was freed from the bondage of legalism she grew up under, and eventually discovered the freedom of experiencing the grace of God in her personal relationship with Jesus Christ.
—Danny Strickland, Lead pastor Dover Shores Baptist Church, Orlando, FL

In *Under Authority*, Kimalee Finelli has written a compelling account of Kate, a woman raised in New England by kindhearted, loving Christian parents who raised their family in a fundamentalist Baptist Church. The story dives into the experience of growing up in a spiritually abusive church in which the pastor controls every aspect of the behavior and thinking of the congregation. The book's well-crafted, narrative form meets a need for quality, personal accounts of abuse in Christian churches and organizations. *Under Authority* belongs on the shelf of every collection of writing dealing with spiritual abuse in such settings and is especially relevant for survivors who continue to struggle, and yet also desire to stay strong and healthy in their faith.

—Ken Garrett, Senior pastor, Grace Church, Portland, OR, author, *In the House of Friends: Understanding and Healing from Spiritual Abuse in Christian Churches*

UNDER AUTHORITY

KIMALEE FINELLI

A Christian Company
ElkLakePublishingInc.com

COPYRIGHT NOTICE

Under Authority

First edition. Copyright © 2023 by Kimalee Finelli. The information contained in this book is the intellectual property of Kimalee Finelli and is governed by United States and International copyright laws. All rights reserved. No part of this publication, either text or image, may be used for any purpose other than personal use. Therefore, reproduction, modification, storage in a retrieval system, or retransmission, in any form or by any means, electronic, mechanical, or otherwise, for reasons other than personal use, except for brief quotations for reviews or articles and promotions, is strictly prohibited without prior written permission by the publisher.

This is a work of fiction. Names, characters, businesses, places, events, locales, and incidents are either the products of the author's imagination or used in a fictitious manner. Any resemblance to actual persons, living or dead, or actual events is purely coincidental.

Letters shared in the text used with permission of those to whom they were written.

All Scripture quotations are from The Authorized (King James) Version. In the Public Domain.

Cover and Interior Design:
Editor(s): Judy Hagey, Deb Haggerty

PUBLISHED BY: Elk Lake Publishing, Inc., 35 Dogwood Drive, Plymouth, MA 02360, 2023

Library Cataloging Data
Names: Finelli, Kimalee (Kimalee Finelli)
Under Authority / Kimalee Finelli

330 p. 23cm × 15cm (9in × 6 in.)

ISBN-13: 978-1-64949-963-9 (paperback) | 978-1-64949-964-6 (hardcover) | 978-1-64949-965-3 | (trade paperback) | 978-1-64949-966-0 (e-book)
Key Words: overcoming; religious trauma; Christian fiction; church abuse; cult survivor; forgiveness; authoritarian leadership

Library of Congress Control Number: 2023945469 Fiction

TO ALL WHO HAVE BEEN HURT BY A
RELIGIOUS ORGANIZATION:

You can heal from your trauma and discover the one true Jesus who loves you unconditionally.

ACKNOWLEDGMENTS

To my beloved husband, Paul, whose unending love and support carried me through the writing of this story.

To my dear friends and family for their encouragement.

To my editors with Elk Lake Publishing: thank you for believing in me.

Special thanks to "Jan DeConner" and "Burt and Renata Tyner" for the copies of the correspondence between you and the reverend.

Final thanks belongs to "Mrs. Liz McKenzie" who once believed in a certain "swivel head" and gave her an A on her first short story. That silly girl has never forgotten you.

CHAPTER 1

TWIN RIVERS JUNCTION

Flutters of uneasiness crept over me as I glanced out the passenger window. The white lines of the highway slipped by—just like the past twenty years of my life. With every whoosh of the tires, memories flooded my mind. The rewind button of my life had been pushed, and there was no stopping it.

What am I doing?

The realization I was back in my hometown hit me, and I could hardly breathe. Everything became quiet. The windshield wipers swayed back and forth in slow motion. My family's idle chatter faded into a distant echo. The rental car's engine sounded as if it had stopped humming too.

You have to breathe sometime, Kate.

My anxiety mounting, I forced my attention back to the window, taking slow gulps of air. I recognized the familiar landscape. Deep forests thick with tall pines stretched out behind vast fields over Twin Rivers Junction. Weighted with snow, evergreen branches bowed toward the earth as if in reverent prayer. Flurries of mountain snow danced off the windshield, revealing the old ski resort in the distance with its white trails beckoning highway travelers.

Ah, a good memory. I can handle this.

The butterflies in my stomach forgotten, I released the air from my lungs and relaxed. It was still beautiful here, even after all these years.

Then why did you stay away? a voice in my head asked.

I let out another sigh, ignoring my nagging conscience. I allowed myself a few moments to be caught up in the beauty of it all. Didn't I deserve that much?

I surveyed the valley. Once dominated by the surrounding mountains, it had finally come into its own. The small grocery store on the hill now competed with a new Walmart. Not far from the grocery store stood the old True Value Hardware. I could picture the owner growling in disgust as he looked out the window to see a Home Depot in the finishing stages of construction across the street in what was once a beautiful meadow.

Further on, the veterinary clinic where I worked as a teen announced a new doctor. We passed a bank and drugstore. I let out a surprised grunt upon coming to a new traffic light. Local drivers appeared none too fond of this addition since they drove through without stopping.

"Finally, Twin Rivers Junction." Pierce pointed to a sign up ahead.

Turning, I studied my husband for a minute. As handsome now as he had been on our wedding day, it seemed strange to be here in New England with him now. Yet that odd feeling left as I felt a surge of love and gratitude toward him. Traveling nearly three thousand miles to be with my parents for Christmas with three teenagers in tow made him a superhero.

His face lit up after seeing the sign for Twin Rivers Junction, the town I was born in. "See, hon?" He grinned. "I knew we weren't lost."

"Okay, I've been gone a long time, but this place is still small. I can remember how to get to my parent's place—I think."

"Where's that cool bridge you told us about, Mom?" a voice called from the backseat. My new to being a teen wiped a sleeve across his mouth as he finished the bagged snack in his lap. Squeezing the wrapper into the pocket of his jeans, he leaned forward in anticipation.

"Move, dufus, we can't see," one twin grumbled from the third-row seat. Just as I was about to tell her to settle down, her sister started in on the how-much-longer routine. Even as teens, they hated being cooped up in the car. To listen to them, one would think a two-hour ride from the airport was a death sentence.

"Really, you two," I called back to them. "We'll be at Grandma and Grandpa's house in about ten minutes, then—"

"I see it," my son interrupted. "The bridge. There it is."

After passing a quaint Victorian-style bed-and-breakfast on the right, the road curved to the left, revealing an old-fashioned covered bridge. To my family, it reflected something out of a storybook. But I was disappointed to see it had not been well cared for over time. The red paint was faded and chipped. Rust covered the metal roof. The whole thing appeared ragged and in dire need of repair.

"Is it safe?" Pierce muttered.

"Of course," I said, hoping I was right. "Hey, did you know this bridge is not the original one? When I was in high school, they rebuilt it because someone had set fire to the old one. They never caught the people who did it, last I knew."

"Arson in a small town," Pierce mused. "Anything else interesting happen here?"

I shot him a look of surprise, and he grimaced. "Sorry, babe. Dumb question." He reached over and took my hand.

With the comfort of his warm hand engulfing mine, we drove across the bridge. Long forgotten, it surprised me how the echoing clatter of the old boards beneath our tires comforted me. My mind drifted back to a day when my father was teaching me how to drive.

"All right, Katie, slow down near the bridge and turn your high beams on." My father pointed to a switch on the left of the steering wheel.

I remember gripping the steering wheel of my dad's old Volkswagen and doing as he instructed. I stopped the car at the entrance of the bridge. The dark evening made the bridge seem like a black hole.

"No one's coming," he said. "Go ahead."

I remained right where I was. Even though I had been over this bridge a million times, nerves got the best of me. I had never been the one behind the wheel. One wrong slip and ...

"Katie, you can't just sit here. Go," my dad coaxed. "You'll be fine. Just stay in the middle."

Releasing a nervous sigh, I eased the car onto the bridge and heard noises under the tires I'd never heard before. *Bump, bump, bump* went the wooden beams as we rolled across them. Images of the boards splintering and splitting came to mind. So did a horrible picture of us trapped in our car and falling in the icy river below. I cringed but kept driving and saw I was almost through. As I pulled off the bridge, something small skittered across the road in front of the car. I hit it.

"What was that?" I jerked the car to a halt.

My dad cranked the window down and moaned. "You hit a skunk. Now my car's going to stink for a week." I could tell he was trying to be mad, but we both ended up laughing.

As my husband drove past the local campground on the left, I recalled the daily rides to school with my younger brother. *The school.*

And the church. The voice was back.

I froze.

"Kate?" Pierce chased away my thoughts. "You okay?"

"I guess so. I ... I don't know, honey. It's so familiar it scares me a little. But some things are different too."

"Such as?"

"You for one. The kids. The what-was-once and the here-and-now. It's like I've stepped back in time, but I'm someone else now. I mean, I'm still me, but ..." I looked out the window with a shake of my head.

"You're not a little girl anymore," my husband said. "This was your home for a long time, and your dad wanted you to be here this year. Your mom—"

"I know. Mom's health is a big concern." My worry centered on my mom and the unsettled feeling I had about being back in this town after such a long time away. So much had happened here—long-forgotten things I thought I had put behind me.

I decided to put on a cheerful face. "Guess what?" I called. "We are here."

I motioned for Pierce to make a right turn after the familiar broken fence. We pulled into the driveway of my two-story childhood home with its weathered shingles and tiny attic window. Aging black shutters flanked the windows on the front of the house, which had been converted into apartments for extra income when my siblings and I were little. Our family lived in the larger part of the house, a rectangular section in the back. I only called it *the back* because it was not visible from the road. My dad's auto repair shop sat across the driveway. He earned a living fixing cars while my mom homeschooled my youngest brother and sister. For a moment, time stood still. I was a teenager again, coming home from a ball game or other school event. *This place is a time capsule.*

To my right, the old, overgrown crabapple tree still towered between my dad's shop and the barn. Without effort this time, a smile spread across my face as I recalled crabapple fights with my siblings. Thrown hard enough, those things stung if you got nailed with one.

Even the smell of lilac blossoms found its way from my memory to my nose. The weathered wooden swing Dad made by hand still hung from the enormous evergreen that blanketed the backyard like a green canopy.

And then there was the small barn. Pathetic and dilapidated, it still stood upright, with its roof dipping in the middle from years of heavy winter snow. How much time had I spent in there organizing tack and brushing the winter coat of my horse Chipper? Sadness rippled through my core at the thought of her and all the other horses I'd ridden. In the troubled times of my youth, horses were my greatest comfort and escape. Accepting my gentle caresses, they would lean into me. "Tell me a secret" they seemed to say. Twitching their ears as if yearning for a juicy tidbit of information, they kept my secrets confidential.

Loud noises from the back of the rented SUV interrupted my memories, forcing me back into the present. Emerging from the house, my dad threw on one of his heavy coats as he made his way toward us.

"Heard you coming." He smiled and laughed as the kids hugged him. He shook hands with Pierce, then put an arm around me as we headed indoors.

I took a moment to study my father. Now in his eighties, he despised his age being a topic of discussion. His hair had turned white, but he was proud to say he had a full head of it. He appeared thinner and lines had deepened in his face since last Christmas when they came to see us. Was it only a year ago? For the first time, my mother could no longer travel because of her health.

"How's Mom doing?"

"She's having a good day today," he replied. "Excited you're here."

Stepping inside the kitchen of my childhood home, my nose filled with the familiar scent of my mother's brew, as I used to call it. After filling a small saucepan with water, she would place fragrant tea leaves, cloves, and orange peels inside. Left to simmer for hours, the whole house smelled delightful.

Before I could go any further, my father held me back. "Katie, you don't know how much it means having you home. I know how hard it was for you to come back, and I'm proud of you for coming all this way." He paused and crinkled his eyebrows. "You okay?"

A barrage of thoughts swirled around my head. *No, you're not fine,* my conscience spoke to me again. *Being back in this town brings up old memories you spent years trying to forget. You're uncomfortable, and you want to run again, don't you?*

"I'm good, Dad." I took a deep breath. "Let's go see Mom." He seemed pleased with my answer and led me into the den, where my mother rested comfortably in a recliner.

During the short walk through the house, an icy sensation crept up my shoulders.

You can't run away this time, the voice taunted.

CHAPTER 2

SHADOWS IN THE DESK

I was running. Trying to get away. Chased by someone. I couldn't see a face. Was it one person? More? Why were they after me? Twigs and dried leaves crackled beneath my feet. Angry, low-hanging branches slapped me in the face in the quiet woods of—

Where was I? Panicking, I realized I was not on the familiar trails around my parents' property. The outline of a large white building near two other smaller buildings emerged through the thick trees. My throat squeezed tight as I recognized those buildings. I wanted to scream, thrash, run, or freeze—all at the same time. But I found myself running again.

"Katie!" a voice behind me called.

No, No, NO! I wanted to scream. But I couldn't.

Someone rubbed my shoulders. I sat up and gasped, then looked into my husband's concerned eyes.

"Are you okay? You were moaning in your sleep. I've never heard you do that before."

Lightheaded, I exhaled and tried to focus. Relief washed over me as I looked around my old room at the top of the stairs. It now contained a comfortable queen bed for guests, even though I guessed we were the first to sleep here in many years. My old worn dresser and vanity lined the back wall of the small room. I was sure some childhood things of mine or my sisters were still inside the drawers. My parents were sentimental and rarely threw out or gave anything away that was not actual trash. If it had a use, it was here to stay. After all, who knew if we might need it one day? Feeling in better spirits at the humor in this, I smiled at my husband, who still looked at me curiously.

"I'm fine. I was moaning?" I remembered running in my dream, but that was all. Everything else disappeared, like a fine mist.

"Yeah, you were." Pierce tousled my messy hair.

"Coffee?"

Pierce produced his cell phone. "Hang on, I'm calling room service." He grinned when a pillow bounced off his shoulder. "Let's go downstairs, say good morning to your folks, and plan what we're going to do today."

"Sounds good." I rubbed my eyes.

Over a delicious breakfast of my dad's classic sourdough pancakes, we discussed options. The kids wanted to go snow tubing at the ski resort, which was only fifteen minutes away. The thought of snow tubing seemed fun, but I longed to get back on a pair of skis again.

Memories of skiing as a teen flooded my mind. One came into focus.

"Don't do that, Jolee!" I shouted.

"What? This?" My best friend from kindergarten rocked the chairlift.

"Quit it." My stomach churned.

Afraid of nothing, my friend threw her head back and laughed. The motion of the chairlift and her sudden movement made her lose her grip on the ski poles. Down they went, falling onto the trails below. Thankfully, they did not hit any skiers.

I forgot my nausea and laughed. Jolee looked surprised, but soon she was chuckling too.

"Nice going," I said. "How are you gonna get down the mountain?"

Always up for a new challenge, Jolee put her nose in the air and brushed her reddish blonde hair aside. "No problem." She adjusted her woolen ski cap. "I'll even beat you to the bottom."

"No chance." I gave a nerdy snort. "Not without your poles."

"Let's go see." Jolee pointed, showing our turn to dismount the lift. Standing quickly, we skied our way over to our favorite trail.

"What's the matter? Don't feel like doing the Blue Diamond?" I teased, knowing that Blue Diamond was the steepest and most dangerous trail at Tanger Mountain. Large red warning signs discouraged anyone who was not an advanced or experienced skier from taking the run.

With a sarcastic salute, Jolee faced one of the less treacherous trails. She turned into a crouch position with her gloved hands on her legs and picked up speed within seconds.

"Cheater," I muttered as I positioned myself the same way. Feeling confident with my ski poles, I was sure I would catch up with her soon. When I spotted her, she was flying yet seemed at ease with her speed. But there was no way I was going to let her win. I whizzed down the trail without consideration for other skiers who were practicing calculated zigzag patterns. One of them yelled a warning, but I paid them no attention. I was gaining on my friend, pleased to see she had slowed down a bit to get around a bend in the trail, using her arms like an airplane for balance. I sneaked up behind her, so close our skis almost touched.

"Behind you!" I shouted.

Jolee jerked to see me over her right shoulder. Her speed and turning motion made her zip over to the right of the slope. Arms flailing, she collided with the large pipelines used to make snow for the trails. Half buried under the snow, Jolee had no way to see them or stop in time.

I skidded sideways to a stop, sending snow spray in front of me. Jolee lay face down in the snow on top of the pipes. I inched my way over, frantically calling her name. Our trail was empty, so there was no one to help. As I made my way to her side, she lifted her head and grinned wickedly.

"You're dead," she said in a low, evil voice.

"Come catch me first, you loser." I returned her grin and continued my flight down the mountain.

"Mom." My son sounded impatient. How long had he been calling my name? "Are you coming snow tubing with us or not?"

"Of course, I'm coming." I smiled at him—grateful he was still too young to realize my smile did not quite reach my eyes. I tried to push Jolee from my thoughts, then considered how odd it was to remember something so long forgotten, relive the wild adventure of that moment, and then feel the loss of those days that were gone. Regret crept its way up my back. I shivered.

You couldn't have saved her. The voice again.

Yes, I could have. I didn't try hard enough. I shot back.

She didn't want to be saved, my conscience reminded me.

Later that afternoon, I stood with my eyebrows raised and mouth gaping at the sight of my brother's old room. In front of me were mounds of boxes, old furniture, luggage, and even the old toy shelf my brothers used to put their books and model airplanes on. Only a narrow pathway down the middle was clear enough to walk through. My eyes opened wider at the sight of the childhood toys still there, along with the empty fish tank. "Quite a sight, isn't it?" My mother's voice startled me.

I whirled around. "Mom, what are you doing up here? The stairs ..." I was under the impression she could no longer climb the stairs because of her arthritis. Nearing eighty, my mother still held herself with poise. Cut just above her shoulders, her straight hair was a mixture of gray with a hint of leftover brown. Her brown eyes had soft lines around them instead of deep wrinkles like most women her age. "My secret?" she used to say. "Stay out of the sun." She would then slather my fair, easily burned skin with sunblock.

Ah, those glorious summer days.

Now, she waved me off. "I'm fine. It took me a while to get up here, but I wanted to see what you were doing." She looked inside the boys' room, her cane by her side. "Or should I say, what your father has been doing? I see he has consolidated things and just dumped them in here." She shook her head.

"Some things don't change." I chuckled. "I'm going spelunking."

Mom laughed. "What?"

"Going in search of buried treasure. You do realize this place is stuck in a former time, right? I mean, you never got rid of anything."

"We always knew you would come back one day."

Another memory hit me. Right before I left for college, I bubbled with excitement at the prospect of attending a faraway school that promised a new adventure, not to mention leaving Twin Rivers. I was desperate to get out of this town. I talked of all the things I planned to do when my mother looked at me with an odd, peaceful expression. "One day, the mountains will call you home."

One day did come, but how long had it taken? I now felt guilty for not coming back sooner. Had my parents kept our childhood things all this time? Simply waiting for the day we would return?

"It's all there," she said. "Old toys, clothes, books. Whatever you left behind."

"Why did you keep it? Why didn't you give it away or something?"

"It wasn't mine to give away. I knew you kids would come back for it when you were ready."

Speechless, I looked around at the stacks in the room, imagining all the things I would find in those boxes. I became a little girl again, ready to go on an exciting hunt for hidden treasure. I glanced around, unsure where to begin.

My mother laughed and told me to have fun.

Spying a worn-out desk near the window, I pushed several boxes out of the way and wedged myself in the middle, where I could open the top. Inside were several piles of old family photographs. I pulled one out and smiled at the images of my little brothers making silly faces. Another photo was of me on Chipper, sporting a black riding hat and boots. I closed my eyes. The smell of horses came into my nostrils, and the feel of leather made its way into my palms. As if my hands were being controlled by a mere memory, I found myself turning my thumbs upward and letting imaginary reins slide through my fingers. I remembered every inch of the saddle, stirrups, and bridle. I felt the wind in my face as I recalled riding her or my neighbor's horses through the open fields, starting off at a rising trot, a canter, then into a full gallop.

It's as if you never got off that horse. The voice broke my trance.

I missed horses more than I wanted to admit. Forcing myself out of my reverie, I sifted through more photographs.

Several were family shots. My little sister's birthday party. Thanksgiving dinner. A few hikes up Rattleback Mountain, where we would give my parents a hard time about the excursions they dragged us on. I lived in a place surrounded by mountains. Did we constantly have to "go up" for a better look?

At the next photo, my mouth fell open. A church potluck dinner showing the grinning face of my father, along with other church folks holding plates stacked high with their favorite foods.

Church.

I dropped the photo like it had burned my hand. Old memories of the church my family and I attended forced their way to the surface as if they were reaching through the photographs, trying to speak to me. *Did you think you could just walk away from us forever?* Their smiling faces seemed to demand an explanation.

Images of white buildings nestled on a hill flooded my mind. The rectangular-shaped church was visible from the road. Behind the church sat a taller, square building. The Christian school. Directly behind the school stood a large gymnasium. The church itself was the smallest of the three structures. The faded gray steps led to ordinary windowless steel doors. The church windows were also dull, not pretty stained-glass windows like most churches. Tall windows lined each side of the building like cold statues looming out of a snow-covered mountain.

The realization hit me hard. *My dream.*

I sucked in a breath and turned my attention to the next photographs in my hand. Me holding my pet rabbit. My brother Marty chasing our youngest brother Mark through a field. A few pictures of my grandmother with us on her lap.

I held up the next photo and couldn't help the tears that stung my eyes. Two of my close childhood friends with our arms around each other after singing a trio together for special Sunday morning worship. I stood in the middle with Jolee and Rachel on either side.

"Rachel," I whispered. The pain of losing her friendship hit me all over again. As if memories of Jolee earlier that morning were not enough. I held the picture for a long time.

We look happy here, I mused. Jolee seemed to be laughing at me. I could almost hear her saying, "Yeah, we're happy in this moment. 'Cause we didn't know anything else." I studied Rachel. Her beautiful shoulder-length blonde hair and smoky blue eyes were the envy of everyone in our class. She had a perfect smile, perfect skin, perfect grades, and the perfect family.

After all, she was an Abbott. And her father, the Reverend Rhuttland Abbott.

My hand trembled as I set the photograph in my lap and stared out the window. The afternoon had turned chilly as the distant sun dodged behind clouds, casting dim shadows to dance around the evergreens. When did this happen? The sun had been out earlier that morning on Tanger Mountain. Had the gray clouds and dark shadows appeared as I remembered Reverend Abbott?

Don't be ridiculous, I chided myself.

Regardless, the day was no longer balmy and bright but gloomy and cold, stretching its icy fingers through the window. The room felt much cooler than just moments ago. Was it my imagination?

Shivering, I reached into a nearby box and yanked out an old sweatshirt. Somewhat warmer now, I tried to shake off the odd feeling I'd had when I saw pictures of Rachel and other church folks. "You are all gone from my life now. I have moved on," I told them flatly, holding their pictures up at eye level. "At least I got out. What's your excuse?"

The only sound I heard was the echo of their empty laughter.

CHAPTER 3

THE RETURN

Cold air clawed at my face as I stepped onto the overgrown trail that bordered the back side of my parent's property. After pulling up my hood, I clutched two large books close. The snow crunched under my boots as I made my way to the warming hut, slightly off the trail where my parents used to keep their kennel of Siberian huskies. The trail had narrowed since I was a child. Dense pines and shrubbery crowded the pathway that eventually ended at an ancient, unused railroad bed.

The sled dog trail. I smiled at the memories. Suddenly, I was a young girl again sitting on the wooden dog sled, bundled against the winter chill. In front of me, three sets of harnessed dogs were connected to the main line. Each dog is positioned in a particular order, with the point dogs in front, swing dogs in the middle, and wheel dogs behind. Out in front of the point dogs was the lead dog, awaiting his signal while the others howled in eagerness.

"Hike!" My father's booming command broke through the husky's baying. His voice sent a ripple through the dogs ahead of me. Their anticipation fulfilled—they were free to do what they were born to do—run with all their might. The lead dog barked in response and led the way down the trail, with the point dogs setting the pace for the rest of the team. The wheel dogs were mostly a blur as the wind and snow stung my eyes. Large and powerful, they pulled the hardest and did most of the work. I thought they were simply magnificent.

A bend in the trail appeared. "Gee!" my dad called to the team. The lead dog followed his direction and guided the team to the right while my dad leaned his body to the left to keep the sled balanced.

"If you want to come, you need to stay in the sled." He placed the wiggly dogs in their harnesses.

I nodded. "Why do you say *gee*, Daddy? Why don't you just tell them to go right?"

"When it's cold, your lips freeze, making it harder to form the words left and right. So, we use more guttural sounds like *ha* and *gee* for left and right. Dogs are trained to understand. I can speak without moving my mouth."

Lost in memories, I stumbled onto the stone step leading into the warming hut. The small building showed severe neglect. The roof struggled to hold its weight and the outside was in dire need of paint. New England seasonal changes were harsh on anyone's home, and this poor hut didn't stand a chance. I took the key off the hook above the door and chuckled at its reason for being there.

"We have to keep the door padlocked so bears won't sneak in," my dad used to say with a grin. "But don't worry, the mountain lions scare the bears away."

The door creaked as I opened it. I went to stoke the potbelly stove.

Thirty minutes later, I sat cross-legged on the lower built-in bunk bed. Handmade by my father, each bunk folded up and attached to the wall to save space. On the opposite wall, the wood stove was heating up the room.

Since the cabin was too small to hold any other furniture, my dad had built compartments under the floorboards for storage. Several cans of food were stored there in case of emergency. A saucepan hung on a wall hook behind the stove, along with two mugs.

The comforting silence helped me relax. After lighting a few candles, I watched the flames leap back and forth, creating shadows. The only sounds were occasional popping noises from the stove, coinciding with the creaking sounds of the evergreens outside. I loved the peacefulness it gave me.

"You want to go where?" Pierce had asked earlier as we got the kids ready for some outdoor event.

"I need to be alone for a while," I explained. "A lot on my mind."

He placed his hands on my shoulders. "Kate, you've been quiet these past few days. I can see you're troubled."

About old ghosts? The voice again.

"And," Pierce continued, "I think it's been harder for you to come back to Twin Rivers than you're realizing. Whatever you need, do it."

Taking a deep breath, my gaze fell on the two books I had brought with me, an old photo album and my mother's thick journal from so many years ago. I gingerly traced the leather imprint of her name on the bottom right-hand corner of the journal. *Jan DeConner* gleamed at me in faded gold cursive writing.

Inside the cover was the date 1986. Amazing. Had my mother's own hand penned these words thirty years ago? I turned the page, revealing her sermon notes from one Sunday in January 1986.

Church, you are dead!

The sermon jumped off the page.

Now learn this: the church is corrupt. When a church takes a step toward compromise, corruption sets in.

Images of Reverend Abbott's face found their way back into my memory. I closed my eyes against the inevitable—remembering him. Everything about him, beginning with how he looked and ending with the lives he ruined. I could almost feel his stony gray eyes peering into the depths of my soul.

His eyes. Full of contempt, his cold eyes appeared almost colorless with their lack of empathy and warmth. A single glance could chill a person to the core. Using this and his height, he seemed to find enjoyment by watching his humble congregation shrivel in intimidation.

We were all weak. So helpless.

My eyes fell again on my mother's notes from that day. I was eleven years old but had no recollection of this sermon. I frequently distracted myself by letting my thoughts wander, the Reverend's words drifting above and away from me. The safest place for me was my peaceful imagination, where I could be free.

I read on.

What is corruption? It begins with pastors not using the King James Version of the Holy Scriptures! They substitute words and translations, a departure from the Word of the Lord! Revelation 2:4. God expects repentance! Revelation 2:5. I will remove the candlestick out of thy place.

He was here in the cabin, preaching at me. Even the candles shivered. I could hear the low, warning tones while he read the Scriptures. Then his voice rose into a loud caveman-like shrieking. His fists slamming the pulpit, waking many a young child trying to snooze on their mother's shoulder.

They must repent! Read 2 Thessalonians 3:6. God commands us to separate ourselves from the workers of iniquity. Will you turn from evil ways or remain in sin? Be not deceived. God is not mocked! You will pay the penalty for your corruption!

I had to look away from the notes to catch my breath. My mother kept a detailed sermon notebook. It was nearly word for word, and I marveled at her ability to do this by hand. I wondered what she had felt when she penned the Reverend's words.

But why such thorough sermon notes? Was she taking them for herself? Or in case her mind decided to wander away into her imagination? Why keep them after all these years? Did she have to answer to someone? I knew it wasn't my dad. He took his own notes, which were minimal compared to hers.

"They never spoke about the sermons," I murmured.

That's not entirely true. Not at the end, the voice responded.

"But they should have sooner," I cried out. Then more questions came. As they had come for years with no answers.

They should have realized what was happening, so how could they not have known? Why did they follow a man who insisted he was placed there directly by God when all other evidence pointed to the exact opposite of what a pastor should be? Why did they believe him? Why didn't they leave?

That last question haunted me. *Why didn't they just leave—sooner?*

Much pain and heartache could have been avoided. Maybe not for the other families, but at least for mine.

Anytime I'd ever been brave enough to approach the subject, my father became silent while my mother broke down in tears. I eventually decided to stop bringing it up for my mother's sake. Years passed before they could reach a plateau of courage just wide enough for them to grasp and pull themselves out of Reverend Abbott's brainwashing and control.

A man like the reverend did not allow a member of the congregation to leave without his permission. In the physical sense, they could, yes. But then he found ways to make them pay.

And pay they did.

With a deep sigh, I compelled myself to read on. But why? Was I looking for something? If so, I didn't know what. But I could not deny being spellbound by my mother's journal. It beckoned to me. I could not put it down or push it away.

Like you've been doing all these years? Pushing things away? the voice asked.

I closed my eyes and rubbed my temples, wishing that nagging voice away. After a few minutes, I focused again on the printed pages. Under the date, my mother had written something I had missed.

Special music: June Britton, autoharp solo.

"The Britton family," I whispered. "Glen and June Britton."

As if unlocked by an invisible, magical key, another door creaked open into the recesses of my memory. A heavy curtain lifted, revealing June Britton sitting on the church stage with her autoharp resting on her lap. Her long brown hair fell over her shoulders in waves. Pretty green eyes glittered out over the congregation. I watched in awe at her ease handling the instrument in front of her, even with her obvious pregnancy coming close to full term.

June played a few bars and began to sing, her voice reflecting her soft, gentle manner. With a smile, she sang higher, never once missing a note with her voice or her instrument. I imagined it to be pure happiness that carried her through her solo, unlike other church musicians who had their solemn faces buried in a hymnal. June had a special joy about her, genuine and refreshing. I looked forward to the Sundays when she was scheduled to sing. But then, I watched poor June through the window of my memory, sitting there performing for Jesus with no knowledge of how the reverend would later destroy her family.

"Oh, June," I murmured. "What has become of you now?"

Are you finally ready to go back? the voice prompted.

I laughed bitterly in the quietness of the cabin. The sound of my voice rang strange and foreign. Why would I want to go back to a place I've spent years trying to forget?

You must find what you're looking for. My conscience. Again.

Images of people I knew long ago seemed to surround me. Their faces loomed before me in the dim light. Old friends, church members, and other familiar faces danced as if being conducted by the flickering candle flames.

I gasped. "What do you want?"

"Come back," they seemed to say.

Gooooo, the wind wailed outside among the evergreens.

I rubbed my eyes. What was happening to me?

Silence was my only answer. I hated how my conscience always seemed to be right. Yet I knew I was supposed to be here at this moment. I wasn't sure why, but I had to find out. Was I ready for this? Was I ready to dig out all that I had forgotten, buried, or ignored?

Yes, it was time.

I opened the photo album from Cross Christian Academy. Once again, church members from long ago looked up at me. Old classmates and friends called to me from the school steps. They beckoned from the basketball court. A dozen expectant faces turned from their lunches in the school cafeteria to stare at me. I looked from my mother's journal back to the photo album, trying to figure out where to begin my search for resolution.

But what exactly was I looking for?

Leaning my head back on the bunk, I closed my eyes. A deep peacefulness settled over me. The past had found its way back to me as if the hands of the present were using their enchanted fingers to wind the clock backward slowly ... slowly ... until it stopped.

I felt light, almost weightless. Without explanation or warning, I imagined myself floating. Higher I soared up and out of the small cabin into the majestic sky.

What was happening? How did I get here? Panic reached me, but my hypnotic state nudged it away.

The scenery below changed. Out of the fog emerged three familiar white buildings.

Oh, God, I prayed. *Not here.*

"Katie," someone called. I tried to speak, but no sound came out. Who called? What was I supposed to do?

Gooooo, the wind cried out again. A strong gust lifted the branches into the air, and the icy evergreen leaves released me into the clouds.

My conscience spoke to me again. *It's time to return, Kate.* This time it did not taunt me but encouraged me. Peace rushed through my body.

Without hesitation, I knew what to do.

CHAPTER 4

THE REVEREND SPEAKS

"Katie!"

My eyes fluttered open. In shock, I took in my surroundings. "How did I get here?"

You needed answers, the voice reminded.

I took in gasps of air and tried to calm my nerves. I was leaning back on an old stone bench not far from the familiar three white buildings. An apple tree above my head nodded as it was greeted by a crisp breeze. I caught the beloved scent of apple blossoms. But at that moment, they made me nauseous.

What's happening? I willed my body to stop shaking. The open soccer field to the left revealed ugly brown patches of grass. Wait, was it springtime? Even though it seemed the snow had melted, a raw snap remained in the air. Shivering in my thin dress, I placed my hand on the cool stone bench and jerked back when it touched something.

My mother's journal.

This is real.

I tried to get my bearings. I was seated outside the church building facing the parking lot. A loud truck lumbered in just then and a couple emerged looking frazzled. The truck doors slammed, and they hurried into the church.

Everyone else must already be inside. Is it Sunday?

The answer smacked me in the face. In front of the church was a parking spot reserved for Reverend Abbott and his family. His newer model Cadillac sat regally for all who passed through the main church entrance. Sunlight gleamed off the car, making the other station wagons and minivans look like pathetic hunks of junk.

I gave a disgusted snort.

"There you are." A figure emerged around the corner of the building.

I swallowed hard at the sight of my old friend. "Rachel?" I whispered.

"What are you doing?" Rachel demanded. "You better get inside before someone sees you. Are you trying to cut Sunday school?"

It was as if I had been looking through a camera lens devoid of focus for many years, only to have it suddenly pop into crystal clear view. I blinked several times and stared at her. Her beautiful, red, A-line dress tied in the back and came past her knees. A matching sweater with tiny, embroidered flowers hugged her shoulders. Even her shoes looked exquisite. Blonde hair framed her face as she cocked her head to the side, waiting for me to answer.

"Of course not." I scrambled to my feet and grabbed the journal. Rachel was my friend, but I never trusted her, fearful she might report certain things to her father.

Reverend Abbott was not a man to be crossed. Children were to be in Sunday school, church three times a week, and enrolled in the Christian school. "Disobedience will not be tolerated!" He'd slam his fist on the pulpit, sending shudders through his congregation.

Rachel snapped her fingers. "Katie? Let's go." She led me into the school library.

Embarrassed at being the last ones seated around the long conference table, I noticed several pairs of eyes glaring at me.

"Katie. Rachel." Mrs. Sullivan, our Sunday school teacher, waved in our direction. "How nice of you to join us. Please enter more quietly next time you plan to be late." Her cold, dark eyes rested on me.

"Sorry," I mumbled, which earned me a curt nod from Mrs. Sullivan.

I pulled out my Bible and pretended to follow along with her great and fabulous instructions for us wayward teenage girls. I disliked Mrs. Sullivan, my teacher from fourth through fifth grades. She had always been passive aggressive with me, even downright nasty at times. I was sure her biggest thrill in life came from humiliating or embarrassing her students.

One of my worst experiences with her came during a second-grade recess. Since our school lacked funds for playground equipment, we drew on the sidewalk with chalk or played tag, kickball, and other games. One day, a friend and I were throwing rocks into the air to see which of us could throw the highest. A dumb and unsafe game at best, but we were bored. We stopped when Mrs. Sullivan came marching over toward us, followed by another classmate who was crying and holding her arm.

"Katie DeConner!" She was red with anger. "Did you throw a rock at another student?"

"No, ma'am. We were just throwing rocks up in the air and—"

"You were seen by several students. Do you know the punishment for telling lies?"

"I'm not lying. I didn't throw a rock at her. We were just—"

"Go to Mr. Fisher's office. You will be suspended for lying to a teacher."

I hung my head and made the long, shameful walk to the principal's office.

From the pulpit, the reverend preached the teacher was always right. "Never question the teacher, as students have the tendency to lie. Foolishness is bound in the heart of a child."

Unable to say a word in my defense, I was suspended from school the next day, along with a secondary punishment at home—as instructed by the reverend. "In the event a student breaks a rule at school," he said, "he or she is to receive a punishment both at school and at home. We teach instant obedience, and disobeying rules will be handled with swift consequences."

His orders were obeyed without question.

My thoughts screeched to a halt as I realized Sunday school had concluded. We were told to head to the church building for the main service.

I slid into the pew where my parents were getting settled in their seats. "Here, Mom." I handed her the journal.

"Oh, you had it. I was looking for that." She placed the book beside her.

I took my usual spot close to the end of the row. I liked sitting by myself, so I could get lost in my imagination once the preaching started. Kids and teens were discouraged from sitting with one another during church so as not to distract the pastor.

"Trust and obey," the congregation sang just a few minutes later. I looked around as everyone held their hymnals. Using a screen and projector was considered a near felony here. How dare the church conform to the ways of other churches who do not fear God the way Cross Independent Baptist Church does. "For there's no other way," the singing continued. I glanced to my left to see my mom's close friend, Renata Tyner, belting it out in her soprano voice.

"Oh, Katie," she would say to me during our once-a-week piano lesson. "Wouldn't it be incredible if you married a pastor one day? You could sing and play piano in church and be in full-time ministry together." Her eyes would drift upward in bliss.

Putting aside her ludicrous dreams for my future, I didn't mind Renata and her family. Her son Kyle was around my age and a friend, even though kids at school teased him for being a nerd. He got his talent from his dad, a big-wig computer programmer at IBM.

While rumor had it the Tyner family was quirky, they were one of the kindest families in the church. Renata ignored odd looks for arriving with armloads of unnecessary items like extra shoes, pillows, or books. Church leaders frowned upon her husband's occasional absence from church because of his job. Kyle didn't seem to care if the other kids liked him or not. Renata remained a loyal friend to my mom. I chuckled as she flung her long ponytail over her shoulder and finished the chorus with a smile. "To be happy in Jesus is to trust and obey."

"You may be seated," Mr. Hearn, a poor excuse for a worship leader, said with his usual hoarseness. He made a wave of welcome for the reverend to take his place behind the pulpit.

And just like that, there he was.

Reverend Abbott stretched forward as if to intimidate the assembly before he even opened his mouth. Placing his large Bible on the pulpit, he greeted the crowd with a gruff, "Let's open in a word of prayer."

Everyone bowed their head toward their lap as his spiritual prayer floated over the congregation covering them with a holiness only he could provide.

Untouched and unimpressed, I scanned the sanctuary during the opening prayer. People watching was a little hobby of mine during church. My gaze settled on the family sitting directly behind the Tyner's. Pam Kelley was shaking her perfect-from-the-salon head in disdain at Renata Tyner fixing her ponytail.

The Kelley's. Sophisticated and financially well-off, they were one of the closest families to the Abbotts. As the only elder in the church, Ross Kelley was Reverend Abbott's confidante and messenger. For anything that needed taking care of, Ross Kelley either did it or found a volunteer. He stood by the reverend's side at the end of each successful sermon. With his short stature, balding head, and tiny mustache, he reminded me of that creepy family member everyone likes to talk about.

And I did not trust him for a minute.

With the prayer over, Reverend Abbott's voice rose with authority. "The Word of the Lord says that sin never pays. Sinners never learn!" He lifted his head to scrutinize the large room. "Turn in your Bibles to Second Chronicles chapter two."

A rustle of pages echoed around me. I opened my own Bible but did not follow along. Then I noticed the Tisdales sitting rigidly in their pew, about three rows ahead of me. But where was my friend Jolee? Odd.

"Sin never pays!" Reverend Abbott shouted. "King Ahaziah was wicked and followed in his Father Ahab's wicked ways. We live in a dream world." *Slam* went his fist on the pulpit.

"Our dreamworld as parents is that our own little mirror images will grow up to be great and wonderful. Wake up, church!" Another *thump*, this time from the worn-out Bible. "The truth is our little ones will pick up our bad habits—our own wickedness!" Reverend Abbott pointed a bony finger at us. "If you think your sin will go unnoticed by your kids, you've got to wise up. The world teaches us there is pleasure in sin. But sin doesn't pay. Look at King Ahab."

Not wanting to think about a dead king, I continued to amuse myself by studying people. As much as I stared, no one seemed to notice. Everyone fixated on the speaker. My eyes stopped moving when I saw our newest attendee Dana Terrell was present again. With messy, prematurely graying hair and a ruddy countenance, she sat with a lost look on her face. Her young son appeared to be drawing next to her.

How on earth did they end up here at Cross?

"Sinners, you just don't learn," Reverend Abbott reiterated. "Sinners pray to false gods with no answers because they never learn. I'll give you an example. I got a call recently from a man in another church who knew of me and wanted me to talk to his dying uncle because he wasn't sure his own pastor would tell him the truth. How pitiful is that? But he called me because he knew I would." He puffed out his double-breasted suit and gave a haughty laugh, which the congregation echoed. "When I saw the uncle, I risked it all to tell him the truth. Even knowing he might get angry."

The reverend paused for effect. The room was hooked. They wanted to know how their very own man of God saved that wretched soul. I was curious to know why the reverend was speaking to someone who went to another local church. Wasn't that forbidden?

"But the man said he didn't need God. Not now and not ever."

The assembly recoiled at that horrific revelation.

"And now his stone-cold corpse is rotting in *hell!*" Upon saying that last word, he leaned into the microphone, causing it to whistle. "See?" he said matter-of-factly, pulling back. "Sinners never learn, and now this man is seeing *my* face in hell every day!" He roared. "And regretting the opportunity he lost as he burns in flames for all eternity!"

The room fell into a dead silence. No whispers from children, no pages turning, not even a cough.

What's going on here? I couldn't put my finger on it.

No one else appeared as if something seemed to be amiss. Peering at my parents, I saw my dad looking down at his lap, blinking rapidly, which he would do to stay awake. My mom jotted in her notebook, then returned her gaze to the reverend. I searched her face for any sign of trouble or concern. But her face remained expressionless.

Was it only me? I sighed. If people accepted the reverend's words of prophecy coming straight from heaven itself—as he said—shouldn't I? Shouldn't I be basking in the glow of the Lord like the rest of these folks?

If you really believed that ...

The voice was back.

You wouldn't be asking these questions, would you?

CHAPTER 5

BAD VIBES

As our teacher, Mr. Fisher, tapped a marker on his desk, heads turned—except one. I remained lost in my thoughts.

School began that day with the usual hurriedness of preparing lunches while my mom pored over textbooks with her morning tea in hand. I was amazed at how my mother began early each morning preparing to homeschool my two youngest siblings, Mark and Kyla. Marty and I, the two oldest, attended Cross Christian Academy.

Snickers erupted as Mr. Fisher's marker bounced off my friend's head. Del sat up and looked around.

"No sleeping in class," Mr. Fisher said as the door opened and in walked Jolee. She produced a tardy slip.

A pretty redhead, Jolee was my closest friend. We had known each other since elementary school at Cross. No one could make me laugh like she could. There was also no one more easily provoked than her. With a mean streak that matched her hair, Jolee could be devilish, with revenge being her favorite game.

"Jolee, wait," I called. The hallway bustled with students slamming lockers and giving high fives over the lunch bell.

Jolee eyed the bell. "I'm going to blow up the school's alarm system."

"Hey, why were you late today?" I asked, ignoring her comment. "How come you weren't at church yesterday?"

"What's with the questions? I didn't feel like going to church. Big deal." She pulled me aside. "I'll tell you why I was late today, though." She had my full attention. "Mrs. Fisher stopped me before I made it to her husband's stuffy class."

"Why?"

"She gave me an eye inspection."

My shoulders slumped.

Cross Christian Academy had a very strict dress, honor, and behavior code set forth by the reverend. Any violation resulted in immediate consequences. Music was monitored at school and at home. Dating was an appalling sin and fraternizing with the opposite sex outside of a group setting earned a penalty. Girls were to wear dresses and skirts with no exceptions. If the hem didn't touch the floor when we knelt, we were fined. Eye makeup was against school rules. On occasion, we would sneak eye makeup, doing our best to avoid Mrs. Fisher and Mrs. Sullivan who patrolled the school floors searching for new victims to pay fines. Most schools issued detentions. Cross issued fines, suspensions, and expulsions.

"I got a ten-dollar fine for mascara today," Jolee spat.

"Sorry." I felt her pain. Not that long ago, I joined a group of girls getting hem and eye checks as well. We lined up in the hallway as Mrs. Sullivan marched, arms crossed, as she scrutinized us. Since most of us were careful about our makeup, there were no fines issued that day. I'm guessing this ruined Mrs. Sullivan's quota for the month.

Before turning toward the stairs, Jolee said, "That's not all." We headed to the first-floor cafeteria. "Mrs. Fisher asked me about you."

I stopped. "What about me?"

"She asked if you and Del have a *thing* going on and said if I was caught in a lie, I would be suspended."

I blinked.

"She said she saw you and Del coming up the stairs together, and you were *close*."

"What's that supposed to mean?" I snapped.

"She said your shoulders were touching."

"That's stupid."

"I told her so," Jolee said. "I also said I got off on shoulder-touching, not you."

My mouth dropped. "You did not."

She laughed. "Okay, I didn't say that. But I did say I had no idea what she was talking about, so she let me go." Jolee turned to me with a curious look. "Seems to me she's had it out for you for some reason."

Without answering, I followed Jolee to the cafeteria, reliving troubled memories of Mrs. Fisher. Third grade was one of the worst years of my life.

"You better shape up, buster!" she would often yell at me.

Embarrassed for not finishing my homework or receiving a poor grade, I just looked down at my shoes and said nothing.

"Look at me, girl!" She never called me by my given name. I knew she hated kids like me. I was a dreamer. I never completed my seatwork on time. She would catch me reading an adventure book or daydreaming instead of working on an assignment. Often, I would hear music in my head and was silenced if the slightest hum escaped my mouth. Math was my nemesis, but if I went to her for help, she accused me of not listening in class.

"Oh, don't forget," Jolee said, as we entered the lunchroom. "High school has chapel with that crazy traveling evangelist every day after lunch this week." She laughed as I groaned.

Pastor Sweeny visited our church and school for revival every spring. Traveling from state to state, he would park his motorhome at the church for the week and attempt to save us poor, wicked sinners from eternal hell and damnation as if Reverend Abbott hadn't already done that.

"God's wrath will be upon your heads," Pastor Sweeny spat. Literally. He was known as the "spitting evangelist" because he spoke with such forcefulness that he sprayed saliva everywhere with each sentence. At least he was aware of his problem and wiped his mouth with a hankie. No wonder the front rows in church were always empty when he came to town.

"Which of you will choose the kingdom of Christ?" *Spit. Wipe.* "You?" He would point at a brave soul sitting up front. "You in the back?" He pointed his hankie toward the back of the auditorium. "Those who do not make a choice will burn in hell where your teeth will gnash, and you will suffer the agony of sin!" *Spit. Wipe.*

I loathed his meetings.

During the car ride home later that afternoon, I listened to my brother Marty's endless chatter while I looked out the window.

"Guess what?" my dad said. "They finally finished the reconstruction of Smead Bridge. Now we can get to school in less than ten minutes."

Soon, the beautiful, covered bridge revealed itself. Appearing exactly as it had in its previous glory, it now boasted fresh red paint, set free from the charred burn scars it once bore. Local police were still investigating who had set fire to Twin Rivers's infamous landmark.

"Dad," I said as we pulled into our driveway. "Do we have to go to revival tonight?"

"That begins tomorrow night, but yes. The reverend is expecting everyone to be there."

"'Course he is," I muttered out loud. *Oops.*

My father frowned at me. "The reverend takes care of all of us, and we owe him our respect. As for today, your mother and I have a meeting to attend, so we hired a babysitter."

"Babysitter?" I lifted an eyebrow. "Don't you think I'm a bit too old for that?"

He laughed. "It's not really for you. You can work on your homework while Ms. Dana watches your brothers and sister."

Dana Terrell? Coming here? Interesting. "Why her? Where are you and Mom going?"

"One question at a time. First, Dana put the word out at church that she's looking for odd jobs. She's not married and is trying to raise a boy on her own. She's having a rough go of it. Second, we are meeting with a lawyer about Mom's old boating accident."

Temporarily putting my curiosity about Dana on the back burner, my mind traveled back to images of my mother when she had her sailboat accident. Before my mother had the four of us, she was an avid adventurer and traveler. She would tell me stories of her travels in Europe and all the beautiful places she saw. But one excursion put an abrupt end to her whims. While on the open sea aboard a large sailing vessel, a harness malfunctioned, sending her flying off the boat. A bungee cord snapped her right across the face, leaving an open wound in the shape of an S. My mother was knocked unconscious during her fall and nearly drowned. She became afraid of boats and dark water. She never sailed again, let alone embarked on any more adventures. I wondered if she missed them.

My dad nudged my arm. "Help Ms. Dana out this afternoon. I'm not sure if she's had this many kids at one time before, plus she's bringing her son with her."

"So, do I get paid to babysit the babysitter?" I grinned as my dad shot me a wry look.

"All right." Dana Terrell clapped her chubby hands. Pushing a frizzy curl out of her eyes, she tugged at her tight black jeans. I couldn't help but stare at her thuggish appearance.

"Everyone, line up." She raised her arm, revealing a disarming snake tattoo hiding near the edge of her faded T-shirt. "You too, Katie."

"Let's surprise your mom and dad with a clean house." Dana seemed eager to please. At that moment, I was struck by how nice she was.

Ignoring grunts of protest from my brothers, Dana assigned a few organizing chores for the other kids, then asked me to help her start dinner.

"Already?" I asked.

Dana smiled. "I love cooking, and your mom said it would be a big help."

"What did you have in mind?"

"Fish roll-ups." Dana tossed her head back with a laugh as my eyes grew wide. "Don't worry. They'll be good."

As we prepared dinner, I attempted to get to know Dana. She seemed kind enough, even funny. But there was something about the way her smile faded after she laughed as if a secret sorrow plagued her. Amidst our cutting up the filets of fish, I offered casual conversation.

"So, have you lived in Twin Rivers Junction very long?"

She shrugged. "A few years."

"What did you do before you came to Cross?"

"Do you mean, *why* did I come to Cross?" The woman was smarter than she let on.

"No, I didn't mean—"

"It's okay. I get it. I'm not your typical churchgoer." Dana's eyes took on a darker hue. "I've had it rough, you know."

"I'm sorry."

She turned to me in surprise. "Thanks, Katie. Not much to tell, really. Like anyone cares."

"Uh ... what do you mean?"

"You church people," she said with a bitter tone. "You act like you care, but not really, except your folks. They've been kind. But Ross Kelley showed up at my house and talked me into repenting of my sins, so I won't burn in the lake of fire. Then he convinced me this was the only Bible-believing church in the whole state. He told me all about your reverend too." She ended with an impolite snort.

Intrigued, I nodded for her to continue.

"I'm no dummy, you know. I lost both my parents as a young kid and grew up in foster homes. Got pregnant fresh out of high school. Preston's lousy father hightailed it when he found out. I've lived in the real world. I've managed things on my own for a while now, so I don't need uppity preachers telling me I'm going to hell for smoking cigarettes and having a beer once in a while."

I stood there, stunned at her outburst. Did Dana call Reverend Abbott an uppity preacher? Did she think he was not all everyone worshipped him to be? Was she still smoking and drinking? A yes to any of these questions would result in church discipline for her.

"I'm sorry, Katie." Dana's face flushed. "I shouldn't have said all that to you. You're young. None of this is your fault. Please don't tell your mom and dad."

"I know you think I'm some dumb teenager," I said while Dana measured out the rice. "But can I tell you something?"

Dana dumped the rice into the boiling water with an unsteady hand. "Shoot."

"I think the reverend can be a stuffy preacher sometimes too."

Dana blew out a sigh. "So, I'm not the only one, huh?"

Relieved at my admission, I was more concerned about trouble for Dana. If she talked to the wrong people, she would be headed for disciplinary action, along with repercussion for the crimes of smoking and drinking. This would jeopardize her part-time job at the school, along with other babysitting jobs.

"You probably shouldn't tell anyone else what you told me."

She looked puzzled. "I'll admit it was out of turn for me to say that in front of a young, impressionable teenage girl such as yourself. But why?"

How could I explain? She didn't grow up in this church. She hadn't been attending long. She wouldn't understand what it meant to follow a leader like Reverend Abbott. Dana had learned the hard way what it took to raise an illegitimate child on her own, while sticking it out in a cramped one-bedroom apartment in a not-so-nice area of town. I'd heard that she jumped from job to job in hopes of earning a paycheck while trying to be a decent mom and provider for her only son. People like Dana didn't belong at Cross Independent Baptist Church. People like her never lasted long around the reverend.

"Why, Katie?" Her tone was impatient.

There were things I felt but could not prove. I was never sure of the exact problem. If I couldn't identify it, how could I be so full of questions? I knew I didn't have the tools necessary to explain this to her. And what if I did? Would she believe me? Wasn't I just some young, impressionable teenager?

"I really can't say." I swallowed hard.

"What? Look, I'm sorry for offending you—"

"No, you didn't offend me. Just be careful is all I'm saying."

Dana squinted. "What do you know, Katie?"

"Things I can't explain right now." I knew I sounded weak.

She grabbed her purse and sifted through its contents. "Be right back. I need a cigarette."

While Dana smoked with trembling hands outside the kitchen window, I reached into the warm dishwater and began washing a dirty pan. A moment later, I nearly dropped it when a terrible thought hit me. With no explanation for what I sensed, I knew something was coming. It filled me with apprehension for Dana.

I wondered if I would ever see her again after today.

CHAPTER 6

UNAPPROVED

Later that week, I felt a nudge and turned to see my friend Brynn holding a tiny note folded in the shape of a triangle. After a glance at our English Lit teacher, Mrs. McKenzie, I reached back to receive the note when she turned to write something on the board.

"Shakespeare's Macbeth," she began. "What can you tell me about the influence his wife had in his life?"

With my right hand hiding the unread note, I raised my left hand. It wasn't long before I noticed that among my classmates, I was the only one who seemed interested in the discussion.

Mrs. McKenzie nodded my way. "Katie, what do you think?"

"Lady Macbeth knew her husband lacked the ability to carry out murder on his own, so she convinced him it was the only choice in order to receive the crown."

"Exactly. Now, since fortitude was not Macbeth's strength, his wife was the mastermind behind the killings. Everyone, please turn in your books to page one hundred forty-seven."

Mrs. McKenzie turned to the board again, the names of Macbeth's victims appearing in succession. I unfolded the note and tried not to gasp. Stunned, I crumpled the note into a tight ball. The one class I loved, Mrs. McKenzie's English Literature class, was ruined for the day.

It's now ruined forever, I thought angrily.

I grabbed Brynn as soon as the dismissal bell rang. "What was that all about?"

Brynn stared at me. "Did you read the note?"

"Of course. Was that some kind of nasty joke?"

Brynn shook her head. "My dad told me last night Mrs. McKenzie gave her resignation to Reverend Abbott."

The news knocked the wind out of me. "But why?"

Brynn leaned closer. "My dad told me to keep quiet, but I know you like Mrs. McKenzie, so I'll tell you what he told me. But you can't say anything to anyone. Mrs. McKenzie is sending her daughter to Jehovah Christian University, and Reverend Abbott found out."

I covered my mouth with my hand. Jehovah Christian University was a Christian college but not on the reverend's approved college list. Everyone knew that. No one sent their kids to a college that was not on the approved list. Had Mrs. McKenzie deliberately gone against him?

"When does she leave?"

"Don't know." Brynn shrugged and turned away. "Catch you later."

Alone with my uneasy thoughts, I watched Brynn catch up with Jolee and our friend Karina and the trio instantly started giggling.

How could they just laugh like that? Like nothing's wrong? Like it doesn't matter that the best teacher this school has ever had is now leaving.

Just then, Mrs. McKenzie appeared in the hallway. For a fleeting moment, I considered stopping her to demand an explanation. *Please don't leave me*, I begged. I searched her face for any sign of truth to the news Brynn had shared with me. Running her hand through her hair, she sighed. Her shoulders slumped more than usual.

My mind traveled back to when I first attended her class. At first, she didn't appear to like me much as she kept calling me "swivel head." I soon realized she didn't say it with hostility but a nickname she used—along with a grin—because I could be a little too chatty with my friends during class. How ironic that one teacher could call me buster, and I felt like a nonhuman, while another called me swivel head, making me feel cared for and accepted.

Upon discovering that I loved music, fine arts, and literature, I soaked up any knowledge Mrs. McKenzie shared. How exciting it was to go on adventures with a new story, whether comedy, tragedy, mystery, or drama. Each story was magical, and Mrs. McKenzie helped make it so. For me, it was the best thing that ever happened to me at that school.

One day, we were to write a short, fictional story and receive a test grade. Many of my fellow classmates groaned, moaned, or flat-out gasped their way out of the classroom that day, but not me. Elated, I couldn't wait to get home and rush to my room with a stack of notebook paper and pencils.

A week later, as I awaited my results, my classmates chewed their nails in hopes that Mrs. McKenzie had called in sick that day. Soon, she entered the room calling out a pleasant greeting to several disappointed faces. As she passed out the short-story assignments, I waited for my name to be called.

"Katie DeConner."

I nearly jumped out of my seat. Extending my hand, I was rewarded with something I didn't expect. Not only did I get an A, but Mrs. McKenzie had also handwritten something at the top of my cover page that I will never forget. *Katie, you have a gift for storytelling.*

Tears stung my eyes. Was she serious? I had a gift? I looked up at her to find her smiling at me.

"It's true," she said quietly. "You have a gift, Katie."

From that day on, I worshipped the ground Mrs. McKenzie walked on. The first teacher to ever believe in me. The first teacher who inspired me to want to be great at something. She never made me feel bad about not getting perfect grades in other areas but always encouraged me to want to learn more and do my best.

And now you're leaving me, I thought miserably as she reached for the door to the teacher's lounge. Before she could turn the handle, the school's Bible teacher, Mr. Kunis, exited the room.

"Good afternoon, Mr. Kunis," she greeted.

I watched in disbelief as he walked past without acknowledgment. He must have known about her resignation, or he would've returned her greeting. Was he angry? Had he been told not to communicate with her any further?

Another thought came. Was he scared of something?

Noisy students and other faculty drifted past. My heart sank as I witnessed the confused look on Mrs. McKenzie's face while Mr. Kunis hurried away from her as if she were a poisonous reptile.

Back again in my favorite place, I thought with sarcasm. Sunday evening service was about to begin. Just as I settled in my pew, my friend Sara came by and plopped down next to me.

"Hey," she said, unzipping her jacket. "So? Did you hear?"

I raised an eyebrow at Sara, who turned her attention to her zipper, muttering about it always getting stuck on the ski lift tags that dangled. Sara's parents walked by and found seats in the row ahead. Jack and Penny Kittridge were longtime attendees of Cross. Jack, a church deacon and treasurer, worked as a manager of one of the local auto parts warehouses for Ross Kelley, who owned several businesses in the area. Penny worked as a housekeeper at a motel in Hanford, the next town over. As the biggest family at Cross, with six children, Jack and Penny were loyal to the reverend.

"Hear what?" I didn't know who Brynn had told about Mrs. McKenzie, so I waited.

"About me and Justin."

If there was anything the students of Cross Christian Academy were good at, it was keeping relationships with the opposite sex a secret. An outsider would scoff at our use of the term *relationship*. All it meant was covert note-passing, sneaking into the school's photo lab darkroom to make out, and being in group settings anywhere else. Attaching a formal title to such a relationship meant you were an item. In secret, of course.

"What? You guys are eloping?" I opened my mouth in feigned shock, which earned me a punch on the arm.

"No, you moron. We're officially boyfriend and girlfriend."

"I'm telling the reverend right now." I pretended to get up.

Sara laughed. With a see-you-later, she joined her mom just as the special music from the Abbott sisters began.

"Seek ye first the kingdom of God," Reverend Abbott said twenty minutes later introducing the evening's sermon. "Matthew chapter six tells us this should be our priority. What this really means is your priority is to be a better servant of Christ. So how does one do that?"

The reverend's questions were rhetorical. "It's simple. To be a better servant of Christ, you need to serve God in your local church. If your priority is money, beware of God's warning in First Timothy 6:9, where the love of money is called a temptation and a trap."

He stopped reading the Scripture as someone entered the service. "Oh, look. There he is." He gestured to Barry Cobb, who was trying to slide into the back row. "We might forgive him for coming in late. But I don't think I'm going to."

Was he joking? The congregation looked unsure. Some had a bewildered look while others gave a chuckle. Glancing back at Barry, I felt bad for him. He and his wife traveled forty-five minutes each way to church, and the reverend knew that. Why was he pointing out his tardiness in front of everyone?

Reverend Abbott picked up where he left off. "If you want to give in to the lusts of the flesh and money is your priority, then, by all means, send your kid to a college that will exploit that."

Oh no. I knew where this sermon was going.

"Sure," the Reverend said with a shrug. "If you want to go to a big, famous, secular college, it might give you an edge in the job market. But the Bible says pursuing lusts only brings ruin and destruction. I wouldn't want to risk *my* child in a secular environment. Seek ye first the kingdom of God and his righteousness. That leaves out secular colleges!"

He went on to list his favored Bible-believing Christian colleges on his newly revised short list.

"As schools change," he stated, "so do my rankings. The biggest problem is pride. Glory goes to God and the local church. When you're serving the Lord, it's not supposed to be far away. Some kids go to an accredited college so they can wear it like a badge. This makes them feel independent of their pastor's counsel."

Closing my eyes, I cringed and waited for an imaginary guillotine to drop. What if I considered a college that was not on his approval list? Did I say goodbye to a favored college just because it was far away? Just because he said so?

"Many of you know one of our teachers here, Liz McKenzie."

When I looked over to her usual seat, my heart lurched. She was not present.

He's really doing this, I thought in alarm. Sara sent me a puzzled look over her shoulder.

"I have asked for her resignation because she is allowing her kid to make the decisions in the family. Her daughter wants to attend a college far away that does not believe the way we do. You need to send your child to a Christian college that believes like we do so they don't come home and argue with you about the local church. You want them to come home and say, 'let's work for the Lord.' Some parents, who aren't real parents, just let their kids go wherever they want to go. They are ruled by their kids. What you should be looking for is the kingdom of God! Seek ye first *his* righteousness!"

I realized at that moment this was the first sermon where I heard every word he said. And all I could do was sit in restlessness as questions flooded my mind. I could not get up and leave, not even to go to the bathroom unless I had a dire emergency. I could not stand up and shout. That would only earn me consequences I didn't want.

I stared over to my left at my parents. As usual, my dad's head was bent toward his lap. But this time, he didn't look sleepy. Wide awake, he seemed to glance from his notes to his Bible. My mother wrote furiously in her journal.

Look over at me, I pleaded. *You can't tell me this is right. That this is normal. Why won't you look at me?* I knew my mother noticed me staring at her because her head turned ever so slightly to the right and then immediately righted itself forward again. As always, her face remained expressionless. But wait ...

I saw something. As if a gray shadow passed over her fair countenance. Like a candle being snuffed out, all that was left was a wisp of smoke.

She knows.

The revelation gave me a blast of hope. But she never looked in my direction.

Later that evening, as we drove home, my family remained quiet. Most times, my mom and dad would discuss the message or the agenda for the upcoming week. But not tonight.

From the third-row seat of my mom's station wagon, my brothers chattered. In the seat next to me, Kyla had fallen asleep with her head resting against the window.

"So ..." I said after clearing my throat. "Mom, do we have anything going on tomorrow afternoon?"

"Uh, tomorrow?" She seemed startled. "Just school. That's it."

She wasn't going to talk further, so I sat back on the leather seat and sighed.

My relationship with my mom was a typical mother-to-teenage-daughter one. Sometimes, I could be grumpy or pretend I knew everything. Sometimes, she'd have to get after me for rolling my eyes or being unkind to my brothers. But overall, our dynamic was tolerable. She was submissive at church, as she was supposed to be. Predictable, but also adept at keeping things to herself except when it came to her eyes.

And tonight, your eyes have given you away.

CHAPTER 7

FLICKER OF DOUBT

"Can you get me two tickets, Katie?" Del called from the table beside me.

I handed him a stack and returned to my cash box station. Every year, the high school raised funds for the next graduating class to visit Washington, DC. We held bake sales, candy sales, car washes, and other fundraisers. Tonight's event was International Game Night, where the theme was "Come As You Are Not." People arrived in unique costumes, many homemade. This was our biggest event of the year and the entire church participated.

"You guys okay here?" asked my longtime friend Karina, dressed up as a postal worker. As preschoolers, we'd struck up a quick friendship that continued when both our families joined Cross.

I nodded just as a blonde cheerleader came up beside me. "Where did you get that?" I asked Rachel with amusement. Her pleated skirt was not short like typical cheer outfits but went past the knee. Even on game night, one must not show any knees.

Rachel shrugged. "Borrowed it." She looked over at Del and Jolee, who were trading five-dollar bills for tickets. "How are we doing?"

"Exceptional. Seems like a big hit so far."

"Great. And you're supposed to *not* be ..." She raised her eyebrows at my getup.

"Pure evil, baby," I responded with a grin. I smoothed out my long black cape—an oversized graduation gown—cautious not to smudge my painted face.

Rachel laughed and turned to see her boyfriend Gil Hindman, dressed as a cowboy, striding toward her. Rachel was talented at many things—one of which was keeping this relationship covert. Guess she didn't want dear ol' dad to find out. Not that the reverend was present. The very formal and important man of God at a game night? No, he stayed busy with other things. This time, it involved my parents. I wondered why the reverend phoned them to come to his home for a meeting. And why my parents dropped their evening plans to do his bidding.

"We're done," a nun in a black habit standing next to Del announced. Jolee snapped the cash box shut and adjusted her black and white headpiece. "This thing is itchy."

"Wait a minute." Del pointed at the two of us. "I get it now. Good versus evil?"

"You got us figured out, Del," Jolee said dryly.

Del, wearing a Superman costume, sent me a fond grin. We were also an *item*, but our relationship was more of a strong friendship than anything else. We kept glances or talks brief due to unending adult scrutiny.

Joining a group near the beanbag throw, my thirteen-year-old brother dressed in army fatigues—complete with a super-soaker gun—asked if I had seen Preston Terrell.

"Why are you asking me? Go find your own friends." I sighed as he squirted his gun at me in response.

"Come on," Marty whined. "Help me look for him. He told me Tuesday he would be here tonight and would let me borrow his new game."

"Tuesday? But it's Friday," I pointed out.

"Right. That's the last time I saw him. He hasn't been in school since then."

I shrugged. "Maybe he's sick." But I wondered. Was he *really* sick? He must be to miss out on a fun event such as this. The whole school had talked about this night for months. I soon realized I hadn't seen his mom in several weeks.

You haven't seen Dana since she babysat that day. The voice again.

That got my attention. I turned away from shouts of those winning or losing at the beanbag toss. Scanning the large cafeteria, I saw people dressed in different attire and felt a sense of satisfaction. All our hard work had paid off. But Marty was right. Neither Preston nor his mom were in attendance.

Marty came back over to where I stood, the dark black ribbons of war paint under his eyes smudged. He had a troubled look on his face.

"Well?"

"Mrs. Miller told me he's left the school."

"What?" It was rare for a student to leave Cross Christian, especially before the end of a school year. I looked over at my former kindergarten teacher, Mrs. Miller, who was dressed as a doctor. How would she know?

"Why would he leave?" Marty said. "He said he'd be here tonight."

"I'm sure he has a good reason, okay? Mrs. Miller doesn't know squat. He's probably just sick." I made a move for his toy weapon.

"Nice try," he said, squirting me again before he left.

Left alone with my thoughts, something nagged at me. People moved in front and behind me, but white noise was all I heard. The bad vibe continued creeping its way up my spine. Where were Dana Terrell and her son tonight? Why hadn't they been at church lately? Reverend Abbott was famous for telling his congregation that if the church doors were open, we ought to be present.

"Forsake not the assembling of yourselves together," he preached. This left out staying home and sleeping in even on the coldest New England mornings. If one were to be absent from church, they had better be sick or on vacation. Ross Kelley was usually the one assigned to monitor church attendance.

The vehicle of my thoughts rounded another bend in the road and slowed to one more stop. What did the reverend want to meet with my parents about? He did not say when he called that evening, but it must have been important. My parents were to arrive on his doorstep at seven p.m. My siblings and I had to hitch a ride to school with the Wheatley family, who lived only a mile down the road from us.

"Katie?"

I blinked and snapped out of my reverie. Kyle Tyner stood in front of me dressed in a blue-and-white kimono, undoubtedly borrowed from his father, Burt, who spent many years in Japan as the child of a missionary family. His mother, Renata, had also been to Japan several times, which was evident in some of her home décor.

"Katie, you are always doing that," he said.

I frowned. "Doing what?"

"Going off"—his fingers flew up to imaginary clouds above—"You just seem somewhere else at times."

Only Kyle or Jolee would have noticed that about me. Since Kyle's mom, Renata, and my mom were close, we were always at each other's house for either piano, math tutoring, or Renata's dreadful Subaru was in my dad's shop for repairs. Kyle and I were practically brother and sister.

"I'm a daydreamer. You know that."

UNDER AUTHORITY

Kyle clicked his tongue at my attire in amusement. "I almost didn't recognize you. Of course,"—he nodded to Jolee, who stood by stuffing Doritos in her mouth—"I should have known Jolee would have dressed up exactly as what *she* is not."

"Let her have her fun, Kyle." I shook my head. Poor Kyle. As he was teased for being nerdy at Cross, I feared I was his only friend. At times, I thought the ridicule made him ugly inside. But when I asked him, he became tight-lipped and only wanted to talk about Rachel. I would roll my eyes as soon as her name came up. Was there any young man at Cross who was not in love with Rachel Abbott?

"Thanks for the ride, Mrs. Wheatley." My brothers and sister hopped out of her van. I slid the large door shut and watched her back out of the driveway. Spotting my mom's car, I knew my parents were back from their mysterious meeting with the reverend.

And what, oh what, did they talk about? I mused.

"Hey," my dad called out to us from the kitchen table where he appeared to be reading over some documents. My mother was not with him.

With excitement, my brothers spilled the details of the evening, beginning with the student who had the best costume—Joey Kittridge, Sara's brother, who came in an authentic policeman's uniform, armed with an intimidating flashlight. Then the worst costume, worn by an elementary teacher. As the boys jabbered on, down to the details of the food and games, I noticed how tired my father looked.

The hardest working man I have ever known, my father labored from sunup to sundown to provide for us and take care of the old farmhouse. Year-round, his main trade was his auto repair shop. In the summers, he resurrected the old

Dodge pickup he used to haul around the dog team before he no longer had the time to devote to sled dog racing. The dog boxes long gone from the back of the truck, he tossed in his chainsaw, and off he would go into the forest to cut firewood for the winter. He rarely had a minute to himself except on Thanksgiving mornings when he'd go deer hunting. If he was ever found idle, he was usually asleep.

Tonight, he seemed more drained than after a normal day of work. And where had my mother gone? Why did she not come out to greet us?

"Where's Mom?" I asked.

"Her back is bothering her. She's already gone to bed."

Bed just after nine o'clock on a Friday evening? I had an inkling there was more to it. I made a mental note to find a way to ask my dad about his meeting.

Careful, the voice warned.

An hour later, after some obnoxious noises from my brothers' room had simmered down, I crept downstairs, wincing as the old staircase creaked beneath my feet. I stood still and held my breath, waiting to see if the steps had betrayed my presence. Thankfully, I had not been detected.

The door to the den, which my parents also used as their bedroom, had been left open. Funny. Not many couples had two bedrooms they used in the same house. But at times, when my mother's back ached, she'd beg off climbing the stairs into the chilly bedroom. Downstairs was closer to the woodstove and more comfortable. My dad had handmade a bed for them that looked like a daybed. We used it as a couch during the day and a bed at night.

I peered around the edge of the doorway. The large den was an odd setup, with the worn upright piano dividing the room across the middle. To the left was a messy office with my mom's computer and several filing cabinets. Since the daybed sat behind the upright piano, I would only be seen if they turned around, which they did not. My dad sat on the piano bench facing her direction. I could picture her propped up on pillows and a heating pad.

Just as I was about to make out what they were saying, a cold, wet nose brushed my leg. Dusty, one of our two Labrador retrievers, sat in the doorway, looking at me with his tail thumping the carpeted floor.

"Beat it," I hissed. He skulked off into the kitchen. I would apologize to him later.

"But, Sam," my mother said. "Miles was handling it fine."

Huh. Not sleeping.

"Not really," my dad said. "He left out some key details during the pleadings and almost missed the deadline for the complaint."

"Okay, I get that." She sighed. "He had a lot on his plate that day and was juggling too many appointments. I'm sure we could have worked it all out."

"Perhaps." My dad stared down at the floor. "But then again, he didn't include the facts in the original petition we'd asked him to. Too weak."

"You felt he let us down, so you went to the reverend for advice," my mom said bluntly.

Until about ten minutes ago, I had been pondering questions I could ask that would seem casual about their meeting tonight. *How was your talk tonight, Dad? Everything okay? Oh, by the way, have you heard from Dana Terrell lately?* At that point, if I had not been shut down, my next question would have been, *what was the meeting about?* I guessed I would get no further than that last question, regardless of any good mood he may have been in. But there was a chance now I could gather a plethora of information. Much more than just asking outright.

If you don't get caught eavesdropping, the voice said.

"Had to, Jan," my dad was saying. "You know he asked us to keep him in the loop about how the case is going."

"But why?" my mom asked. "Is he just looking out for us and that's all? Doesn't want us to get short-sighted here? Or whatever you call it?"

"Right," my dad agreed and then fell silent.

I found it interesting my mom did not let the subject drop. If we had been present, she would not have pursued this conversation. Could it be my mom was one way around us kids and more open alone with my dad?

"So, why wouldn't he let us keep Miles?" she asked.

Dad heaved a sigh. "The reverend said he was incompetent."

"But this is not a complicated case, Sam. He drew up our complaint involving fault on the sailboat manufacturer for the malfunction of the safety harness and bungee cord. Evidence was detailed and presented. Simple. I can't see why Rhuttland Abbott is making us fire our lawyer just so he can be our legal representation."

My hand flew over my mouth. My mind reeled, much like that boat had done the day it pitched my mom into the black water, making her hit her head underneath its belly. The reverend had told them to fire their lawyer so he could take his place? But why? For what purpose? I couldn't believe it.

"And now we have to start all over again, is that it?" My mom spoke in an accusing tone I had never heard before.

"It shouldn't be too hard, hon. The complaint will have to be redrawn, showing Rhuttland Abbott as our acting lawyer. Everything else is already taken care of."

"*Acting* lawyer," my mom repeated. "Has the reverend passed the bar exam? What does he know about practicing law?"

"We have to trust his advice," my dad stated. "You heard what he said tonight. God showed him a vision that we needed to receive counsel from him instead of a worldly man out for our money."

"Miles has been a longtime friend. Do you think he was out for our money?"

"Well, no, but the reverend—"

"Isn't he getting a piece of the settlement once we get it? As payment for his time."

My dad said nothing.

I stood there, dumbfounded. Apprehension lurked in the shadows as I heard the conversation between my parents unfold. I had never in all my sixteen years heard a discussion quite like this one. There was no fighting or arguing. No loud voices. No shouting. But what I heard spoke volumes.

What I had witnessed was the first real flicker of doubt about the reverend. I felt like one of those actors on TV. The kind who are in the wrong place at the wrong time, hiding around a corner as they witness a crime being committed. Those were the ones who usually ended up getting bumped off in the end. Forcing my thoughts back into focus, I decided now would be a good time to slither upstairs before I got caught.

Back in my room, I lay in bed staring out my window at the stars. Many of them winked at me as if they knew what had happened just a few moments ago and vowed to keep quiet.

How had Reverend Abbott convinced my dad he was better at the lawyer's job? Was that it? Or did he just want to be in the middle of what was going on? If so, why? What did he care? Didn't he have enough church and school stuff to worry about? Was it just my parents' welfare and well-being he cared about? Why did he think Attorney Miles

Cooper was going to be dishonest about money in some way?

The questions preyed upon me like tiny little monsters that hid under the bed and came out in the obscurity of the dark. Their nagging claws reached for me, unrelenting.

Stop, I begged them.

There would be no sleeping for me tonight, I was sure. My mind would not turn off, no matter how much I willed it to.

CHAPTER 8

THE OBITUARY

"I have a newsflash for you." The voice whispering in my ear jolted my attention. I had not heard Jolee come up behind me.

"Better make it quick. The singing is about to start," I told her. It was Sunday once again, and the church sanctuary was filling up. Mr. Hearn stood at the pulpit, clearing his throat in an unnatural manner while sifting through the hymnal. Seated at the piano was Sonya Abbott, the reverend's wife, waiting for her signal to begin a prelude. There were no other instruments on the platform.

Jolee slid in next to me, tossing her hair over her shoulder. "You won't believe what I heard."

"I can just imagine." I shook my head at her.

"Remember our beloved Sunday school teacher and your pal from elementary, Mrs. Sullivan?"

"Let me see," I said, thinking of Mrs. Sullivan's nasty sneer when Rachel and I showed up late for Sunday school that day. "She wants to know if I'm wearing eyeliner so she can bust me with a fine. No, that's not it. She has caught me in a lie and wants to have me suspended again."

"Worse." Jolee stated. "She'll be coming to the high school to take Mrs. McKenzie's place. Someone else will cover Mrs. Sullivan's fourth- and fifth-grade classes."

Just as I groaned loud enough to earn a frown from my mother, we were instructed to stand. Jolee hurried to her seat a few rows ahead of me, but not before she threw up her hands and rolled her eyes.

Forcing away my angry thoughts, I moved my mouth to the music but did not participate. Instead, I fixed my gaze on the pearl-covered clip that Velma Holtz wore in her graying hair. The couple seated in front of us, Velma and her husband Floyd, were one of the older ones in the church often referred to as the snowbirds. They came to Twin Rivers every April through September and then back to some gorgeous sandy beach in Florida. For some reason, Velma gravitated to my mother and doted on her as if she were a long-lost daughter. They often came over on Sundays after church for my father's pancakes or afternoon tea. At times, my dad worked on their car. Sometimes they brought us small gifts from the beach, such as sand dollars or unusual seashells.

They were also good friends with the reverend.

During the summers, when Velma and Floyd were in town, they'd park their airstream camper alongside the Abbott's vast lake house so they had access to the water or the reverend's boat. I was always curious how this arrangement came about and if they paid rent.

"You may be seated." Mr. Hearn closed the hymnal and motioned to June Britton to begin her solo.

When June smiled, I realized she was probably the only one who got up on the platform to sing who smiled. Looking close to popping with her third baby, June got up from beside her husband, Glen, in the front row and stood behind the pulpit to sing, this time choosing Brynn to accompany her on the piano instead of using the autoharp.

Behind the pulpit. This is a first.

UNDER AUTHORITY

When Rachel and her sisters performed as a trio, they each had spots to the right of the pulpit near the piano. Even now, an empty microphone stood waiting. Sometimes, Sara Kittridge's older sister Denise would perform if she was home from Bible college. On occasion, I would sing a solo, obediently standing where instructed. I wondered what made June want to stand behind the pulpit. Was she self-conscious of her protruding belly?

My questions were soon forgotten as June's lofty voice drifted over us. June had a unique voice that was calming, and I enjoyed her music. Her rendition of a song about rejoicing in the Lord was clear and flawless. I envied her for being able to sing this without any apparent stage fright, along with being pregnant. When her chorus was over, I felt warmed by the words of her song. June waddled back to the front row beside Glen. I studied them for a moment. They had only been coming to Cross for about a year. From what I had seen, Glen was a quiet guy who preferred to sit in the back row. He didn't seem interested in talking with the other men, whereas June was outgoing and friendly. It was common for him to wait for her in the car with the kids after church. Maybe he was shy. My train of thought was interrupted as the song ended and the reverend rose to preach.

He looks upset, I thought, noticing a darker-than-usual expression on his gray face. A curious new line had slid from his ear to his jaw, giving his chin a clenched appearance. Adjusting his glasses, he asked the congregation to turn in their Bibles to Romans 13.

Let every soul be subject unto the higher powers," he read, his voice tight. "The powers that be are ordained of God. Whosoever therefore resisteth the power, resisteth the ordinance of God. And they that resist shall receive to themselves damnation." He looked up, his face still a distinct shadow. "Let us close our eyes and bow our heads in prayer."

I stared down at my shoes. Each Sunday, I became increasingly bothered. What was wrong with me? Did I have a bad attitude about the ritual of church and following rules? Was I a rebellious teenager? Was I bored? Maybe my imagination had taken off again. Wouldn't it be better if I just followed along with what I was told? Maybe I needed to focus a little more on fixing my mindset concerning the church in general before I got myself in trouble.

"The translation of this"—Reverend Abbott was now getting more into his routine as his tone fluctuated in its usual dramatic fashion—"is that God has instructed the church body to surrender to the authority of those he has placed in command of his congregation. Submit or be damned!"

His last words ended with a deep rasp. The microphone trembled.

"Your ministers, your leaders, your teachers are placed by God himself in these positions of governing because God declared it. It's right here in his Word. If you don't believe it, read your Bible. If you still don't believe it, you're probably not a Christian!"

Ministers? Leaders? But isn't he the only one? Everyone else just does what he tells them to.

Who did you think he was talking about? the voice asked.

"Who is ordained of God?" the preacher now asked.

No one said anything, of course. There would be no open discussion.

"Your local pastor is ordained of God," he said bluntly. "Verse four says, 'For he is the minister of God to thee for good.' Go down to verse five. 'Wherefore ye must needs be subject ...'"

Next, the reverend took a step back and extended his palms. Taking on a mocking voice, he imitated a person with doubts. "Well, preacher," he jeered. "I don't want to do that. I don't want to surrender my will, because I want to rule myself." His hands came down, and his voice took on a menacing tone. "You either believe and obey the Word of the Lord or you don't. It says right here in verse two what happens to those who defy God. You face damnation. Do you think God will overlook disobedience? God has ways of dealing with rebellion in his people!"

Goosebumps of suspicion prickled my back. Why had he chosen this topic for today? Had someone overstepped their boundaries? Questioned something? Disobeyed in some way? Was this a continuation of what happened with Mrs. McKenzie? There had to be a reason for him to be so uptight this morning.

"Not only does God instruct us to obey the pastor, but he also commands us to give double honor. First Timothy 5:17 says, 'Let the elders that rule well be counted worthy of double honor, especially those who labor in the word and doctrine.'" Pleased with some wide-eyed faces from his congregation, Reverend Abbott gripped both sides of the pulpit and leaned in for emphasis. "These are God's ministers. Verse 6, back in Romans 13. 'Pay ye tribute also, for they are God's ministers.' Now in verse 7. 'Render therefore to all their dues, tribute to whom tribute is due.'"

I had all I could do to keep from fidgeting. Any efforts I made before the sermon to improve my attitude evaporated. Glancing around the sanctuary, I tried to see if there were any others who seemed uncomfortable with this message. Most everyone in my line of vision remained fixated on the preacher. My mother was, as usual, writing away in her journal. I saw her slide her elbow to the left and grinned when my dad's head popped up. Feeling bad for him, I remembered he stayed up late last night trying to finish a difficult transmission rebuild in his shop as a rush order for one of Ross Kelley's clients.

After what seemed an eternity, the sermon ended. Mrs. Abbott took her place at the piano. While the melody to "I Surrender All" rang out, I did not think about the bigoted sermon. I decided the best thing to do was simply ignore it. All it did was make me confused and maybe even a little angry. I didn't know why, and I hoped I was not becoming one of those obstinate teenagers. But trying to understand the feelings that had come over me made me weary. Since I couldn't say or do anything about it, I would practice the art of ignoring.

They say ignorance is bliss, right? I wasn't sure who said that, nor did I care. I was ready for a little bliss.

The students' favorite time of day—the bell rang, and students scurried to their lockers. I waited for the frenzy of kids to grab their lunches and get out of the way. I disliked sharing the hallway with the lower grades, but at Cross, the elementary and high schools were divided. Once a student finished grade six, they were in high school and moved upstairs.

Could these middle schoolers be any more obnoxious? I couldn't help but snicker at my own brother. Marty flexed an arm muscle at a girl who threw him a dirty look.

"You coming to lunch, or are you just going to stand there?" Brynn called out. She was waiting for me, along with Jolee and Karina. My longtime friend, Karina's personality was an unusual combination of goofy and sensitive. I wasn't always sure what she was thinking, but she was kind. We had some good times laughing as we developed film in the darkroom for yearbook photos.

I waved. "Yeah, I'm coming. Save me a seat."

Descending to the cafeteria, they left me to find my locker and get my lunch. Out of the corner of my eye, I saw Christopher Kelley, a few lockers down, eyeing me.

"What are you up to?" I said, annoyed.

He shrugged. "Today? Just hit six feet tall. Feeling pretty good about that."

Rolling my eyes, I imagined he must have been worried about his height for quite some time. As the youngest of church elder Ross Kelley's children, Christopher didn't look much like his balding, short-statured father. Beyond that, his intelligence was far inferior to his dad's. I supposed being a sophomore in high school explained that.

"What do you have there?" Since gum chewing was not permitted in school, I knew Chris was not stupid enough to get caught with it. He pulled a gnarled wet straw from his mouth and showed it to me. Accustomed to two disgusting brothers, I was quite unfazed.

"Something on your mind, Chris?"

The crowd around the lockers had thinned out. Chris glanced over his shoulder. "So, I heard Dana Terrell worked for your parents."

"She babysat us once. That's all. What do you care?"

"I don't." He shoved the straw back in his mouth. "When's the last time you heard from her?"

"A while, I guess. Why?"

"She's dead."

Since Chris was a Kelley, I didn't trust him. I had a hunch he was trying to bait me. Why would he say such a horrible thing? And why to me? Not for a second did I believe him. Especially as he stood there looking like an idiot with that nasty straw sticking out the side of his mouth. Who jokes around about someone being dead?

"You're full of crap, Chris." I fully expected him to burst out laughing at delivering his first real prank.

But he didn't. Instead, he grabbed my arm as I turned to go. "It's true. If you don't believe me, check the newspaper."

"Are you crazy?" I yanked my arm away just as Mrs. Sullivan rounded the corner. Any physical contact between the opposite sex intercepted by a teacher would result in fines. A double shot for each of us.

"You two," she called, pointing to us. "Get to lunch. Now."

For once, I was eager to follow her command and hurried down the stairs, trying to outrun the disturbing prospect that what Chris said might be true.

"Why did you pick us up today?" Marty asked Renata Tyner as we rode home from school. "Dad working on your car?"

"Not today. Your dad is busy working on Reverend Abbott's car right now. I was visiting your mom, and she asked me to come get you. It's all good."

Odd. Mrs. Tyner had never picked us up before. And since when did Dad work on the reverend's car? His cars were newer, so what kind of repairs could they need?

Kyle spoke up. "Mom, are we staying long? I have homework."

"No, we'll head home as soon as we drop off Katie and Marty." Mrs. Tyner slowed before her approach to Smead Bridge. When she turned into my parents' driveway, my attention went to the open door of my dad's shop and Reverend Abbott's car. The hood was up, and my dad was underneath the car on a dolly. The tinkling of tools echoed on the concrete floor. Knowing the reverend was on our property, I rushed inside the house. After the Tyner's left, I knocked gently on the door to the den, where I was told my mother was lying down with a headache.

"Mom?" I whispered as I stepped into the room. I leaned around the tall piano to see if she was awake.

I found my mother curled up on her side, facing the opposite wall. By her even breathing, I could tell she was sleeping. My mother was not one to sleep in the middle of the day. She must have had one killer migraine. But then, why had the overhead light been left on? As I turned to leave, I noticed her hand covering something.

A newspaper.

I froze, remembering Chris Kelley's remark. *If you don't believe me, check the paper.*

I had to get that newspaper. Adrenaline filled my veins, and I willed my hands to stop shaking. I stepped forward and carefully reached over her, easing the newspaper from underneath her hand. Then I noticed her puffy eyes, which only happened when she cried.

And my mother rarely cried.

A minute later, I had it, relieved I had not startled her awake. Only one piece of newspaper from a few days ago. I backed out of the den and flicked off the light.

Sitting on the stairs outside the den, I unfolded the paper. The adrenaline pulsing through my veins just minutes ago vanished, leaving a wake of dread in its place. I quickly found the news I feared.

Woman Dies of Gunshot Wound to Head
Local Police Suspect Suicide

The shooting occurred in North Twin Rivers Junction on April 21 when a neighbor called 911 after reporting the sound of gunfire. Brad Potter, a deputy spokesman with the Twin Rivers Police Department, provided few details other than the victim was an approximately thirty-year-old female identified as Dana P. Terrell. Sources say Terrell is survived by a young son who has been taken out of state to live with relatives.

An update will be provided as more information becomes available.

I became aware of a throbbing in my head that reverberated throughout my body. I could not stop shaking, yet oddly enough, I could not move.

Dana was dead. She killed herself.

Those ugly, invisible words became the headline instead of the one that had been printed.

As the truth penetrated the fog that had settled over me, I looked up. My mother stood in front of me, hands to her side, her face drained of color. How long had she been standing there? I could see with relief she was not angry with me for taking her newspaper article.

An apparition of Dana Terrell flashed between our eyes, holding our gazes spellbound. Neither of us could speak for several moments.

"So, you know." She spoke quietly as she sat next to me on the steps.

Was she relieved she didn't have to be the one to tell me—that I found the article and read it for myself? Tucked toward the back of the house, the stairs provided privacy from the shouts of my siblings' laughter. Right now, we needed this quiet moment together.

But the quiet didn't last long.

"I have questions," I blurted. Where had that come from? I hadn't planned on saying anything and wondered what my mother would think. Her answer surprised me.

"So do I, Katie." She sighed. "So do I." She pushed a long strand of hair away from her face. Her thick brown hair had fallen out of its usually tidy knot at the back of her head.

Could this be my chance to ask what was going on? Children were not supposed to question authority. Neither were adults, for that matter. Then I remembered the reverend was out in Dad's shop. Once in a while, a customer would ask to use the bathroom, which sat just off the kitchen. What if he came into the house and heard us talking? Saw us reading the paper? Asked what we were doing? What would my mother say?

"How?" I began, hoping the question was safe enough.

"Dana was troubled, Katie," she said in a small voice. I had to lean forward to hear her. Her eyes took on a faraway look.

"I know. But ... this? Killing herself?"

"Mrs. Tyner has spoken with Mrs. Kelley."

Mrs. Pam Kelley, the classy and polished wife of church elder Ross Kelley, apparently revealed Dana had backslidden.

I tensed and narrowed my eyes at my mother. "That's your explanation?" I dared to question her.

Thankfully, she ignored the tone. "Not mine, Katie. Mrs. Kelley's. I told you—I have questions too."

I looked down at the newspaper article clutched tightly in my hand. I could picture Mrs. Kelley now—flawless makeup and expertly styled hair—shaking her head in mock sorrow, telling anyone who would listen that Dana had backslidden, and we must all separate from her until she repented.

Backslidden. A loose term members of Cross gave to those who did not comply or obey the rules the reverend set forth. Once a person became saved by accepting Jesus into their heart, they were to begin an instant transformation within their soul and their lifestyle. Many were able to adapt to the demanding changes that were required. Those who struggled were counseled. People who did not conform were disciplined. Anyone who did not confess and reform their sinful ways was considered backslidden and cast out of the fellowship. No one could have further contact with them unless the reverend was convinced they'd fully repented of their transgressions. Only Reverend Abbott got to decide whether they were to be permitted back into the fellowship. He called out anyone who left the church without his approval, charging them with leaving in an improper fashion and for unbiblical reasons. These people were also to be avoided.

"Backslidden?" I tried to keep the scorn out of my voice but failed. "I know she had a rough history. But was anyone helping her? Or did they just cast her off to the side because she didn't fit in with the rest of us?" I was being bold, but I didn't care.

"I think there were people trying to help her," Mom responded weakly.

"They weren't!" I spit out the words.

"How do you know that?"

"She told me. The day she was here. People only pointed fingers and judged her."

Mom finally looked at me. "What else did you and Dana talk about?"

My mouth snapped shut. There was no way I would betray Dana now.

Mom patted my leg and blew out a long breath. "All we can do now, Katie, is pray for Preston. Wherever he is." She stood and walked away.

For the first time, I was disappointed in her. She knew I had questions, and she walked away. Why? Did fear compel her to withdraw? What if she knew her oldest child was aware of more unsettling things than she could even begin to presume?

CHAPTER 9

UNDERMINING AUTHORITY

The next morning, I yawned and pressed the dial on my electric blanket to the off position. Even in April, nights were chilly. Our mud season began with warmer days melting the snow into slushy puddles and soft brown muck. By far, April showed itself the ugliest month of the year in New England, with sludgy roads and leafless trees.

Except for those who loved to ski, the last few weeks on the slopes were highly sought after as the balmy weather allowed the powdery snow to thaw and pack the trails. This meant faster runs, less spray, and fewer trips to the lodge to defrost. We had just finished our spring skiing at Tanger Mountain Ski Resort with the promise of lifts reopening in the fall for foliage viewers.

Squinting in the early morning sunlight bursting through my window, I spotted my blue suitcase near my bedroom door and sat up with excitement.

Rocky Springs' annual student holiday. All high school students looked forward to the three-day, two-night spring break camp. As always, the school rules applied, but we relished our times at the Rocky Springs Resort. It was our chance to take a break from school, recharge, and blast each other during either our supervised games or unsupervised pranks.

Hiding in the mountains of Arwell Notch, the little town of Arwell was about an hour and a half drive from Twin Rivers Junction. A well-kept secret, the resort could easily be missed as one drove past on the interstate. The beautiful retreat was unique for its privacy. Each dorm, the main lodge, and several outbuildings were obscured by circles of pine, birch, and maple trees. Each spot boasted its own slice of heaven under the protection of the trees, nearby lake, and rocky mountain face.

"Katie," my dad called from the bottom of the stairs. "You up? You need to leave early to get on the bus for camp, right?"

"Be down in twenty," I called, zipping my almost-forgotten bathing suit into my case. The newest addition to the resort was the indoor swimming pool, where my friends and I made fools of ourselves, jumping and splashing in the heated paradise. Next, we cooked like lobsters in the large jacuzzi while trees as tall as skyscrapers danced for us against the blue skies outside the glass ceilings of the aquatic center.

Of course, we disliked the devotional time because it took us away from games and socializing. We had to sit and endure the pressures of saving our souls from eternal hell for the thousandth time. Was there really one among us dumb enough not to have gotten saved yet? At least, we could tolerate preacher Perrin Grayson without much difficulty. A longtime acquaintance of Reverend Abbott from seminary, Evangelist Grayson was one of the few guest speakers the students of Cross appreciated. He delivered his short messages with kindness, not judgment. He even enjoyed participating in games with us, and his gentle manner was refreshing.

A short time after I'd carried my suitcase downstairs and finished breakfast, my dad rifled through the junk mail on the counter for his keys to the Volkswagen. Our kitchen counter, both dumping ground and a launching pad for our daily routines, remained a constant disaster.

"Where'd I put them ..." he muttered. He lifted a pile of hunting magazines, causing a large stack of papers to slide onto the kitchen floor. He bent down to pick them up and announced, "Got 'em. Ready to go?" He stopped and turned when I didn't respond.

I held one of his auto repair orders he'd accidentally left on the counter. Usually, he put these in his office, but this one had been left behind.

The work he'd done on the reverend's car.

"What does N/C mean?" I asked.

"No charge."

"No charge? Like, he didn't pay you?" I asked, incredulous.

"Correct," he replied, offering no details.

"But why? You worked on his car. Why didn't he pay you?" I had never heard of my dad doing a job for free. This was his business, his means of earning a living.

"Katie ..." He held up a palm as a sign for me to stop this conversation.

"But—"

"The pastor gets double honor." My dad's voice took on a serious tone. "This is a decision I made for Reverend Abbott. Sometimes doing the right thing requires a few sacrifices along the way."

The ride to school was subdued. I got on the bus with a smile for my friends but decided to take a seat by myself in the back. Ignoring the chatter and excitement of the group, I noticed Del glancing back at me with curiosity. I sent him a reassuring wave, knowing he was not permitted to sit next to me on the bus.

I turned my attention out the window as the bus jerked forward, torn between enthusiasm about the retreat and my growing distaste for recent events.

Unable to push her away any longer, I allowed Dana Terrell to swim to the surface of my mind. I thought of the things she revealed to me and wondered why she chose to tell them to some random teenager.

Maybe no one else would hear, the voice of my conscience whispered.

We let her down. She tried to do the right thing, but it wasn't enough.

One of my questions had answered itself. The gravity of this understanding surprised me, and I felt somewhat relieved. Dana's death was not about her wanting to end her life. She gave up because those who should have cared gave up on her. They pointed fingers. They decided she was scum, no better than the dirty rags my dad used to clean his oily car transmissions—or so she must've felt when she put that gun to her head.

I knew, somehow, this could not be how God wanted things. He did love everyone, didn't he? Even Dana Terrell. Did he really speak to us only through Reverend Abbott?

The reverend.

Maybe this wasn't about God or the Bible at all. This was the reverend's doing. Despite all the harsh condemnation he grilled into us, there must be a God who loves us equally. A sense of relief came over me. But with it, a grave reality. Even though the source of my struggles consistently pointed back to the reverend, there wasn't much I could do about it. Not without getting myself or my parents in trouble.

I decided to keep track of everything happening around me. My new, self-appointed role at Cross would be the silent observer. Maybe I needed to write things down and tuck them away in a notebook or something.

A journal.

Yes. That would work. My mother kept a journal. Was she secretly doing the same thing? She did admit she had questions, just like I did. Were they questions about Dana or something more?

There must be a way to find out.

Just as I began to plot out my new mission, Rachel Abbott floated over to my seat in the rear of the bus and sat next to me.

"What are you doing?" She tipped her blonde head to one side. "I almost didn't see you back here. Wake up. We're almost there."

"Oh, right." I blinked, hoping I sounded cool. Sometimes Rachel made me nervous because I never quite knew what her relationship with her father was like. Did she tell him things? Was she one of his spies? Did she even have a choice?

"I'm so glad camp is finally here," Rachel continued. "My itinerary includes snowmobiling, eating trash, and watching Jolee come up with some good pranks. You?"

"Totally with you." I laughed as the bus slowed down in front of a glittering gold sign that told us we had arrived at our destination. Several whoops echoed against the yellow roof of the bus. Exhilarated, I allowed the contagious merriment of my fellow high schoolers to drift over me, helping me forget about the reverend. And Dana.

At least for a while.

We were in awe once again of the Rocky Springs Resort main lodge. Upon entering through the heavy oak double doors, the reception desk was on the right. A large sitting area occupied the left side, complete with a crackling fireplace, leather couches, and an intimidating statue of a stuffed bear taller than a grown man. In between his giant claws, the bear held a chalkboard sign that led hungry travelers toward the Cave, also known as the cafeteria.

Furnished from top to bottom with bear décor, the Cave looked as if a giant tree house had been plucked from its boughs and relocated here at Rocky Springs. Stair rails made of thin, gnarled tree limbs served as banisters that led up to an upstairs loft with dining tables for additional seating. Downstairs held an assortment of picnic and farmhouse-style tables. Bear, cave, and mountain ornamentation covered every visible wall space. The owners must've taken years to accumulate and assemble it all here. Each year, we attended this magical place. I was always impressed.

Boy, I need this right now.

After a delicious dinner of chicken tenders, baked macaroni and cheese, and salad, we dispersed for evening games outdoors. But Jolee and I had made other plans. We did our best headache routine to bow out of the game in the field below us. We needed to reflect on what happened just a few hours after we arrived at the resort.

"Are you believing this?" Jolee angrily waved her arm in the direction of the group playing flag football below. Outdoor lights illuminated the field, making the few patches of remaining packed snow almost glow.

Two parent chaperones who were scheduled to be on this trip had a sudden family emergency, so they were not able to participate. Before the reverend called off the retreat, Mrs. Sullivan and Mrs. Fisher volunteered to take their places. Almost every high school student wished the reverend *had* called off the trip rather than have these teachers watch our every move. Many of us believed the entire holiday would be nothing but a drag.

Just then, Brynn caught sight of the two of us watching from our balcony. "Fakers!" she called up at us while Karina pretended to play a small air fiddle.

"Shut up!" Jolee shot back.

As soon as the laughing pair ran back into the game, I sniffed the air hoping to distract Jolee from her bad mood. "You smell that?"

"What?" She made a face.

"Smells good out here." I inhaled the cool air. "It's not that cold. Smells like spring is coming. Maybe it's the mountains."

Jolee wrapped a blanket around herself and sat in a rocking chair. "I don't smell anything. You know, I have a real headache. I got it the second Dead Fish and Sullivan crashed our vacation."

I grunted. "Can't argue that."

"You know those two did this on purpose. They've been itching to come to a camp like this so they can see how many fines they can pass out. I'll bet they have a competition going. Whoever gets the most infractions gets to—"

"Jolee!" I interrupted, cringing at her tirade. "What's wrong?"

"I'll tell you what's wrong. It's my whole jacked-up life."

"What do you mean?" Was she speaking of church and school? Did she see things the way I did? Jolee was not one of the more obedient kids. Her tongue and temper were proof of that.

"Nothing. Hey, did I tell you I have a part-time job?"

"What? Where?"

"After school and this upcoming summer. At the college downtown. Just some simple filing work in the office. I started last week but didn't mention it then 'cuz I didn't know if I'd like it. But it's not bad, really. I've met some nice people."

"What kind of people?" I was a little concerned about my friend having a job at the downtown community college. As the school was infamously known around town for parties and drugs, my parents had mentioned from time to time that this was no college they wanted any of their kids to attend. Like the reverend would permit that anyway.

"I just told you. *Nice* people." Jolee shrugged.

"Like?"

She sighed. "Okay. I met someone. A guy."

My eyes widened. "Are you guys hanging out?"

"Not yet." She grinned. "But I hope to soon. You'd better not tell anyone."

"Of course not. But ... be careful, okay? What if he's a drug addict or something? You're only sixteen. Do your parents know? Your mom?"

"Geez, if I didn't know better, I would think *you're* my mom." Her ill-tempered tone returned just as Mrs. Fisher's air horn blew, signaling the start of the evening message with Preacher Grayson.

"Come on, Katie," Jolee said, with contempt coloring her words. "Let's go *pray*. Pray I don't knock Fisher out with that air horn."

The first level of the ladies' dorm contained a large meeting hall mostly used for events or company conferences. During our student holidays, rows of chairs were placed in front of a small lectern. After a message from the evangelist, we would play more games, eat junk food, and socialize for the remainder of the evening. Staying up late was a given, and we often joked about sneaking out—even though none of us had the nerve to do it. One caught in such a transgression would surely get the fine of their life, as well as the embarrassment of being sent home from camp.

We were hit with a surprise when, instead of us scattering after the final prayer of the evening, Mrs. Fisher went to the lectern and instructed all the students to sit back down. We looked around with puzzled expressions and noticed Evangelist Grayson also seemed confused. An uncomfortable silence settled over the room.

"Mrs. Sullivan, will you come up here, please?" Mrs. Fisher called.

Sporting a deep frown, Mrs. Sullivan hurried over to stand next to her vicious friend. After whispering something in her ear, she nodded and crossed her arms over her chest like she was standing guard. The evangelist stood awkwardly off to one side, clueless to their plan.

"All activities for the evening are canceled," Mrs. Fisher declared sternly. "Mrs. Sullivan and I have heard murmuring and complaining among you. There is an attitude of ungratefulness in the room which will not be tolerated. Boys, you are to return to your dormitory and read your Bibles. Girls, you will remain right where you are."

Everyone exchanged bewildered glances, not sure what to do first. We watched as Preacher Grayson's expression went from confused to surprise. He gathered his Bible from the lectern and gestured for the boys to follow him.

Chairs scraped the floor as the boys stumbled to their feet. Jolee sat next to me, watching the teachers with venom in her eyes. She called them ugly names under her breath. I closed my eyes and prayed no one else had heard.

Mrs. Fisher stood by, waiting for the boys to shuffle out of the room. A few minutes later, a thump came from the corridor, followed by a loud howl. Several of the girls gasped. I wondered who would dare make that kind of ruckus after we had just lost our privileges. The muffled snickers coming from the hallway only made the teachers angrier.

Jumping into action, Mrs. Sullivan threw the door open with such force, it banged on the opposite wall. She screamed at the boys so loud, I was curious if there were any other guests staying at the resort who heard her. Her screeching could be heard all the way down to the pool house. I knew Mrs. Sullivan was mean, but I had no idea she could raise her voice in such a manner.

"It has come to my attention," Mrs. Fisher addressed the girls, "that there has been some backstabbing regarding Mrs. Sullivan's and my presence here at camp this year. My own daughter Krystal came to me in tears this afternoon upon overhearing her best friend making rude comments, along with others."

Oh no. This wasn't good. She was calling people out. All heads turned toward Krystal, seated next to her best friend, Molina. Krystal started crying, most likely from the embarrassment her mother was causing. A high school senior and big crybaby, Krystal often bawled for no good reason. Molina ignored her tearful friend and flushed bright pink.

"Guess that friendship's over," I muttered under my breath.

"How do you think it makes my daughter feel," Mrs. Fisher continued, "when she hears hurtful things about one of her family members?"

Jolee snorted. "Who cares?"

"Shut up." I nudged her in the ribs. I swear, sometimes she was her own worst enemy. Good thing she had me around to protect her.

"Something you want to add, Jolee? Katie?" Mrs. Fisher called over several heads that turned toward us.

Oops. Too late.

"Come now, let's get this out in the open. I understand that you, Katie, enjoy a good rule-breaking now and then. You too, Jolee. Well?"

My jaw fell open at Mrs. Fisher's unfounded accusation. I was so caught off guard I sat there speechless, the color in

Molina's face finding its way to mine. I dared steal a glance at Jolee. She sat rigidly, but I could almost feel the heat of anger kindling inside her. I knew her well, and I was afraid one day she would not be able to control her temper.

"Say nothing," I said between my teeth so only she could hear.

A noise drew my attention to the left, and I realized Rachel was snapping her fingers behind her back trying to get my attention. She looked directly at me and shook her head. I took this as a warning to keep quiet. She appeared shaken by what was going down tonight. I knew she would go home and tell her dad everything, and for once, I welcomed it.

"Ah, I see," Mrs. Fisher said smugly. "We can say things behind people's backs, can't we? But not to their faces?"

She was trying to bait me into losing my cool. I sat quietly, facing forward, unmoving and unblinking. By not reacting, I knew I could beat her at her own game. *Go ahead and make your example out of me.* I told her in my head.

Finding some hidden spunk, I returned Mrs. Fisher's icy look with one of my own. I speculated—with some degree of concern—that Jolee's fire was beginning to rub off on me. Or maybe I'd just had enough.

Soon, Mrs. Fisher looked away and called a demure teen out of the group. She asked her to come to the lectern, then put her arm around the wide-eyed girl and told everyone she was an example of what a godly young woman looked like and proceeded to lavish praise on her.

"Like hell," Jolee croaked out of the corner of her mouth.

Everyone knew the only thing Talma was good at was being a fantastic actress in front of adults. I found it amusing she had somehow secured Mrs. Fisher's outrageous status of approval and made a mental note to give Talma a high five later for such a great performance.

"The remainder of the evening will be spent in prayer and Bible study." Mrs. Sullivan now stood at the lectern while Mrs. Fisher was busy hugging Talma. "You are dismissed to your rooms, but there is to be absolutely no talking." She motioned for us to stand and exit.

The walk to our rooms felt like those old walks of shame I used to make to the principal's office. I could see the girls looking at me, feeling sorry for the way I had just been treated. Molina kept her head down. Krystal looked like a lost puppy.

Over the next few days, we managed to survive without further catastrophe. Preacher Grayson delivered refreshing messages to us in the morning and evening but disappeared for most of the day's programs. Some minor infractions were passed out for accidental hand touching during game time. Any excitement was easily kept on the down-low because it had already gone up in a puff of smoke as soon as Mrs. Sullivan and Mrs. Fisher waltzed in. When the bus arrived back at school on Saturday afternoon, parents, expecting to welcome their tired but upbeat teens, confronted downtrodden faces instead.

"All right," my father said as we drove out of the parking lot. "What happened?"

"That obvious?" My laugh was bitter.

"Not just you. Everyone seemed upset. Even Evangelist Grayson. So?"

Over the next ten minutes, everything spilled out about the weekend. I made no apologies for how I talked about Mrs. Fisher and Mrs. Sullivan, at least being prudent enough to keep my contempt on the back burner—for now. After I finished, I could tell my dad was deep in thought.

Still think Reverend Abbott is right to preach that we should never question the teachers? I wanted to ask. But I didn't. I had a hunch none of this was over just because camp had concluded. Preacher Grayson's somber face came to mind. He was probably talking with the reverend right now, and I hoped he left nothing out. I resolved to be patient and see how all this played out, confident I had done nothing wrong, much to the disappointment of the dirty-dog camp directors.

I spent the rest of the afternoon decompressing by going to the horse farm next door to ride Aaron. While I enjoyed my own horse, she could be fickle at times and not always in the mood to be ridden. In such a snit, she'd try to buck me off. Aaron was one of our neighbor's many horses and my favorite. Since he was older, my neighbor appreciated me coming by to exercise him from time to time. A gentle Appaloosa with a white coat and gray spots on his back end, his gray muzzle felt like silky taffeta. He would close his eyes when I reached one hand behind his head and used the other to scratch his whiskers.

"Hey, old man," I murmured, giving him a kiss. "Miss me? Feel like a walk today?"

Aaron dropped his head and nickered in response as if to say, "Let's go." I grabbed the bridle off its hook and slid it gingerly between his teeth and up over his ears, letting the reins rest behind his mane. After loosely securing the throat latch, I lifted the brown leather saddle over his back and buckled the girth under his belly.

"Not too tight," Shana called to me as she brushed down a quarter horse in the next stall. She was the owner of the farm and the one who had taught me everything I knew. "He's getting fat in his retirement."

"Aw, you hurt his feelings." I laughed as Aaron pawed at the ground, as if in offense.

I clicked my tongue against my cheek twice, as I steered Aaron out into the old rear training field. He trudged along the familiar trail through the tall grass.

"Remember this, buddy?" I asked as we walked. The field had once held a large jumping course. Several fences placed lengthwise at different levels completed a row, and barrels were placed sideways at another. Aaron and I used to like jumping barrels the best. I could still remember the anticipation of the jump as it approached. I held my breath and gave him enough slack in the reins to gain the momentum to execute the jump. He always delivered, and we made a great team. Unfortunately, since Shana had downsized her farm, she no longer trained or jumped the horses as many of them had gotten too old. Today, the field was absent all its obstacles, leaving the grass to grow tall where it had once been trampled flat by horse hooves.

"Too old for that sort of thing now, huh?" I patted Aaron's neck. "Sometimes I feel like I'm getting too old for certain things too." I then proceeded to empty my heart of all I had bottled up. Aaron just walked and listened, his ears occasionally twitching to remind me he was still paying attention.

An hour later, I walked Aaron back to the barn. I removed his tack and brushed him down. I led him to his stall, patted his neck, and thanked him for one more ride. He plodded over to his feed bin. As I closed the lower half of the Dutch door to his stall, I exhaled, feeling calmer than I had in weeks.

"Okay. Thank you, sir." My father held the phone in the kitchen as I entered the house. My mother tended to something on the stove that smelled amazing. I watched my dad as he hung up the phone and turned to me.

"That was Reverend Abbott," he said. My mother turned with a spoon in hand and crinkled her eyes together. "You're not going to believe this," he continued, "but he wanted you to know, Katie, that he is very displeased about what happened at camp."

"Really?" I was surprised. And then again, I wasn't.

"As you know, Mrs. Fisher and Mrs. Sullivan were not supposed to be there. They just stepped in to fill a need. Evangelist Grayson had some very unpleasant things to say about them and the way they handled things. He even left to go back home. He was going to preach tomorrow at church, but he was so upset he's decided not to come back."

"Oh," was all I could say, disappointed to hear he would not be preaching, but I couldn't ignore the guilty pleasure I felt at Mrs. Fisher and Mrs. Sullivan getting into trouble with the reverend. I wondered what sort of repercussions this would have for them. I doubted we'd be so fortunate as to have them fired.

"Apparently," my dad was saying, "the reverend is also upset that Perrin Grayson left the way he did and is equally upset with your teachers. He had not given them the green light to act the way they did, so he views that as undermining his authority."

"Well," I said, treading with caution. "In some ways, I guess he's right."

"He also wanted me to mention to you that this subject is now closed and not to be discussed at school."

"All right." Did my dad—or Reverend Abbott, for that matter—really think the student body would not talk about this? Preacher Grayson leaving and stating he would not return was a big deal. Members of the congregation were going to have their opinions about that. Looks like the reverend would have to dig out his fire extinguishers and do some damage control.

A feeling of satisfaction came over me. Pride that I kept my own irritation in check, plus the bonus of knowing Mrs.

Fisher and Mrs. Sullivan were going to get chewed out by the Reverend.

My mom eyed me. "Everything okay?"

"'Course," I smiled. I could not discuss things that had transpired at camp or even my own decision to begin keeping a record of the happenings at Cross. I would do this alone and in private.

And I was ready for the challenge.

CHAPTER 10

TROUBLED

I was getting concerned about Jolee.

Something was wrong. I could sense it. No longer laughing or joking, she'd flare up like a Fourth of July sparkler and burn herself out within minutes. This happened more than usual, leaving me to dance on eggshells around her. Hoping she wasn't depressed, I tried to cheer her up.

"Hey, Jo," I'd call to her as we headed to our lockers after another dull literature class delivered by Mrs. Sullivan.

"What?" she'd respond, seeming uninterested.

"Want to come by my house after school?"

"Umm," she'd say, fumbling through her backpack. "I'm working today."

"I thought this was just a part-time job."

"Some other time." She'd wave to me as she left.

Brynn and Karina had noticed too. She didn't want to hang out with anyone these days and wasn't passing along her customary gossip. As usual, everyone went about their normal business, laughing and chatting. They couldn't care less about Jolee since the two friends she normally gravitated to were Brynn and me. Besides, her bad habit of speaking her mind had earned her a reputation.

Trouble. That's what people called her. I could see why they thought that, but if they got to know her a little, they'd see this was just her way of joking around. Everything else was merely a façade.

To hide what? I often wondered but never asked.

After several unsuccessful attempts to be witty like Jolee, I finally gave up and asked her what was going on.

"Nothing," she replied. "Hey, can you do me a favor?"

"Of course."

"If anyone asks, I'm going to your house today."

"You are?"

She rolled her eyes. "No, but if my mom calls or whatever, I'm at your house. I have somewhere else to be."

"Like where?"

"I'm going to hang out with Robbie."

I frowned. "Who's Robbie?"

"Really, Katie?" She sounded annoyed. "My boyfriend, okay? We've been seeing each other for a few weeks."

"Oh, is this the guy you met at—"

"Yeah, at work. Satisfied? Just help me out this one time, okay?"

"Uh, okay. Sure." I didn't know what else to say, so I caved. I suspected this Robbie guy was older if he was already in college. That meant he had access to stuff she didn't. Stuff that was prohibited by Cross—or by law, for that matter. I groaned. What was Jolee up to? What would I say to her mom if she called looking for her? I figured the best thing to do would be to say she was in the bathroom with a stomachache. I had never been a fan of lying because the rules at Cross and even at my home were so tight that the chances of getting caught were high. But I was worried saying no would push her further away from me.

She'd better not get me in trouble, I thought as the final dismissal bell rang and school let out for the weekend.

I froze on the church stairs from the basement area, where I used the restroom before service began.

Another Sunday, another sermon, I had whispered in the bathroom mirror a moment ago while I smoothed out my long curls. After losing the battle with my hair, I was about to run up the steps to the sanctuary when I overheard voices on the landing. Since Jolee no longer transported juicy gossip, I had to find my own entertainment.

But this wasn't funny. Crouching down behind a post at the bottom of the stairs, I leaned against the wall and looked up. From my vantage point, the three ladies standing on the landing could not see me, but I could see and hear them.

"There now." Mrs. Kelley tried to soothe June Britton, who wiped tears from her face while trying to stifle sobs.

"You're doing the right thing, June." This from Sally Gordon.

Great. Sally the idiot.

I had sized-up Sally during a midweek prayer meeting. While the men convened in the basement for prayer, the women spread out over the sanctuary in small groups. Sally ended up in the same prayer group as my mother, Renata Tyner, and me. She was overbearing and acted ridiculous when talking about our *wonderful* reverend. One might think she was infatuated with him. My mother sent me a sharp look when I made a gagging sound—which I quickly covered with a cough.

"Oh, Katie," Sally gushed. "Are you sick? Let's pray for you tonight."

Clueless.

"You did the right thing by leaving him," Mrs. Kelley was saying now, her hand resting on June's shoulder. "If Glen chose not to come back to church, then we must separate from the ungodly works of darkness."

I caught my breath. June left her husband?

"And" Sally put in, "the fact that God provided a home for you and your babies with your parents is proof his presence is at work here."

"But I still love him," June cried.

"The Lord will sustain you," Mrs. Kelley chided. "The reverend asked you to come forward and apologize so you can be welcomed back into the fellowship. God's kingdom is our destination. Things of earth will fade away and never last."

I knew by now I shouldn't be surprised at any unusual developments at Cross. But I found myself astonished by this line of thinking. How could these people believe the things they said? Were they condoning June for leaving her husband? Had he done something wrong? What was really going on here? What awful thing did June do that she needed to apologize for? Had she been church disciplined? And why did Glen choose not to return?

I squeezed my eyes shut in heartfelt pain for June.

After the assembly finished singing "What a Friend We Have in Jesus," everyone reached for their King James Bible, ready to hear what grandeur Reverend Abbott would cast over them today.

Except the reverend did not approach the pulpit, elder Ross Kelley did instead. He asked everyone to remain seated and listen to something June Britton had to say.

Wide eyes turned to the front of the church where June, no longer pregnant, rose and stood to the right of the pulpit in front of a free-standing microphone. I could see her legs shaking near the hem of her skirt. My heart dropped to my feet. The Bible I held quickly followed.

"Uh ..." June cleared her throat, her eyes glistening with leftover tears. "I wanted to ... to come up here today to publicly apologize for something I did." She looked over at Mrs. Kelley, who nodded for her to continue. "Um, not very long ago, I came to sing but ..." She faltered, trying to remember the words she had been coached to say. "I realize now I made a mistake in standing behind the pulpit, which was not my rightful place to be."

So, that's what had bugged the reverend. I knew something was off about that day but couldn't put my finger on it. June was the first woman I could remember who had stood behind the pulpit. Women were not to do that at Cross. Women were to be silent in the church except for standing next to the piano for scheduled music. The pulpit was a holy place reserved for men of God. Things were beginning to click into place, like jagged, thorny, hurtful pieces to a large, complex puzzle.

"With this apology, I have repented, and uh ... ask that my communion with you be restored." June heaved a big sigh when Mr. Kelley came to stand beside her.

"You have been forgiven," he told her. "You may be seated, June."

The reverend then rose from his sovereign chair behind the grand piano. He made his way to the pulpit, where he would spend the next hour pounding and speaking about God's intolerance for sin.

In my seat, I seethed. I'd perceived many things over the years—confusion, disappointment, surprise, and fear. But now I was angry, and this worried me. I knew I needed to be careful about hiding my anger, so I would not be observed and questioned.

And then another new emotion occurred. I felt sick at the escapade of June being forced to apologize in front of the church. My stomach fluttered as I imagined the trepidation June must have experienced before and during her apology. Poor woman. Not only had she recently given birth, but she'd also lost her husband.

Wait a minute. Had June Britton been coerced into leaving Glen? Because he refused to be a part of what was going to happen today? My stomach did another flip at the thought. I glanced over at my mom, this time not disguising the exasperation on my face.

She turned toward me. Usually, she kept her attention focused on the reverend and her journal. But there was something different about her expression today. *Am I seeing things?* I wondered as my eyebrows shot up. Her eyes narrowed, and her eyebrows crinkled. Was it my imagination?

And then, eye contact. This time it wasn't some fleeting glance. The look was real, and it said a lot. I was comforted in the knowledge I was not alone in how I felt. Maybe my chances for a real discussion about Cross Independent Baptist Church were improving.

I wondered if my dad—in the back room near the foyer working on the sermon recording and getting a final tithe count—heard June's apology through the sound system. Most of the time, this was Jack Kittredge's job, but he was not in service today. Strange. My dad did not usually get asked to do Jack's job. The sermon recordings were handed out to those who missed church for an excused reason so they could keep up with the reverend's preaching. Those who claimed ignorance about a topic of discussion were frowned upon.

So, what about those who cry foul about a topic of discussion from the reverend? I wondered.

Anyone who questioned the reverend was subject to church discipline.

Over the next few days, I worked hard at keeping my attitude in check. During Mrs. Sullivan's boring English lit class, I kept my nose in the textbook. The same went for Mr. Fisher's geography class while the rest of the students were falling asleep. When it was time for music in the sanctuary with Mrs. Abbott, I found satisfaction through singing and earned lead soprano for the small church choir. Warmed by compliments of my vocal abilities, I walked with the others to the school cafeteria after chorus and felt a new lightness in my steps. I began to wonder if music would be a way for my voice to be heard over the mounting heap of mistrust, confusion, and frustration that surrounded me at Cross.

Not long after I sat down to eat lunch, Jolee appeared, boiling mad.

"What's wrong?" I asked, frowning.

Jolee pointed in the direction of the other girls. "It's everybody. Karina just follows Brynn around, then there's Little-Miss-Perfect-Pastor's-Daughter Rachel, with Maryanne and Jessica tagging along. They're all idiots. Look at them."

I turned around to see the girls chatting and eating lunch. For years, Jolee maintained a deep resentment of Rachel. But I was aware there was more to her rage today than just a few silly schoolgirls.

"How about you tell me what's really bothering you," I said flatly.

"You might not like what you hear."

"Try me."

"Randy Sturbridge touched me in an inappropriate way."

I swallowed. "Excuse me?"

"He's been harassing me." Sparks ignited her eyes. "He's tried to fondle me a few times before."

"Randy? What?" I couldn't process it. My gaze traveled to where the boys sat on the opposite side of the room. Randy was laughing with his pals at their lunch table. I had known Randy for many years. As kids, we used to go sledding down Roganfield Hill when his dad used to run a tiny school in the next town over. Not long after the school property was sold, both our families joined Cross. Randy was a senior and his talents were the envy of many. At seventeen, he'd reached his second-degree black belt status in martial arts and had won several competitions. He spent most of his time perfecting his karate skills. He was also an accomplished skier and gave lessons up at Tanger Mountain. I was having a hard time believing he would touch Jolee. Usually, he directed his casual flirting toward Rachel or her friend Maryanne.

"Are you sure?" I asked, doubtful.

"Of course, I'm sure. Do you remember last month when we rode up the ski lift together? That's when it began."

"Oh," I remembered how she ditched me to ride up the lift with Randy. But he didn't seem interested in having her as a passenger.

"I've already told Principal Fisher about it," Jolee said.

"You what?"

Principal Fisher appeared. To my dismay, he strode over to our table and asked to see me in his office. Of course, the usual chatter in the room hushed. I felt eyes burning a hole in the back of my head. Frustration toward Jolee for dragging me into her drama rose to the surface.

"Thank you for not wasting any time coming to my office," Mr. Fisher said several minutes later. He slid a hand over his thinning hair, ensuring his comb-over was intact. Seated in front of his worn desk, I thought about the times I'd found myself here in elementary grades, particularly the third grade when his heartless wife sent me to see him. Those days, he'd just sigh and assign homework on the student desk in front of the window. He never treated me poorly, and for that, I was grateful.

"It has come to my attention that there has been an altercation between Jolee Tisdale and Randy Sturbridge."

He cleared his throat. "She has listed you as a witness to the allegations against Randy."

"A witness?" I responded, surprised.

"Yes. Jolee states that you saw Randy grope her on the ski lift during the first week of April." He pushed his glasses up the bridge of his nose and waited.

"Umm ..." I fumbled. "Well, I didn't see anything, not really."

"But you did see the pair on the ski lift alone together, correct?"

"Well, yeah. But—"

"You are Jolee's closest friend, are you not? I have seen the two of you together often. Has she told you anything concerning Randy?"

"Just that he touched her or something. She didn't tell me details."

"All right." Mr. Fisher jotted something down in front of him. "So, you're confirming the allegations?"

"All I know is what she told me. That's it." I shrugged.

"Do you believe her to be telling the truth?"

"Well ... I don't think she's ever lied to me before if that's what you mean." Deep down, I wasn't sure if I believed my best friend to be telling the truth. Would Jolee lie about something like this? Even to me? If so, why? What fueled her anger these days? She'd been distant and irritable for weeks, so maybe this was it. But could Randy do such a thing? I didn't see it as a possibility.

"That should be all for now, Katie. You may head over to your next class." And with that, I was dismissed. The first chance I got, I would question Jolee again as to what her problem was with Randy and why she had pulled me into it.

Thankfully, the rest of the week went without incident. Jolee had been standoffish with me about any further probing into her issues with Randy. Since I had not been called back into Mr. Fisher's office, I assumed the incident had blown over. That is until I bumped into Randy on the staircase after PE class.

"Why'd you do it, Katie?" His green eyes were angry.

"Do what?" I drew back in surprise.

"Did you know I'd get expelled?" He spit out the words. "Two months before graduation. How long have you known me?"

"Expelled? What are you talking about? Does this have something to do with Jolee?"

"You know it does!" he bellowed. "And you helped her. I never laid a hand on her. I can't even stand Jolee."

"I didn't help her," I insisted, feeling nauseous. "Mr. Fisher questioned me, but I didn't say I saw anything because I didn't. All I know is what she told me."

"You know me. And you just believed anything she told you. Guess what really happened. Jolee came on to me. I turned her down, and she was furious. She must've wanted revenge, and she got it. And she used you. How does that feel?"

"Randy, I ... I didn't know." I pleaded.

"Too late, Katie," he said in a calmer voice, now laden with disappointment.

One of my oldest friends turned on his heel and marched out the double glass doors, never looking back. Randy did not even say goodbye. He would never return.

And I barely made it to the girl's bathroom before I vomited.

I spent the rest of the afternoon in my room reading one of my favorite mystery books. When I tried to focus on the words, they blurred together from the tears that clouded my eyes.

Randy, my old sledding buddy, was gone. News of his expulsion for inappropriate conduct with a female student had gotten around the school. Jolee refused to look at me, but I saw a mixture of contempt and satisfaction on her face.

What was happening to my best friend?

I now knew she had fabricated the charges against Randy. What I didn't know was why, and she refused to speak to me. What had I done? Not only had I lost one friendship, but another seemed to be slipping away as well.

"Katie?" my mother called up the stairs. "Phone call for you."

"Hello?" I said into the receiver a minute later, hoping to hear Jolee's voice. I had been waiting for her call. I deserved an explanation.

"Katie?" a familiar voice said. "It's Mrs. Tisdale. I'm looking for Jolee, but your mom said she wasn't there. Is she on her way back home?"

Just great.

I took a moment to calculate the outcome of what this twenty-second conversation would mean for me later. Jolee had cost me a dear friend because of her lies. She had told her mom she would be at my house when she wasn't. For all I knew, she'd done this dozens of times, except now it caught up to her. How many lies had Jolee been feeding me? For how long?

How does it feel? Randy had asked right before he walked out.

Horrible. And I was not going to allow it to continue.

"I have no idea where Jolee is, Mrs. Tisdale." I stated.

"But she's been at your house every Friday." Mrs. Tisdale sounded confused.

"No, she has not."

"Oh." Concern crept into her voice. "So, you don't know where she is then?"

"Working, maybe?" I gave no other information because I had none to give.

"Working? Up at the college? But she quit that job."

I exhaled, weariness washing over me. Jolee's lies were stacking up, and now they were affecting everyone.

After hanging up with poor Mrs. Tisdale, I sank into a chair. Outside the dining room window, the tall evergreens nodded to me in the gentle spring breeze. "I'm losing her too," I mumbled.

Where are you, Jolee? Why are you pushing your family and friends away?

And then, another question came, along with an uneasiness. What has Jolee gotten herself into? And what repercussions would there be if that question were answered.

CHAPTER 11

COBB'S CAMP HELL

"Mom," I groaned. "Are we almost done here?"

I had been pushing the shopping cart through the grocery store for forty-five minutes. Not that helping my mom was a big deal, but listening to my younger brothers beg for sweets had gotten on my last nerve. The next thing I knew, the two of them were smacking each other on the arm.

"Almost done. Boys, settle down," my mother said as she crossed things off her food list.

"Hey, it's Mrs. Cobb." Marty pointed.

We turned toward the freezer doors where Mrs. Cobb stood with her own full grocery cart and four kids in tow. I grinned when I saw one of her little boys sneak a container of ice cream under a cereal box.

The Cobb family had only been here about a year. They had inherited a large piece of land in the mountains just north of Twin Rivers Junction. The tract held a hunting camp, and the Cobbs wanted to turn it into a retreat for families to reconnect. The camp had been in a state of disrepair, and Mr. Cobb was working night and day fixing up the grounds so they could begin having guests. Rumor had it all six Cobbs were living in a tiny fixer-upper on the property. I marveled this didn't seem to bother them one bit. They were happy and smiling when we saw them at church.

"Hi, Darlene," my mother said. "How are things at the camp?"

"Slow progress but coming along," Mrs. Cobb replied. Her face looked unusually tired. Dark circles hung underneath her eyes.

"That's good news." My mom smiled.

"We should get going," Mrs. Cobb said. "We need to finish homework."

"Oh, that's right. You homeschool. How is that going?" my mom asked, seemingly oblivious to Mrs. Cobb's abnormal demeanor.

My mother must have been curious to learn how homeschooling went for others because she had made the decision to homeschool my two younger siblings. Kyla started off poorly in kindergarten while attempting to sit still in a seat all day. The teacher had thrown her hands up in exasperation.

My youngest brother Mark, the quiet genius in the family and currently in sixth grade, was bored. Schoolwork was too easy for him. He completed any seatwork and homework in minutes and then sat with nothing to do for the rest of the day. The day Mark left class and showed up on the school roof to help the roofers patch a leak was the day my parents decided maybe he'd be better off going at his own pace.

"Between homeschool and working at the camp, we stay busy." Darlene was saying. She said goodbye and left.

Intriguing. Something was off with Mrs. Cobb. She didn't seem to want to talk with us today. Upon first meeting them, I was impressed at how this hardworking family had so much to be happy about. The Cobbs didn't have money. They didn't wear new things or drive a fancy car.

They didn't go on vacation. They felt led by God to start a Christian retreat so others could enjoy these luxuries. Their ministry was selfless in every way. I admired the sacrifices they made to follow their dream.

"Mom," I said later as we put groceries away, "did Mrs. Cobb seem kind of upset about something to you?"

"I don't think so." She stuffed lettuce and tomatoes into the refrigerator and muttered something about cleaning it out one day.

I sighed and dropped the subject. If she hadn't noticed, maybe it was just me? Maybe I had become too suspicious of everybody at Cross.

Still, I couldn't ignore the worried look I had seen earlier in Mrs. Cobb's eyes. And, as always, I could do nothing.

Finally, a quiet spot all for me. I set my textbooks down on the table and flicked the light on. The early May sunlight had not yet reached the school library windows on the west side of the building, making the room seem gloomy. I was eager to get my homework done during study hall so I could have a free afternoon. Most of my other classmates had gathered in the school cafeteria to discuss yearbook layouts. Since I only worked in photography, I was more than happy to dismiss myself from potential arguments.

I heard a sound behind me and realized I was not alone. Sara Kittridge's older brother Joey rushed past me and out of the library. I turned in the direction he had come from but didn't see anything. Just as I pulled out my notes for history, I became aware of a hushed noise coming from the rear wall of the library. I glanced around, but only saw shelves of books. If someone was there, they were hiding.

"Hello?" I called. No reply.

Knowing I'd never be able to concentrate on my homework without finding the source of the noise, I went to investigate.

"Leah?" I looked down in surprise at Brynn's younger sister sitting on the floor in the corner, crying. Her pretty blue eyes were red, and she wiped tears from her face the instant she saw me.

"You all right?" I asked. "I thought I just saw—"

Leah pulled me down next to her. "Oh, Katie, it's just awful."

"What is it? Are you okay?"

"It's not me. It's Sara. She's in trouble, and so is Justin." Leah took a deep breath. "Sara and Justin got caught."

My eyes grew wide. "Doing what?"

"Kissing. They kissed, and someone saw them and told Mr. Fisher. The reverend is furious and has issued a punishment for them."

"Wait." I held up my hand. "The reverend has issued a punishment? Why? I thought Mr. Fisher took care of the school stuff."

"Mr. Fisher must run everything through the reverend first. Didn't you know that?"

I didn't. The only thing that surprised me is I hadn't picked up on this until now.

Leah cleared her throat, calmer now. "The punishment is worse than a suspension or even expulsion."

"What is it?"

"Sara and Justin are suspended from school for one month, but that's not all. Joey just told me they have been ordered to work every day of their suspension up at Cobb's camp. Unpaid, of course. Since it's such a far drive, they have to stay at the camp and do labor every day. They can't come to school or church. A whole month. School will be nearly out for the year by the time they get back." Leah's face twisted.

UNDER AUTHORITY

Astonished, I leaned against the bookcase. A month's labor up at Cobb's run-down camp? That seemed severe. And why? Just because of a silly little kiss? I thought the school issued fines for physical contact between couples.

The reverend has issued their punishment, Leah had said.

He's making an example of them.

Labor? A month? Could the reverend see this through? Did he expect the Kittridges and Cobbs to go along with this extreme sentence? The entire situation seemed ludicrous.

Then, I realized it was already happening. Something had been bothering Mrs. Cobb at the grocery store. She had not said one word, but her distressed look ...

She couldn't tell you. The voice again.

She doesn't agree with it, I concluded. In fact, this could be tormenting her. And she can't do a thing about it.

I took a deep breath to calm my nerves. Leah stood up and handed me something.

"What's this?" I asked.

"Joey gave it to me. It's from Sara."

"How'd he get it?"

"He had to bring homework lists and books for Sara, so she passed him this note before he left."

"You okay with me reading it?" The folded paper burned a hole in my hand.

"Just don't tell anyone." Leah looked worried.

"I won't," I assured her. Since the library remained quiet and unoccupied, I opened the note and read.

Leah,

I have to be quick in case I'm caught writing this. But I want you to know I'm okay. The Cobbs are quiet and treating me well. They have separated Justin and I as they have been instructed. I get up early and help

them with anything they need, then do my homework at night. I think Justin has been doing more of the heavy stuff around the camp while I've been helping Mrs. Cobb with a lot of cleaning, painting, and even aiding her younger kids with their schoolwork. The bad part is at night when I'm alone in one of the cabins and it's chilly in there. I wonder how Justin is doing, but of course, we're not allowed to communicate. I don't even know where he is on the property.
I'm calling it Cobb's Camp Hell. See you in a month.
-S

I slid the note back to Leah, who stuck it in her skirt pocket. We both stood staring at the books around us, but I didn't see a single title. All I could see was Sara.

Leah sniffed. "I just don't get it."

"Get what?"

"Why such a harsh punishment?" Leah's voice rose. "It's not fair."

"Better keep your voice down. I agree it's not fair. It's crazy. But we don't make the rules, Leah. Reverend Abbott does."

Leah looked spent. I felt bad for Sara's best friend, who hadn't done anything wrong yet felt the effects of the punishment. And what about Sara's and Justin's families? Again, I wondered what their parents were thinking. Had they agreed to such a steep consequence? Had they gotten a chance to give their opinion on the matter? And what if they had disagreed with the reverend's choice? Maybe that would've gotten them sent to camp too. The irony of that happening made me laugh.

It struck me that a natural and happy thing like laughter could also be fueled by scorn and bitterness.

UNDER AUTHORITY

My emotions were bothering me. Try as I might to ignore them, it was getting more difficult. I noticed things with others, such as what they wore right down to their demeanor. If someone changed their hair at church, I saw. If someone wore a pair of new shoes, I noticed. If anyone was absent, I was aware of it. If a member wore a smug expression, I saw it. If a person looked upset, I could tell. If somebody was sad, I felt it. Could this be a gift or curse God had given me? A gift because I was observant and felt the energies of others. A curse in many ways because if something was wrong, I could not help them.

Who will help you? The voice spoke again.

And now my concern turned to myself. All my years at Cross returned to me then, and I was carried back to the moment when my parents first joined the church.

Until the age of six, I had never attended church with my parents. Sundays were for fun with Daddy and Mommy. Daddy didn't have to work on cars those days. Mommy didn't have to work at the dog hospital. And I didn't have to go to the babysitter's house. I was the happiest little girl playing with the huskies and horses and jumping in piles of leaves. At least until those two men showed up at the front door in scary dark suits one night after dinner.

"Ross Kelley," one of the suits said, thrusting a hand forward after my dad invited them in.

Why did he do that? I wondered. We were not supposed to talk to strangers. I was supposed to be in bed, but even as a little girl, I had to know who these strange people were in my family's house. Barefoot, I sneaked over to the stairs, slipped down a few steps, and peeked out the top railing. Good thing my great-grandma's huge desk blocked everyone in the living room from seeing me. I had a good hiding spot.

"We're here to invite you to our church, Cross Independent Baptist, over on Yeltan Road." This came from the one with the icky mustache. "Ever been to church before?"

"Uh, no. Not really." My dad shook his head.

"Do you know what it means to be a Christian?" This from the tall suit.

My dad answered the same way.

"Do you know God has saved you from your sins?" The mustache in the first suit spoke again. I didn't like him very much.

What's sin? I wondered. I yawned and decided this conversation was boring. I went back up the steps to my room.

That next Sunday, my mom and dad put a dress on me and took me to church. Thinking we were going to a wedding, I was excited at first until I realized how hard it would be to just sit and listen to another suit get up and talk about weird stuff.

And so it began ...

Now, here I was, ten years later, still feeling much the same way I did when I was six, except now I dragged a set of Samsonite baggage behind me. And in it, many years' worth of tormented feelings I'd tried to stuff away, hoping they'd just get lost.

But they hadn't. Instead, they grew as if the lock on the suitcase had finally burst open because it couldn't take its load anymore. I stared into its contents, seeing all my raw feelings reflected at me.

And this was why I struggled now. I knew nothing here was imagined or misread. Everything was real. But what could I do? Stuff it all back in the suitcase? That wasn't working. I needed to talk to someone about it.

My mom's voice came back to me. *I have questions too, Katie.*

Ask her, the voice said.

Later that evening, after dinner was over and my younger siblings were busy playing or finishing homework in their rooms, I waited for my dad to go in his office so I could snag my mom in the den. Was there really any good time to bring up concerns about Cross? I realized with a flutter in my chest I had no plan whatsoever for what I would say. Maybe I should raise a more recent issue so as not to overwhelm her with too much information.

"Mom, you busy?" I announced my presence as I entered the den where she sat reading on the day bed. Next to her, Dusty brushed the bedspread with his tail.

"No, what's up?" She set aside her book and gave me her full attention.

"I'd like to talk with you about something." I cleared my throat. Why would I be nervous? I had talked to my mom before, and we were in the comfort of our own home. I felt foolish.

"Sure." She scooted Dusty over to make room for me.

"Um, have you heard about anything going on up at Cobb's camp?" A question. That seemed safe enough.

"Just that they're working hard to get the camp ready. You heard Mrs. Cobb at the store the other day." She shrugged.

She doesn't know.

Choosing my words carefully, I told her about Sara Kittridge and what happened with Justin. I told her I thought Principal Fisher had decided on a consequence, but now the reverend had chosen their punishment for their wrongdoing. Making sure to leave frustration out of my voice, I told her their sentence. My eyes never left hers for one second as I wrapped up my story.

My mother remained silent.

What are you thinking? I watched her face.

Her countenance reflected much like that day at church when the reverend preached about—or rather against—Mrs. McKenzie. I knew my mother's face like the back of my hand. I knew when she was happy or if she had something on her mind. Her mouth might be good at staying zipped, but her eyes told a different story. This proved to be one of those times.

The warmth I'd seen on her face when I first sat down vanished, replaced with a dull stare. Her lower lip stiffened, and I could tell she had some inner dilemma.

Just tell me, I silently implored. Why did she sit there and say nothing?

"Any thoughts?" I coaxed. "I think this is what was bothering Mrs. Cobb on Saturday. She's such a nice lady. I could tell she had something on her mind, but—"

"How do you know?" Her voice broke through my rambling. But oddly enough, she seemed to be making a statement rather than asking a question.

"You mean, how do I know about Sara and Justin? Well—"

"No." She waved away that answer. "I'm aware kids talk at school. I want to know how you know things."

"What things?" I stalled. I didn't know how to answer her in a manner that wasn't going to get me or anyone else in trouble.

"Things that make you want to ask questions."

"Uh, I don't know. I just know that ... I have them." I imagined myself climbing one of the trees in the back field and had just stepped on a very thin limb. *Crack.*

Was that the crack of a branch breaking underneath my weight or my imagination hoping to hear a different fracture? Like one in the foundation of Cross Independent Baptist Church?

She fell quiet again, and I reached over and scratched Dusty's ears. He lifted his head and set it down on my leg so he could enjoy the attention.

"We are not permitted to question the reverend," Mom reminded me.

"I know," I said. "But you have questions too. You told me."

"I shouldn't have said that."

"Why? This is home. I'm not going to run off and tell anyone."

"You need to drop this, Katie."

"Are you serious?" I stopped rubbing Dusty and stood, barely able to hide my frustration. "How can you ask me to forget how I'm feeling. You said yourself you notice things. I do. I can't help it, and I can't help how I feel."

"Sit, Katie."

I did as I was told.

"Listen" She leaned a little closer to me. "We both have questions. But getting answers to these questions might be tricky. Give me some time, okay?"

"Okay."

"And this is just between us," she said as I stood to leave.

"Okay," I said again, my pulse quickening.

Was it really going to happen? After all this time? Was this her way of validating that something was wrong at Cross? Would my mother find out what's been going on with Reverend Abbott? How? She'd need to be very clever at asking questions or word would get back to the reverend. Would he impose church discipline on her?

You know he would, the voice responded. *He'd make an example out of her too*.

Nevertheless, I felt hopeful that answers would come one way or another.

Careful what you wish for, the voice warned.

CHAPTER 12

THE COVER-UP

Something was bugging my dad. Always the happy-to-help-you kind of guy, my father was not often without a smile on his face unless he was in his office paying bills and muttering something about money flying out the window.

Most mornings, he'd lumber up the stairs and make his rounds to our rooms, saying a chipper "wakey, wakey" or "rise and shine." We were so accustomed to it that not hearing it was puzzling. His manner had been more of a gruff "time to get up."

"Dad," Marty was saying on the way to school. "So, can we?"

"Uh, sorry, bud." Dad forgot his turn signal and took a left. "Tell me again."

While Marty pleaded his case again, I thought about reasons my dad would act differently. Could it be finances? Work? Couldn't be. My dad had vehicle repairs waiting for him. I knew his health was fine. So, what could be bothering him?

What bothers you? The voice of my conscience prompted.

Church. Reverend Abbott.

My brain reversed to the last service and stopped with a click.

"At the end of the message today," the Reverend told the congregation, "We will have a brief church meeting. I will be speaking to you about a disciplinary matter. Now, turn in your Bibles to 2 Corinthians 6:17."

I tried not to snort. Meeting? That meant the reverend wanted to notify his congregation of something important. We never actually *met* or were allowed opinions on matters concerning the church. The only one permitted to give their own assessment was Elder Ross Kelley. Of course, he never went against the reverend.

The reverend continued. "When you read the phrase, 'thus saith the Lord,' it should grab your attention. 'Wherefore come out from among them and be ye separate.' Separate how? Well, it's clear. Distance yourselves from those who sin."

I wondered how many folks were imagining scenarios of who sinned and who would get church disciplined next. I hoped it wasn't Jolee. I suspected she had fallen into some sketchy things that would get her in trouble at some point. And I still didn't know much about Robbie. I didn't have any answers because after she found out I didn't cover for her when her mom called, she refused to talk to me. I was desperate to know what she was involved in so I could try to help her. For a long time, it seemed that the embers of Jolee's anger at the world would ignite into a sea of flames, scorching everyone around her. Had she been caught? Had Reverend Abbott found out something from his spies? Would he really preach against the son or daughter of a member?

"Now, turn to Hebrews 13:7 and 17." Pages rustled. "We are instructed by God to remember those who have the rule over us. You might ask, what does this mean?"

Of course, no one asked. They wouldn't dare. There was no speaking allowed during a sermon. The reverend's hand came down hard on the pulpit. "It means to obey and submit! Obey your pastor! Obey your church leaders because we must give an account of you all."

Noises stopped.

"God has commanded us to separate from sin so that we're not tempted to join in. Yield not to temptation. The world tries to entice us into sin. There are many kinds of sin. The sin of fornication. The sin of adultery. The sin of disobedience. The sin of stealing. God's laws and commandments are there for believers to follow and obey."

Looking down at my empty notebook, I had every intention to take notes but couldn't bring myself to pen the words coming from Reverend Abbott's mouth. Instead, I drew meaningless lines and jotted down a few Bible verses. My mom took notes in her journal as usual. Before the message began, Mr. Hearn had asked my dad to sit in the back office near the foyer to monitor the sermon recordings. For some reason, Jack Kittridge was absent again.

"The actions of one of our church members have required my attention." His voice took on a more somber tone, as in one of disappointment.

All eyes were glued to the reverend.

"We have church officers here. You know many of them. Kenton Hearn leads worship. Ross Kelley is our church elder. Earl Simpson and Sam DeConner are deacons. And our church treasurer is Jack Kittredge." The Reverend closed his Bible and set it aside. "The treasurer is responsible for gathering the tithe and counting it after each service. This is the Lord's offering, is it not?"

It's Jack. I gulped. *He's done something wrong.*

"I have asked for the resignation of our church treasurer Jack Kittredge."

Hushed gasps rose over the crowd.

"Questions have been raised about the accuracy of the funds he oversaw. When confronted, Jack admitted guilt for his sin."

Exclamations were tossed back and forth to one another, along with a few whispers. Reverend Abbott frowned at the congregation. "Jack has been disciplined for his actions. He will be out of our fellowship and in silence for the duration of six months. He is not to be communicated with, and he will not be in our services. There is to be no gossiping about this. He would appreciate any prayers you can say for him at this time."

My eyes narrowed as my fingers gripped the underside of the pew in shock. I willed myself to remain calm and breathe. What was going on with the Kittridge family? First, Sara is sent to work at a camp for a month, and now her dad? Both her brothers, Joey and Jordan, had seemed detached lately. I couldn't imagine the toll this was taking on their family, especially Mrs. Kittredge. She must feel humiliated with so much negative attention. If only I could see her face and try to read it. But like her husband, she was not present in church that day. And who could blame her?

"Uh, Katie?" My dad had turned around in the car and tapped my shoulder, pulling me out of my thoughts. "You going to keep sitting there?"

"Oh, sorry." We were at school. How long had I been sitting there staring off into space? "Dad, is everything okay?"

"Sure," he replied. "See you at three."

My steps were slow. The scent of lilacs drifted over me, but I couldn't take pleasure in their delicate sweetness. Something was disturbing my dad beyond Jack Kittridge taking money from the offering plate.

Pull yourself together. You have school, and you have got to put the Kittridge family out of your mind.

Just as I reached the doors, they burst open. The entire high school class poured out past me.

"Katie, let's go. You're late." Rachel looped her arm in mine, forcing me to make an about-face. I followed the group away from the school and down the short path to the church building.

"Why is everyone going into the church?"

"She's amazing." Kyle drooled. "She got Mr. Fisher to excuse us from geography so we could practice our special music for graduation."

Loud shouts of praise for Rachel echoed throughout the group. She grinned and curtsied.

"What special music?" I asked.

"Better to practice our music for graduation during school hours rather than *after* school, don't you agree? Come on, I need you as soprano. Besides," her voice lowered to a whisper, "they love that I got them out of geo class." Rachel danced over to the grand piano on the platform.

I grinned. Why not? After all, the senior's graduation ceremony was right around the corner. At least I could enjoy some music for a while and postpone any nagging thoughts that insisted on hanging around.

I knew they'd be waiting for me later.

Dangling the Volkswagen keys in front of my dad later that evening, I said, "What do you think? It's Friday night, and I'm supposed to get some driving time in."

Harding's Driving School was run by Bruce and Kerry Harding, one of the younger families in the church. Since they had one of the few driving schools in the area, they hit all the local high schools in the region, whether private or public. Their business did well, and it often meant a lot of time in the car teaching teens the art of driving.

I had a good arrangement with them. Free driving school for babysitting. But I still had to get in my practice hours so I could take the test for my license. The reverend discouraged teenage driving, but he didn't have much ground to stand on by outlawing it. Would he really discipline a high school teen for obtaining a driver's license? He had his nonsensical rules and beliefs, but when it came to practical things like real laws, he was clever about what he dictated.

My dad sat at the dining room table and pretended to be deep in thought. "Well, let's see. Drive with a teenager. Hang on, I need to go find my old football gear."

I clicked my tongue at him in mock offense since we knew he had never taken any interest in football. Just then, Marty appeared in the doorway and wanted to know where we were going. Nosy boy.

"Just for a drive," I told him sweetly. "And I'm the one driving."

"Never mind." He pretended to run for his life.

"Need anything at the store while we're out, Jan?" my dad called into the den.

"Milk, please," she called back.

The evening was cool and pleasant as we drove away from Smead Bridge down past where the old fairgrounds used to be. I loved cotton candy there as a little girl and petting bunnies and goats. My favorite attraction was the gigantic Ferris wheel that towered over everything. But it was all gone now.

"I miss the old fair that used to come to town," I said to my dad as the last of the overgrown field disappeared in my rearview mirror.

"You do? Surprised you remember that."

"Why did it never return?"

"The people who ran it decided Twin Rivers did not provide enough business for them. The last few years it was here, it got smaller and smaller until no one showed up anymore. That land has been for sale for quite a while now. Guess no one wants it."

"That's sad." Just as I was about to make another comment, I realized we were approaching a bend in the road. That meant we were about to pass Jack Kittridge's house.

Our casual conversation came to an abrupt halt. I slowed the car as their old, gray-shingled house came into view. It seemed a small house for the size of their family, but their kids' ages were so spread apart it was almost as if they were a family of five, not eight. The three oldest kids were grown and had moved out of state. Joey, Jordan, and Sara were the youngest three, and Jordan was about to graduate. At times, I'd spend an afternoon at their house hanging out with Sara. Her mom taught us how to make homemade pickles. If Mr. Kittridge wasn't at work, he would be in his garage tinkering on his motorcycle. Which is right where we saw him as we drove by.

My dad raised his hand to wave but quickly put it down. He must have remembered we were not supposed to communicate with Mr. Kittridge. Thankfully, Jack did not look toward the road. I pushed harder on the accelerator so he wouldn't see us and think we had been sent by the reverend to check up on him. No doubt other people were doing that for him.

The next few minutes were quiet. At the end of the road, I came to a stop and pointed at the glowing yellow McDonald's sign in front of us.

"What do you think?" I asked my dad. "Sundaes?"

He checked his watch. "Sure, we have time."

Several minutes later, with sundaes in hand, we slid into a booth. I made sure to check the restaurant before we sat down. No one from church was present.

"Okay, Dad, what's been going on with you?"

"Is that why you wanted to take me for a drive tonight?" He chuckled, but his face looked grim.

"I saw your face when we passed Mr. Kittridge just now."

"Oh, that." He rubbed his chin and looked away.

"Yes, that. What do you think about all this?"

"I think it's all very unfortunate."

"That's it? Just unfortunate? First Sara, now her dad? What's going on with the Kittredges? Did someone see Mr. Kittridge steal money out of the offering?"

"No." My dad sighed. He removed his glasses, set them on the table, and rubbed his eyes.

"No? No, what?" I knew my dad was not pleased by my questions, but until he told me to stop, I would go ahead and ask them.

"Katie," he put his glasses back on and looked at me. "You're getting older now, and I'm going to tell you something you cannot say to anyone else."

My dad was going to talk—after all this time. Nothing could have made me leave my seat. My spoon froze midair. "Got it."

"No one else knows what I'm about to tell you. I shouldn't even tell you, but you always ask so many questions when you shouldn't."

"I promise. This conversation stays here."

He took a deep breath and glanced around the restaurant. An older couple sat toward the front. A group of scruffy-looking college-age boys laughed at something one of their buddies said. Other than that, the McDonald's was empty.

"Jack Kittridge didn't take a dime."

I almost dropped my spoon. "What?"

His face took on an almost grief-stricken look. I was not accustomed to seeing my dad like this.

"The theft was a cover-up." His voice was tight. "Jack did something much worse than take money from the offering. The reverend is trying to hide it from the members."

"What was it?" I asked calmly while my nerves raced.

"Your classmate Sabrina has an older sister, right?"

"Uh, yeah. Kendra. Why?"

"Jack had a sexual relationship with her. She was only seventeen at the time. It was consensual between them, but she was still under eighteen."

My head spun like a ballet dancer practicing her pirouettes. *Jack Kittridge cheated on his wife? With a girl young enough to be his daughter? Right under the reverend's nose?* I thought about Sabrina's older sister. She was in her first year of college, so this must've happened a few years ago.

"Kendra is over eighteen now, so how did this all come up?" I asked.

Dad frowned. "I don't know the details. I'm not supposed to know any of this."

"Then how do you know?"

"Mr. Hearn has been asking me to sit in the sound room and make sure the sermons get recorded. A few weeks ago, they were in the counseling room behind the baptismal."

"Who?" I was confused.

"Sorry. The reverend, Ross Kelley, and Jack Kittredge. Mr. Kelley had a lapel microphone and must not have realized it was on. As you know, Reverend Abbott likes the pulpit mike."

The picture of what really happened came into focus. Mr. Kelley said a prayer before the service that day, so it made sense.

"You overheard something you were not supposed to hear," I concluded.

"Exactly."

"And they don't know you heard."

"No, they don't know." He gave me a warning glare.

"And they won't know," I said. "So why not just come out and say what Jack really did? Why act like he stole money from the church?"

"Because he could do jail time, that's why."

"So, the reverend's actually doing him a favor?" I was a tad suspicious of that.

My dad gave a contemptuous laugh. "Not exactly. There's something in it for him."

"Like what?" This was getting more bizarre by the minute.

"For keeping Jack out of jail, the reverend has asked him to pay a fine to the church for what he did."

"A fine? To the church? Why?"

My dad lifted his shoulders and showed me two empty palms. "Why, indeed?"

"To make money then? Like you and Mom?"

He frowned. "What do you mean, like us?"

No use backpedaling now. "I overheard the arrangement the reverend made with you. He's acting as your lawyer now."

"Overheard that, huh?" His frown deepened.

"And I haven't said a peep to anyone. But back to Mr. Kittredge. How much does he have to pay the church?"

"I didn't hear that part. I was uncomfortable in that room. I slipped out the door and got some air before they came out."

"Does Mom know?"

He shook his head. "Nope, it will just upset her."

"Yes, I think you're right. Are you upset about how this was handled?"

"I don't agree with it." He paused for a minute. "Jack did something foolish, for sure. But the punishment isn't fitting the crime."

"What about Kendra's parents? Are they angry?"

He shrugged. "Don't know. I seem to recall Ross Kelley mentioning something to Reverend Abbott about Kendra moving down south or something. Who knows for sure?"

I suddenly had another thought. "What about Brynn's dad? He's a cop. Do you think he knows about this and is just turning the other way?"

My dad scrutinized me with a wary expression. "You should be a detective yourself."

"Sorry, can't help it."

"I don't think he knows anything about this. He is bound to that badge he wears. Mr. Kelley does a good job of protecting the reverend."

I nodded in agreement. "What are you going to do?"

"Nothing. I have no proof. It would be my word against theirs."

"But Jack must pay the reverend. He'll tell his side of the story. Won't he?"

"No. He doesn't want anyone to find out. He is embarrassed and afraid of jail. He wants this whole thing to go away as quickly and quietly as possible."

And the reverend made that possible.

I decided it was time to be bold with my father. "So, Reverend Abbott gets away with it." I wondered how my dad would take such a statement.

"For now, Katie." His voice was firm. "And you will say *nothing*."

"I promise you."

We looked down at the swirly mess in our plastic cups. Time to go. On the short ride to the grocery store, I stayed quiet and thoughtful. Sure, Mr. Kittridge made a big mistake. But what the Reverend did was far beyond normal, fair, or legal.

He's doing illegal things now.

Not just now. The voice again. *What about things you don't even know about?*

What surprised me was how grateful I was that my dad opened up and trusted me enough to tell me what was happening.

I knew what this meant. Change was possible.

CHAPTER 13

THE BRIEFCASE

"Katie?" my mom called. "Your dad was looking for this earlier. Can you take it out to him?"

"He's in the shop?" I took the checkbook from her.

She nodded. "I heard a customer come in. If they're still here, just leave it on his desk."

"Oh, I didn't hear anybody drive in."

"They came in early while you were still asleep."

"Who comes in early on a Saturday? That should be a crime," I joked.

Just as I reached the door of the shop, I saw the sign that Dad had tacked on the outside door for his customers. His errands were quick ones—taking us to and from school and his regular trips to the auto parts warehouse. The sign indicated he'd be back within an hour.

No big deal. I'll just leave this on his work desk, where he'll see it as soon as he gets back. The sharp odor of transmission fluid, coolant, and motor oil filled my nose the moment I stepped into the small corner of my dad's garage that he designated as his office. The area—comprised of a tall counter where my dad drew up his repair orders—was about the size of a powder room. He'd place them in order of service date on the hanging wall rack. Opposite the counter sat a well-worn bench for customers who had to wait for their car. A large assortment of old magazines lay nearby and judging from the dust that had accumulated on them, I guessed not too many customers were interested in the sport of hunting wild game.

As I set the checkbook on the open repair order on the counter, I happened to glance down and saw a name that made me do a double take.

Ross Kelley.

Strange. I couldn't remember the last time my dad had done work for him. He sent other business dad's way but not for himself since he preferred to drive newer cars that didn't need repairs. I craned my head around the open doorway of the cramped office and saw a large, unfamiliar car. That's when I heard a strange scuffling noise. I blinked. Did I just see that car shudder?

Creeping closer to the vehicle, I realized the full-size sedan appeared brand-new. The fluorescent lights overhead made the silver paint gleam like a full moon in the middle of the darkness of oily rags, dirty tools, and unused car parts. If this car were brand-new, what was it doing here? And where had that noise come from?

"Mr. Kelley?" I called out.

No one answered.

Deciding there was no harm in checking it out, I ran my hand down the car's smooth finish, stopping at the handle. As I clicked open the driver's door, I stepped back in surprise and stumbled over a box full of oil filters.

Crouched down in the soft, rippled seat, my brother burst into fits of laughter.

"Marty!" I yelled. "What's your problem?"

"I don't have a problem," he retorted. "I'm hiding."

"Hmm," I said, placing a finger on my cheek and pretending to be deep in thought. "In Mr. Kelley's new car? Did he say it was okay?"

"Uh, no. Have you seen Mark?"

"No. Why?"

"We're playing manhunt. He's supposed to be looking for me," Marty huffed. "Kinda getting tired of waiting in here."

"S'cuse me for interrupting your stupid game," I said. "But did it occur to you that you shouldn't be in here messing around with Dad's customer's cars?"

"It's just Mr. Kelley," he protested. "And I didn't touch anything, not even his suitcase."

I stared at my brother. "What suitcase?"

Marty pointed to a dark rectangular shape on the back floorboard. I opened the door and saw Mr. Kelley's black briefcase resting there. My heart skipped a beat at the sight of it.

Don't, the voice warned.

Grasping Marty's arm, I ushered him out of the shop and told him to get lost, or I'd tell on him for snooping. Of course, I had no intention of doing that. If I could get rid of him, I could do some snooping myself. I wondered if the briefcase contained work-related stuff or church. More than once, he had brought the briefcase with him on a Sunday. There had to be something important inside related to the reverend and the church. If it was pertaining to his job, he would have just left it there or at home. I had to know for sure.

While my thoughts assembled themselves in my head, I stood with my arms folded next to the open door of the car, glaring down at the black case. My imagination created terrible images of sirens going off the moment my fingers clasped the handle. Lights flashed, but these lights were twirling red and blue. As the ghostly form of two police officers apprehended me and forced me into handcuffs, I pleaded for help but was led away to jail.

Shivering at the preposterous scene in my mind's eye, I shook off the images with a nervous laugh. How would I get caught? My dad was out with Mr. Kelley and wouldn't be back for a while.

Just a quick look.

Leave it alone, the pesky voice of my conscience warned again.

But I couldn't.

I ran to the oversized door and peered out one of the tiny rectangular windows near the top. The driveway remained empty except for my mom's car. But she wouldn't come looking for me. She was too busy tending to her own things in the house, along with minding Kyla. Knowing I had only a matter of minutes, I hurried back to the briefcase. I hit the tiny brass buttons on the left and right—hoping fate was on my side, and the case was not locked.

The clasps snapped open. I lifted the lid as if a large cobra were coiled up and ready to strike. Instead, I was met with the strong smell of peppermint candies which lay on several manila folders.

Little kids at church liked Mr. Kelley because he always kept a full pocket of peppermint candies. They squealed with delight and offered a chorus of "Thanks, Mr. Kelley!"

I had not been one of those kids.

I tilted the briefcase to slide the candy out of the way, then reached for the first file. This contained what looked like order forms for one of his businesses, so I closed the file and reached for another. This one was labeled CIBC— Cross Independent Baptist Church.

Sucking in a breath, I jumped up and looked out the shop window again. No cars. I rushed back to the bench and grasped the file again. The first thing I saw was a series of documents I did not understand. But I had heard the terms *complaint, plaintiff,* and *defendant* before, and Cross

Independent Baptist Church's name was on the line that read *defendant*.

I gasped. *They're being sued.*

I wanted to take my time and read over all these forms, but I knew my father and Mr. Kelley would be back soon. What would they say if they caught me with these forms in my hand? What would they do?

You'd be church disciplined, came the silent reply.

As if pulled by an invisible force, my eyes traveled to the small square machine near the office.

The copier.

I can do this.

After scanning the driveway once more, I raced over to the copier and pushed the power button. My heart sank as I remembered this old thing took a while.

"Only a few pages then," I muttered.

I tapped my heel impatiently while the machine hummed to life. Before long, the glow around the power button turned green, indicating it was ready. I placed the first document on the glass, slammed the lid, and hit Copy. The light beam took its time sliding from one end of the glass surface to the other.

My heart rate increased with every second that went by. Was this thing ever going to get to the other end and spit out a copy?

Finally, I exhaled a long breath as a copy of Mr. Kelley's form dropped into the tray. I grabbed it and set it next to me on the workbench. As fast as I could, with my hands trembling, I slid in another important-looking form.

Last one. No time for another.

After enduring another eternity, I had the second document in hand. I took the two copies, folded them in half, and tucked them into the back section of my jeans, then smoothed my sweater over the top.

That's when panic the size of a baseball lodged in my throat.

Two car doors slammed shut just outside the garage door.

Blood rushed to my face, and I went into scramble mode. I leaped at the copier to shut it down. I then snatched the original documents, placed them in the manila folder, and rushed back to the car. I placed the folder labeled CIBC underneath the business folder.

They're coming! The voice shouted.

I no sooner had the briefcase closed and the door shut when the door to my dad's shop opened. Mr. Kelley was chuckling as he entered. I flew into the tiny room used for washing and rebuilding transmissions at the far end of the shop.

"Well," my dad said. "If all you really needed was a new air filter, this one was a good choice."

"Great. Thanks for giving it a look over," Mr. Kelley replied. "I'm not usually one for a used car, but this one was a steal at such low mileage and only a year old."

"Hi, Dad," I called cheerfully, rounding the corner into view.

"Hi, Katie." He cocked his head to one side. "Were you looking for me?"

"Mom sent me out here to give you your checkbook. It's on your work desk." I prayed they wouldn't notice the tremor in my hands.

"What were you doing in the transmission room?"

"The boys are playing manhunt. I was looking for them, but they're too cagey for me. I simply can't find them." I shook my head, hoping I looked disappointed.

"What's a manhunt?" Mr. Kelley asked.

His sudden attention unsettled me. The folded papers in my jeans were itching to commit treason. Pretending to stretch, I reached back there, reassuring myself there was no risk of them falling out and revealing my misdemeanor.

"Oh, that's another name for hide and go seek," I told him. Not wanting to engage any further with the men, I excused myself, feigning the necessity of finding my brothers. But once outside, I bolted into the house and up the stairs to my room. Removing the papers from my pants, I hid them behind my grandmother's picture in the beautiful antique frame I kept on my vanity.

"Keep them safe for me, Nana, okay?" I whispered.

She smiled back at me in response.

The afternoon would be long as I awaited an opportunity to analyze the copies, sure they would spell out nothing but trouble.

Much later that evening, after my brothers were asleep, I set my book down and reached for the picture frame. I pulled out the two papers tucked inside. All afternoon I felt restless as I thought about the papers.

I was also nervous. Was it the guilt for what I had done? Did this make me nothing better than a common neighborhood thief? Had I committed a criminal act?

I looked up at the ceiling, trying to reason with myself. *No one knows about this. Only you. And after you read these, you'll burn them, and no one will ever find them.*

Feeling more relaxed, I opened the first page. The large bold type at the top of the page read *WARRANTY DEED*. Underneath this heading:[begin legal document]

> Calvin Iverson, whose address is 183 Yeltan Rd, of Twin Rivers Junction, for undisclosed consideration, hereby sells and conveys to Cross Independent Baptist Church and Rhuttland Abbott, whose address is 189 Yeltan Rd, Twin Rivers Junction, the following real property in

Rivers County in Twin Rivers Junction to wit: Lot 186, Lot 187, Lot 188, and Lot 189 of Yeltan Road. Twin Rivers Court Filing, Twin Rivers Junction, Rivers County.

Scanning the rest of the document, I saw an underlined portion that spoke of a fee required because consideration was over $500. Following that were additional legal terms regarding conditions, restrictions, limitations, reservations, encumbrances, existing easements, and all other matters of record. The form was signed and dated by Mr. Iverson along with an official state seal and witnessed by a notary public.

I mulled over the form. A man named Calvin Iverson sold the Reverend the property the church sat on. But why did Mr. Kelley have this? The date on the document was the late '70s, making it old news. What was he doing with this now?

My eyes then fell on the other form lying open on the vanity. The document was the first page of what I guessed to be the formal lawsuit against the church. The upper left-hand corner had the name Wesley Iverson along with his address.

DISTRICT COURT OF TWIN RIVERS JUNCTION
CASE NO: 134007-091
WESLEY IVERSON,)
PLAINTIFF,)
VS.)
COMPLAINT
CROSS INDEPENDENT BAPTIST CHURCH,)
DEFENDANT)

Plaintiff Wesley Iverson brings forth the following causes of action and alleges the following:
1. Plaintiff is an individual and resident of Twin Rivers Junction.

2. Defendant is a corporation and at the time of this complaint, a resident of Twin Rivers Junction.
3. On or about June 12, 1979, Plaintiff's father, Calvin Iverson, now deceased, contracted with the Defendant for an agreement of the price of land for sale located at 189 Yeltan Road, Twin Rivers Junction.
4. On or about June 12, 1979, Plaintiff's father Calvin Iverson, now deceased, contracted with the Defendant and signed a contract stating the terms of the sale.
5. Terms of the property for sale on 189 Yeltan Rd were lots 186,187,188,189.
6. On or about September 19, 1983, a building was erected by the Defendant, on the lots belonging to Calvin Iverson, which are lots 184 and 185.
7. Following the beginning of construction, the Defendant produced a non-legal document showing the sale of the lots including the lots 184 and 185.
8. The deceased, Calvin Iverson, had in his possession a legal document that showed the sale to only include lots 186,187,188, and 189.
9. Following Cal Iverson's death, Plaintiff has discovered evidence that his father Cal Iverson had attempted to resolve.

COMPLAINT-1

I turned the page over, knowing it would be empty but wondering what the rest of the complaint had to say. Disappointed at not seeing the legal form in its entirety, I let out a frustrated sigh. If only I'd had more time, I could have copied the whole thing.

But what did it all mean? Why was Calvin Iverson's son suing the church?

Placing the forms back into the picture frame, I sat on my bed where my blue-eyed Siamese lay sprawled out, sound asleep. "What do you make of it, kitty?" I asked, my fingers stroking the soft fur on the side of his neck. He stretched and purred in response. "Big help you are." I pushed him over to make room for me to sit.

What were the facts here?

Rhuttland Abbott purchased land from Calvin Iverson. Except, it appeared that he built one of the three buildings on a portion of Calvin Iverson's land and not on the land that was in the original agreed-upon sale. Why?

Did Calvin Iverson agree to sell him just those four lots? The deed I copied only listed four lots. Was there a different deed out there somewhere? Was it in the files Mr. Kelley had, and I just didn't have enough time to find it?

If the Reverend already had in his possession the agreed-upon lots, why on earth would he build on other lots? Did he take something that didn't legally belong to him? And how did he come to have in his possession a different document than Calvin Iverson?

Had I unknowingly climbed into a fraudulent web of misappropriated contracts and records? Once again, I was plagued by a stream of unanswered questions. Yet again, the nagging determination to find these answers only fueled my ambition to untangle this new enigma I had discovered.

CHAPTER 14

THERE WERE OTHERS

Staring into the open woodstove, the weight of my transgression slid off my shoulders. The blaze gobbled up the two documents like a hungry animal. Within seconds, my fear of someone finding the pages diminished into gray dust.

They're gone. I sighed in relief.

Only your proof is gone, the voice of my conscience reminded me.

Glancing over my shoulder, I made sure no one was coming down the stairs. Thankfully, with the weather growing warmer, my parents had moved back upstairs. That morning, I was able to sneak downstairs and destroy the papers before anyone else woke up. Now that it was six o'clock, I felt fortunate my mom was not already awake and having her tea.

I reached for the handle of the old wood stove and closed it. Relieved the forms were no longer in my possession, I could not shake the persistent questions.

I had to figure out a way to learn the answers to my questions. Naturally, I couldn't go to Mr. Kelley and ask. That was a good way to earn myself a spot working up at the Cobb's camp for the summer. The mere thought produced a cold chill.

My thoughts then turned to Sara Kittridge. Her time at the camp was over, and she would be permitted to attend graduation ceremonies. But no one was allowed to ask about her duties at the camp. Same for Justin. But why?

I went into the kitchen to make coffee. My dad would be surprised to see me up early and the coffee perking. If he asked why, I would tell him it was the last day of school, and tonight was the senior graduation ceremony. The entire church came for graduations. Not only to support the students, but also to enjoy the special music the class had planned as their farewell before they left for Bible college.

"What are you doing in here? I smell something burning."

I whirled around to see my dad standing there, blinking at me. He stretched and made an exaggerated yawn.

"Oh, sorry. Just trying to make some coffee and ..." I pretended to be fiddling with the coffee pot.

"Katie?"

"Yeah?" My heart picked up speed. He must have smelled smoke. Would he ask me what I was doing with the woodstove in the middle of June? I thought I had been careful to make sure the smoke stayed in the back and up the chimney.

"That thing works better when you plug it in." My dad chuckled before heading for the bathroom.

As soon as the door shut, I took extra care to wash out the pot and, within minutes, had the pot brewing. I took a bagel and slid it into the toaster while I waited for the coffee to finish.

Outside the window behind the kitchen sink, my gaze shifted into the field where trees had once stood over the horse pasture and beyond. About every fifteen years, my mom and dad contracted with a local lumberjack to have their property cleared and the logs taken to be cut and shaped into lumber. My dad was compensated for the trees, but when the job was over my mother could not walk out on the trails without shedding a few tears, sad to see so many tree stumps scattered about when they had protected the land belonging to my parents. But one tree still stood.

"Grandpa Pine," my mother dubbed it. "Never ever let him be cut down." She yanked the bright-orange ribbon into a firm knot around its wide trunk. Grandpa Pine was the grandest tree we had ever seen, towering over everything else on the property. We guessed it to be several hundred years old due to its massive height and size.

A loud popping noise to my left alerted me that my bagel had finished cooking. One glance and I groaned.

"All right." My dad was out of the bathroom now and shaking his head. "What did you burn this time?"

"Well, Katie," my mom said as we drove home from graduation. "How does it feel? You're a senior now."

"It's cool" I said, reflecting on the evening's events. Rachel graduated and was going to Christian college in the fall. I didn't like that she was leaving, amid the turmoil going on with Jolee.

She'd approached me in the choir room minutes before the ceremony that evening. "Where's Jolee?"

"I don't know," I told her, my eyes wide.

"She'd better hurry, or we're going to be an alto short, and I need her." Rachel rolled her eyes and asked everyone to get in place. Her older sister, Samantha, home from college for the summer, handed Rachel her black cap and gown along with strong words about getting dressed right away.

A few minutes later, we were positioned on the risers in front of the congregation ready to sing. As the last few stragglers entered the church and took their seats, Brynn nudged me.

"Jolee is late," she whispered.

"I know," I said, keeping my gaze forward. This was the first time I could recall a student skipping out on a graduation ceremony, a required school event. And as one of the best alto voices in the school, Jolee's absence was noticeable. Rachel kept glancing at the empty spot next to Brynn. I felt a rush of anger at Jolee. How dare she ruin this night for Rachel when she had worked hard preparing a short program of Bible readings and special music. She had even written some of the musical arrangements herself.

"You're gonna have to sing loud to make up for it," I murmured to Brynn.

"Hey, where's your dumb friend Jolee tonight?" Marty's voice interrupted.

Mark joined in too. "Yeah, she is dumb. And ugly." Both boys erupted into laughter.

Any other day I would've corrected them for being rude. But not tonight. On this night, the whole junior-senior class was upset with her.

I pulled my thoughts together. "My dumb friend Jolee didn't show up tonight, and I don't know why."

"That's strange." My mom frowned. "She's been acting off lately, huh?"

I said nothing as we pulled into the driveway. I went up to my room to change out of my skirt into some soft pajamas before plopping on my bed. A lot more than Jolee weighed on my mind. One of the most beautiful graduation programs I had ever seen at Cross—thanks to Rachel's musical talents—and her dad had to go and ruin it with his preaching.

Who preaches about the deepest, darkest, hidden sin at a graduation ceremony? How about some congratulations or simple encouragement on beginning a new season of life? At one of the reverend's approved Christian colleges, of course.

"Katie?" my dad called from the bottom of the stairs. "Phone."

My eyes narrowed. Probably Jolee. *She'd better be in the emergency room.*

"Yes?" I said into the receiver. I knew it was her and didn't even bother with a hello.

"Uh ... hey, Katie," Jolee said in a weak voice.

"What's up?" I said in a clipped tone, uninterested in her excuses.

"Okay, look." She sighed. "Don't be mad at me for not coming tonight. I wasn't feeling very good."

"Neither was Del, but he came. Why didn't you call me? Everyone was wondering. I think you owe Rachel an apology."

"Whatever," she retorted, her temper rising. "I don't owe Rachel anything. I didn't call so you could chew me out, okay? Sorry I wasn't there is all."

"Okay, fine. So, what's wrong?"

Seconds passed. But in those fleeting seconds, I realized I had spooked her in some way and before I could stop it, she slipped away from me again. Instead of responding, Jolee uttered what sounded like a moan, as if she was about to say something and then changed her mind.

"Nothing." She cleared her throat. "I'm fine. Just a virus, and my throat hurts."

"Okay," I said, knowing there was more to it, but also not ready to push her away even more. "Don't worry about tonight. I'll let Rachel know you're sick."

"Thanks," Jolee replied.

"Jo?" I said before she could hang up. "If you need anything, let me know, okay?"

"Sure." She hung up.

She's hiding something, the voice said.

I knew that. But what? This guy she's been secretly dating? I thought that ended once her mom found out she'd been lying about where she was.

And where exactly was she?

Then it dawned on me. I had assumed since she was not feeling well, she was calling from home. I reached up and moved the dining room curtain away from the wall where the phone was plugged in, revealing the caller ID. The number that glowed from the tiny screen was not from Jolee's house. I knew her number by heart, and this was not it.

"All she ever does anymore is lie," I muttered.

My mom walked past me into the kitchen. "Everything okay?"

"Uh, yeah. That was Jolee. Said she was sick and had a sore throat." I yawned and stood. "Think I'll head back upstairs for the night."

"Be sure your sin will find you out!" I could picture the reverend's hand coming down hard on the pulpit, followed by the echo of splintering wood. How many times had poor Mr. Simpson, the overworked general contractor and carpenter, taken the pulpit into the back of his truck on a Sunday after service for repairs. Countless.

Lying in bed awake yet again, the reverend's unwelcome voice kept creeping back into my ears and chasing away any hopes for a decent night's sleep.

Go away, I'm tired, I asked silently of the reverend. But he kept barging into my thoughts and dreams.

"There is no rest for the wicked." The reverend's voice hovered over the room as he delivered his graduation message. "God has swift judgment upon those who sin!"

UNDER AUTHORITY

Several of us who had finished singing had to sit in the front row as there were no other empty seats in the sanctuary. After all, this was the yearly graduation ceremony and since many relatives had been invited to attend, the room was packed. Quite unlucky for us rising seniors. Sitting in the front made the reverend even more menacing than usual.

"The second half of Deuteronomy 24:16 says that every man shall be put to death for his own sin." The Reverend paused to chuckle and look around. "Aren't you glad we don't put people to death here?"

Here? What was he saying? Brynn glanced over at me, eyes wide.

I kept my own gaze forward. The reverend seemed to be pausing for effect. What kind of game was he playing? Didn't he realize how many visitors were in the room tonight? Was he truly so brazen he didn't care?

"Thankfully, today's culture provides more of a process for crimes. You commit a crime, go to jail. Can you imagine being put to death for a lack of faith?" The Reverend waited to see if anyone would dare to speak out of turn. Of course, no one did.

"So, what exactly is faith, you ask?" He paused again. "It's believing without seeing. Simple as that. Just believing. Not asking questions. Not demanding proof."

And not questioning authority. Prickles in my lower back caused me to sit up straighter. *That's it. Again.* My pulse quickened as my thoughts rushed back to when I first became suspicious of the reverend that day on the bus as we drove to camp. *No one is to question his authority. This is how he gets things done when and how he wants them.*

But not you, Katie, the voice said.

"No. Not me. Not ever." I surprised myself by saying this out loud and jumping out of bed. As I stood in the darkness with my thoughts darting back and forth between Jolee and the reverend, my stomach growled, reminding me that I hadn't eaten since long before the graduation program.

"Great." I needed to eat something quickly so I could go back to bed and sleep. I slid my feet into my slippers and tiptoed downstairs. As I reached the kitchen, I saw a ripe bunch of bananas sitting on the counter.

"Katie?" my dad called around the corner from his office. What was he doing still up?

"Yeah?"

He appeared in the doorway, looking tired. "I'm finishing up some paperwork. I thought you were in bed. It's after eleven."

"I *was* in bed. Can't sleep."

"That's not like you. Something weighing on your mind?" he asked.

I stared at him for a moment. "Always."

"This about your friend Jolee? About not showing up tonight?"

"Yes. And ..." I shrugged.

"And what?"

"Who is Cal Iverson?" I blurted. Where had that come from? Had I just asked that question out loud? Me and my big mouth.

"Huh?" My dad scratched his head. "Why is this name keeping you awake?"

"It's not. Not really. I just didn't enjoy the reverend's sermon tonight, plus Jolee was missing in action, then I did hear someone say that name or something." I hoped he bought my feeble explanation.

For now, he seemed to. "Well, Calvin Iverson was the original owner of the land where the reverend built his church. He sold a lot of it to the reverend back in the late

'70s right around the time we bought this house. I heard he passed away."

"Yeah, I heard that too. Was he just old?"

"Uh ..." Dad paused.

"What is it?"

"What have you heard about Calvin Iverson?"

I shrugged again, wondering why he seemed to be stalling. I thought of the documents regarding the lawsuit but was careful not to say a word about them. I knew my father would be very upset if he ever learned what I had done. "Just that he sold that land to the Reverend a long time ago or something."

"You probably heard some gossip because ..."

"Because?" I coaxed.

"Cal Iverson committed suicide not long ago," Dad said in a low voice. "Not sure why, but it was all kind of odd. He was friends with the reverend many years ago. Then one day, he just wasn't."

And yet another death.

I felt the blood draining out of my face and gripped the counter next to me. My dad must have noticed as he reached for my shoulder.

"Katie? Did you hear something about this guy?"

My mind raced. The cabinets swayed around me. My father was asking me something, but all I saw was his mouth moving. I heard nothing. Before I knew it, I had been ushered into a dining room chair in the next room. The white noise around me subsided enough for me to realize that both my parents were hovering over me with looks of concern shrouding their faces.

"What's wrong with her?" my mother demanded.

"I don't know. She mentioned a rumor she heard at school and then turned white as a ghost. I thought she was going down. Brought her in here."

I was only half listening to my dad explain to my mother what we had been discussing mere moments ago. Two words kept ping-ponging back and forth in my head.

Another suicide.

Bounce.

Another suicide.

Bounce.

"Katie!" My dad snapped his fingers in front of my face. I blinked, and he came back into focus. "Are you okay?"

"Uh ... yeah. Think so."

"You need to tell us why you reacted that way when I told you about Cal Iverson." They waited.

"I just hadn't heard how he ... uh ... died. That's sad."

My dad wasn't buying it this time. "Nice try. Start talking."

I sat up a little straighter. "How do you know it was suicide?"

"It was mentioned at the deacon's meeting."

"Who told you?"

My dad frowned. "Ross Kelley, why?"

I closed my eyes. Of course. "Why didn't you tell me?"

"I didn't think you needed to know. You had never met Mr. Iverson. You were just a kid when we started going here. I doubt you even remember him before he parted ways with the reverend."

"Why *did* he part ways with the reverend?"

Dad looked at Mom, then back to me. "I guess I don't really know."

"I do." My words were a whisper.

"What?" He looked shocked.

"He was suing the reverend. Or maybe his son was." It was dangerous for me to admit what I knew, but my dad was in the dark.

"What are you talking about? How on earth could you know something like that?"

"I can't tell you. I'm sorry." How could I tell him about the photocopies? What if I did and somehow, he felt obligated to tell Mr. Kelley? No way.

"What do you mean you can't tell me? You're not making any—"

"Come on, Katie." My mother patted my knee. "Talk to us."

"I will not tell you how I found out, okay? I can't."

They both frowned but nodded. I let out a shaky sigh and told them about the lawsuit in general and Mr. Iverson's son Wesley. I was careful not to reveal I had seen the partial documents, just that I knew of the lawsuit against the church. As I told them what I had heard, I wished I had been able to view the rest of the documents in the file. Maybe all this would make more sense.

My dad sat back in his chair and stared at the wall behind me. He said nothing for several minutes. I had a nagging question I needed to ask but wanted to give him a chance to process this. My mother appeared to be praying.

"Dad?" I said. "How did Mr. Iverson end his life?"

"Gunshot."

I sucked in a breath the same time as my mother. Her mouth fell open, and her gaze went from my dad to me. Just when I thought nothing else could surprise me, what my mother said next sent me reeling.

"There were others." She covered her mouth with her hand as soon as the words escaped.

"Jan!" my dad exclaimed.

"What?" My mother pointed an accusing finger at him. "You know it's true. She knows things too. She's not stupid, Sam."

I sat rooted to my chair, my eyes wide in a stunned stupor. I had never heard my mother speak this way to my father. Women at Cross were to be obedient and submissive to their husbands. Was my mother right? I had not heard before now of others who had committed suicide under strange circumstances. Could this really be happening?

"Who?" I pressed. "Besides Dana Terrell?"

A long moment passed.

Finally, my mom spoke up. "Do you remember the Wendell family?" I could tell my dad was not pleased, but he didn't try to stop her.

"Yeah, I do." I was in the sixth grade but remembered the Wendell family being preached against for leaving the church for what the reverend called *unbiblical reasons*. "What happened to them?"

"They left because they were angry with Reverend Abbott. He wanted to church discipline their daughter."

"What was her name? I forgot."

"Kathy. She was a senior in high school and allegedly caught in a lesbian act of some sort with someone who didn't go to Cross. Reverend Abbott found out and planned to discipline her and expel her from the school. Except ..."

"Except what?"

"Her father got involved and confronted the reverend about it being a lie. But as you know, questioning a decision the reverend has made is not permitted. So, he expelled Kathy from school. The Wendell family left the church without notice. Reverend Abbott told everyone they left for the wrong reasons and were to remain separated from then on."

"Poor Kathy." My mom closed her eyes as if reliving the event. "She swallowed a lot of pills right after this happened. She was only eighteen."

"And then there was Robert Raker." My dad's voice sounded calm, yet sad. Not at all what I was used to hearing from him.

"Who was he?" I asked, trying to keep my own voice calm.

"He and his family were members of the church when you were in about second grade, so you most likely don't remember them. He and his wife had some sort of dispute with the reverend. Robert also committed suicide. Don't remember the details of it. But his wife moved to another state after that, and one of his kids eventually came back here to Twin Rivers. You probably don't realize that you know him. He's the one who drives the skidder and cuts the trees. Wally Raker."

I couldn't believe it. That last year when the timber had been cut around the property, my siblings and I watched in awe as Wally drove the enormous skidder, plowing through and over anything in its way. I had no idea who Wally Raker was at the time nor his past connection to Cross. "Did you know them? The Rakers?"

"I only know Wally. I met his dad many years back and had a few casual chats with him," my dad said. "We had only been going to Cross at that point for just over a year, so I didn't get to know him. He seemed like a good guy from what I remember."

"Well, something terrible must have happened for him to ..." I couldn't finish that last part. "No one talked about it. No one said why or how he died?"

"I don't think so." My dad seemed to be having trouble remembering the situation. "I just didn't know him well, I guess. The family disappeared afterward."

I sat staring at my parents. I had to say something—now or never. "I need you both to admit something."

They looked at me curiously but didn't balk or act surprised. "Yes?" my dad said.

"Please tell me you now realize something is wrong here. Something is wrong with Cross." I took a deep breath and just spat it out. "And something is very wrong with Reverend Abbott."

My throat began to ache with a suppressed sob at the pain I saw enter my mother's face. Her lips pursed together, and she bowed her head into her lap in what I guessed to be an attempt to hide tears. Except that I had already seen them shimmering in her eyes. After a moment, she lifted her head and looked over at my dad who had become silent and thoughtful. "Sam?" she pleaded.

He nodded at her and then at me. "Yes, Katie. You're right."

There it was.

My heart soared up into the clouds. The burden of being plagued by confusing thoughts, unsettled feelings, and unanswered questions drifted away as I floated upward.

Something wasn't wrong with *me* after all.

Of course, the questions remained, but right now was all that mattered. At this moment, I had my parents' acknowledgment and support. They were no longer pretending. No longer ignorant or in denial of what was happening. After all this time, I finally had the validation I had been searching for.

But even as my concerns were affirmed, my spirits sank as another question crept forward.

What happens now?

CHAPTER 15

RUNNING

"Kate?" A familiar voice called.

I shook my head. I was warm and comfortable. The soothing sounds of the trees rubbing elbows with one another and the crisp snapping of tiny frozen branches falling to the snowy ground beckoned me back into slumber.

"Kate?" The familiar voice again. Closer now.

"Mmmm," I murmured.

"Open your eyes, Kate."

I burrowed under the covers of the sleeping bag, not wanting to wake up just yet. I wanted to drift more, in the clouds ...

Wait, what? Adrenaline hit me.

"Dad?"

His face and gray hair came into focus. He removed his glasses and cleaned them on the sleeve of his flannel shirt. "You always were a heavy sleeper. Feeling a bit jet lagged?"

I glanced around. The warming hut. The pot belly stove. My mother's journal and photo album. "How did ..." I didn't know what to ask first.

Dad put his glasses back on. "That's better," he said. "Well, when you weren't in the house after everyone got back from the slopes, we wondered where you'd gone."

I must have slept much longer than I intended. My dad followed my gaze over to the wood stove in the corner and grinned. "Good thing you got that going. Otherwise, you'd be chilly by now because it's already burned itself out."

"How long was I asleep?"

"No idea. I'm guessing you were here all afternoon."

"How did you know where to find me?"

He pointed to a picture hanging on the wall close to the stove. "I figured you'd want to come say hello to him."

I lifted my eyes to the portrait above the makeshift table and sucked in a breath. How had I not noticed this before? Had I really been in such a state over finding my mother's album and journal that I forgot about this precious photo?

I rose from the bunk and lifted the dusty frame off the wall. I held it in my hands, allowing the memory to pull me back into the thrill of the ride. My very first solo dogsled team. "Deeno." My eyes misted as I touched my sweet dog's photograph. I marveled at the feelings that rushed over me.

"You were drawn to that pup the moment you saw him," my dad reminded me.

"It was his nose." I smiled down at the picture of the husky. "He had a pink nose, remember?"

My dad laughed. "You two were inseparable from the start."

"Can I keep this?"

"Of course. You all right?"

I rubbed my eyes and sent my dad a reassuring nod. "I'm fine."

"You forgot about the photo," he pointed out. "Meaning you must have come here for another reason." He gestured toward the two books.

"Oh, those." I sighed and sat back down on the bunk.

"Why do you have those here, Kate?"

Tell him, my conscience pricked.

"I don't know."

He blew out a breath. "All of that was so long ago."

So much for him not recognizing those books. And like dandelion seeds wandering in a summer breeze, my mind followed them back to my dream about Cross Independent Baptist Church and school.

"I had a dream. I remembered things as if I went back in time to relive those days."

"Anything to do with those?" He again nodded to the album and journal.

I let my shoulders slump.

"Let it go, Kate. It was another life."

"I know, Dad. I get that. One I've said goodbye to. That's why it's been so hard for me to come home and—"

"Kate, don't."

"Let me finish." I put up a hand in front of me. "For so long, it was about Cross and the reverend and all the things that went wrong there. And what did I do in the end?"

"You left."

"I ran away, Dad."

"Why are you being so hard on yourself? You decided to go away to college, to the one *you* wanted to go to. You made a great life for yourself. You made good choices, and I don't understand why you're doing this to yourself now."

"You're right, I did all that, but ..."

"But what? Don't you know how proud we are of you for getting out? For leaving to find your own happiness?"

"Thanks, but being back here has brought up so many memories of things I left unresolved."

My father stood up and stretched. "We should get back to the house. It's almost dark and everyone will worry."

But before we left the now-cold hut, he touched my arm. What he said next only made my troubled heart ache even more.

The morning after Dad found me asleep in the hut, I woke to jubilant chatter from my children floating up the stairs. Christmas morning. I hadn't spent this special holiday in Twin Rivers Junction in many years. Determined to make it a memorable one, I got out of bed and stood by the window, hoping to see some new snow. I was rewarded with flurries that put on a show. They seemed to be having a contest to see which one of them would get to the ground first.

Pierce came up behind me with a steaming mug of coffee and a hug. "Merry Christmas, babe."

"Merry Christmas to you too." I smiled.

"You coming down? Everyone else is up already. I think your mom was up before the kids."

"Not surprised," I told him. "Let me get dressed. I'll be there in a few minutes."

I thought of my mom as I slid into a pair of jeans and warm sweater. Oh, the fun things she used to do all those Christmases we had together. I guessed she was making up for lost time and had something up her sleeve for the kids this morning. One of my fondest memories worked its way into my mind.

"Now listen up," my mother would say as she handed each of us folded pieces of paper. Behind her, lights from the Christmas tree blinked on and off, matching our wiggles of enthusiasm at yet another Christmas scavenger hunt.

"You each have your own map to find five goodies. They could be anywhere in the house. If you come across someone else's, you must put it back and no hints. Ready?"

And we were off. My siblings scrambled around looking inside bins, underneath tables, and even on top of the bookcase in the dining room. I scoffed at them, knowing

Mom was a lot smarter at hiding surprises than that. Checking my map, I gathered up my goodies one by one. A can of Pringles with my name on it hiding in a potted plant in the living room. A new pair of gloves stiff in the freezer. Some bath soaps in the pocket of my bathrobe hanging on the back of the bathroom door. A chocolate bar slipped into a cranny near the stairs. A decorative writing journal covered in musical notes hiding in the piano bench.

The memory made me smile as I pinned my hair into a clip at the back of my head. "Good things," I said aloud. "I wonder if she's still up to some old tricks." I took the now-empty coffee mug and went downstairs to greet my family.

Just after lunch, my mom and I plopped down in the living room with tired, yet happy sighs. We had spent most of the morning amid a hurricane of wrapping paper, ribbons, packages, bows, and a tornado of tissue paper.

"You spent too much on the kids, Mom."

She gave a little laugh and eased back on the antique rocker, holding a hot beverage between her fingers. "This is good, Katie," she said, sipping from her mug.

"Kate," I corrected.

She shrugged and looked out the window, then seemed to be smiling at the trees.

"See something?" I asked, taking a sip of my own tea.

"Oh, not really. Just remembering my dad."

"Oh."

"Did I ever tell you he used to be a pilot?" she asked.

"He was in the air force, right?" I rested my mug on my leg. "He had pictures of his medals on the wall."

"True. But he was in the air force only four years. Did you know he lost his pilot's license after he got out?"

I was intrigued. "What happened?"

"He and a friend decided to take on a dare." She chuckled. "I think he was dating my mom at the time. From what I was told years ago, he and an old air force pilot buddy of his were working at a small municipal airport giving biplane tours."

"Wait." I waved a finger in the air. "He went from being an air force pilot to flying tour planes for fun?"

"Just on weekends for extra money. He was in school finishing his degree during the week while your Nana was busy with her job as a night shift nurse at the hospital. Anyway, he and his friend were given a dare. Whoever could fly their plane under the Merricade Bridge in Manheimer."

My eyes widened. "I know that bridge."

"Yes, it's still there. Your grandfather and his friend took the dare because there was a cash reward for the pilot who could make the drop under the bridge without wrecking. They both flew underneath and came out on the other side like it was nothing."

"You're kidding, that's impressive."

"After they safely landed the planes, some not-too-happy authorities were waiting for them at the airport. They had to fork over some fines, along with their pilot's license."

"For how long?" I asked. "Did Grandpa ever get his back?"

"No, he would've had to take the test again after a year, so he decided to pursue his degree in counseling and get his masters. He said goodbye to flying for good."

An image of my grandfather pasting together models of fighter jets and setting them up on shelves for display came to mind. "Bet he missed it."

"Yes, but he never regretted what he did," my mom said with a smile. "Always said it was one of the most adventurous things he ever did."

"That sounds just like Grandpa."

UNDER AUTHORITY

We were quiet for a moment then, both of us missing him. I knew my mom was thinking of that Christmas Day all those years ago when I was still a teenager. On that night, she got a call from my uncle that Grandpa had passed away after celebrating Christmas with his family.

"He went to sleep happy and never woke up," she said, seeming to read my mind. "I think he was ready to go and knew it was his time."

"Poor Nana," I murmured. "She had a hard few years after that."

"Yes and no," Mom said. "She was relieved he went peacefully but knew she was alone then and had her own health concerns."

She felt alone. The voice echoed in my mind.

My eyes narrowed as more memories entered the room. They waltzed in, prancing in front of me. Unwanted and unwelcome. One image in particular, Mrs. Pam Kelley, stood out from the others. Ross Kelley's wife. My grandmother's only friend at Cross.

"She deserted her."

"What did you say?" My mother stared at me.

"Nothing." I did not realize I had spoken aloud.

"Who were you talking about?"

The remaining tea in my mug had grown cold, so I headed toward the kitchen for more. As I turned to go, my mother surprised me by grasping my hand.

"Not yet. Sit by me a bit."

I did what she asked.

"What was it, Kate? You changed just now."

I avoided her eyes. "What do you mean?"

"You shut down on me."

I ran my hand over my forehead and slid a few strands of hair that had escaped the clip away from my face.

Sitting up straight, I attempted a little laugh. "Sorry. Just remembering Nana."

She shook her head. "I think it was more than that."

"Well, I remembered when Grandpa died and we were all there for her but the one friend she had at Cross—Pam Kelley—she just left Nana to fend for herself."

A flicker of recognition shifted over my mother's face. Her eyes fixated on the twinkling tree lights. I watched them too. On ... off. On ... off. Much like the light that had shone in Mom's eyes just a moment ago. On, now off. Suddenly, I felt the weight of an elephant sitting on my chest. I bit my tongue in frustration. Why did I have to say anything about Cross?

Watching the rise and fall of my husband's shoulders as he slept, I shifted in the well-worn cushioned chair in the corner of the bedroom. The darkness of the past midnight hour engulfed the space, replacing comforting evening glows with oppressive shadows.

You've been here before. That voice. Again.

"Leave me," I whispered.

I couldn't remember the last time I struggled with sleep. My days were full of teaching, running kids to and from school, dental appointments, activities, sports, errands, and everything else. By nightfall, I fell into bed and slept well.

But not since returning to Twin Rivers.

I felt as if I'd stumbled across a time machine and here I was—back in the place I had escaped. Back in the same house I grew up in. Back among persistent ethereal beings of the past.

I should never have come.

Squinting in the darkness at my husband's computer bag, I spied the plane tickets for our return flight in the front pocket. They were dated for the day after New Year's Day. Another week. I was not sure I could bear it.

And you want to run again, don't you? The words had been haunting me ever since the car ride from the airport to my parents' house.

And why shouldn't I? I've been done with this place for over twenty years. Time for me to go back home.

Determination lifted me out of my chair. I tiptoed back to bed, relieved to have a plan. Tomorrow morning, I would change our plane tickets to head home a few days early. My parents would be disappointed, but I couldn't dwell on that.

I'd left them before. They would understand why I was doing it again.

And yet as my eyes began to close, my father's words came back to me. The words he spoke as we left the warming hut the previous day. Words that caused my newfound willpower to drift away beyond my reach.

CHAPTER 16

GONE

After slamming the rental car door with a thud, I put my seatbelt on and forced myself to breathe. I stared at the silver emblem in the middle of the steering wheel.

A minute later, I was backing out of the driveway.

I had to forget any ideas about rescheduling our return flights. I couldn't leave to run back to my safe territory.

Is it possible for someone to feel transported back into their past and then go on with their life as if nothing ever happened? As if former ghosts were never seen? As if old wounds were never reopened? As if attempting to ignore the pain would make it vanish?

I admired people who made it their life's goal to achieve this endeavor. How did they manage to rise above their heartache instead of building walls and creating a false world where they kept out anything and anyone that reminded them of their pain?

Like I've been doing all these years.

"Don't run away twice, Kate." My father's words had been reverberating in my head for over two days now, ever since we left the warming hut on Christmas Eve.

Turning onto Main Street, I was welcomed by my childhood town with views of the pretty shops and small park in the middle. The gazebo to the left had been replaced by a much bigger one. On the other side of the brick walkway, the snow-filled fountain waited for spring to come. I was surprised that little had changed in all this time.

Alvin's Bakery still sat on the corner, fortunate not to have been taken over by a Starbucks. Just a few stores down stood the Tanger Mountain ski shop where I used to rent ski gear. I was pleased to see these stores still here and flourishing. Time had brought in a few new restaurants, a realty agency, and a few new names on old banks. Even the post office had received a face lift. A minute later, I parked in front of my favorite store and went inside.

As if taken from an old Western movie set, the Makawee Country Store remained unchanged with its front entrance guarded by an enormous hand-painted Indian chief carved out of wood. Along the length of the building sat an old-fashioned carriage hitched up to two life-sized, spotted ceramic horses. I wondered where these items came from and marveled at how many years they'd spent there.

Upon opening the door to the old store, the jingling bell alerted the employees to a customer's arrival. I smiled, remembering when Jolee and I used to come here. She always snarled at that bell.

"All bells are annoying" she would say.

I felt as if Jolee were with me now. After passing multiple barrels full of penny candy, I walked by the racks of homemade jams and sauces. The store smells reached into deeper parts of my memory, giving me a sense of comfort. Beyond the specialty foods area, rows of moccasins waited for tired feet to try them on and take them home. An old upright player piano with a stained-glass front still occupied a wall near the children's toy area. With the tinkling sound of a quarter dropped into it, the out-of-tune piano would plink out a happy ragtime tune. I smiled as the sounds kept me mesmerized. Unique gifts ranging from household items to tools lined shelves as I found my way deeper into the store looking for the snug candle room tucked in the back—Jolee's and my happy place.

When we came here, we could pretend we were not in Twin Rivers. That's what this store with its Native American Indian themes and Western décor did for us. For short periods of time, we could let loose and even act a little silly, suspending the burdens we carried from being under the dictatorship of Reverend Abbott.

I could almost hear Jolee's voice even now. "This one smells delicious. I want a spoon." She would bury her nose further into the glass jar she held in front of her.

"A spoon?"

"Yep. I want to eat it." Jolee read the label. "Cinnamon bun. I'll bet you I could eat it."

"Do it. I dare you."

"Okay then," she said, her jaw tight. "You're going to watch me eat this candle." Taking the end of her car key, she dug out a chunk of the brownish colored wax and popped it into her mouth.

I stifled a laugh. I couldn't believe what I was seeing. What kind of person eats a candle?

"Don't swallow that," I whispered, looking around to make sure no one was watching.

Of course, she looked me right in the eye and swallowed. I held my breath, waiting to see how long it would take her to gag.

"See? I won." She stuck her tongue out at me.

"You are so gross, Jolee."

Just then, the candle slipped out of her hand and fell onto the floor with a loud smack. We froze, wondering how long it would take for a store employee to come running.

The glass jar did not shatter, but rather split sideways into two large pieces.

"Hide it," Jolee commanded.

"What? We can't do—"

"Come on, Katie. Let's go." Jolee snatched what was left of the broken candle and stuffed it behind a row of items on the bottom shelf. We hightailed it out of there.

"Hi there." A woman's voice startled me out of my memory. "Did you find one you like? Don't they smell so nice? All our candles are twenty percent off through the end of the month."

I spun out of my trance to see a lady wearing an apron and straightening a few jars on the shelves. Glancing over her shoulder at me, she tilted her head toward my hands. "Oh, cinnamon bun. That's one of our most popular sellers."

I looked down to see what I was gripping, alarmed that I did not remember taking the candle off the shelf. I thrust it at her as if it were on fire and about to burn my hand. "No, thank you," I said quickly. I couldn't get out of the store fast enough.

The unexpected memory of the day Jolee broke the candle left me feeling dazed.

Drive, the voice ordered.

Back in the car, I turned onto Main Street and then onto Tanger Mountain Highway. But instead of turning right onto Quinella Road, I sped on by—and sailed right past Yeltan Road, where Cross Independent Baptist Church inhabited the hill a mile away.

Fifteen minutes later, I crossed into the small village of Dornell. A tiny dot on the map, Dornell consisted of one blinking yellow light near a gas station. Ahead stood a small corner market for those who didn't feel like driving into Twin Rivers for a gallon of milk.

Muscle memory controlled me now. I turned left at the blinking light onto Pointe Street and up over the hill. Another left. Then a right. I slowed the car as a familiar black mailbox with a faded painted flower on the side came into view. Snow crunched under my tires as I pulled into the long driveway. The rear end of the car sashayed as the tires searched for new traction.

"Huh," I mumbled. "Doesn't look like a plow has been through here."

The red house came into view, and I jerked the car to a stop.

Jolee's house.

No one's here.

No one's been here in a long time, the voice said.

Standing in front of the small house, I was sad to see it abandoned. Shaped like a shoebox, the house was never in great condition to begin with. Although Jolee's dad was a hard worker, his farm equipment business kept him away from home a lot. Her mom stayed busy with her job as a store clerk in town. Still, the place had once been cozy and warm inside. Jolee had the single upstairs room to herself while her mom and dad shared the smaller, downstairs bedroom. The narrow kitchen consisted of fifties-era appliances and a table off to one side. The living room was just big enough for one couch and Jolee's upright piano.

The house looked so forsaken that a twinge of sorrow came over me. The roof sagged toward the middle, suggesting years of torture from heavy snow. The peeling red paint made the house appear as if it had been constructed of badly cooked bacon. The front porch had shifted on its foundation, the aged concrete cracked in several areas.

What was I doing here?

Thankfully, the porch held my weight. I knocked on the front door, knowing no one would answer. Trying the knob, I was not surprised to find it locked. Even the few downstairs windows were boarded up.

Where had the Tisdale family gone?

They left too. The voice again.

So that's it then. There was nothing left here. Just as I thought about leaving, a creaking sound from the back of the house pulled my attention away from the car.

"Anyone there?" I called out.

Creak.

My boots crackled on the snow as I sought the noise. But all I saw was an old, free-standing bench swing that had been left behind.

"Jolee's," I whispered, remembering how much she liked it.

I sat on the rusty swing praying it would still hold. It screeched in surprise at being touched, but it held together. The metal hinges soon found their way again, and the squeaks subsided.

Rocking gently, I removed a hat from the pocket of my heavy, fur-lined coat and pulled it down over my head. I leaned my head back and looked up at the clear sky, astounded by how peaceful it was here, and at the same time knowing it had not always been a place of harmony. Regret settled in around me, filling the emptiness and lingering just long enough to crush my spirit.

I should have saved her.

She did not want to be saved; the voice again reminded me.

I should have tried harder. Whether she liked it or not. My eyes stung with tears. After all these years, the pain remained strong.

I just let her go. My head began to ache as a gusty breeze swept past me. The trees along the back ridge of the field groaned at having their limbs and branches stirred.

UNDER AUTHORITY

Goooooo, they entreated, as if repeating my last thought.

"She's already gone!" I cried out. "She's dead because I didn't save her when I had the chance."

Jolee Tisdale, my best friend. Gone. A young girl's promising chance at life, ending so young.

My heart swelled with anguish. Tears burned my cool cheeks. I rubbed them away angrily with my gloves. I leaned back again on the swing and felt wearier than I had in a very long time. My eyes felt heavy.

The only sound was the soft whine of the metal swing gliding back and forth.

Back and forth.

Someone pounded on my door.

"Katie, get up. Mom wants you. And you call *me* lazy."

Marty?

I sat up as my bedroom came into focus. Blue walls. Sheet music I had hung in place of posters. My Siamese curled up at the foot of the bed.

Home.

My hand flew to my forehead. The weight of the headache I'd woken up with bore down on me. Upon touching my face, I was surprised to find my eyes moist.

Had I been crying in my sleep?

More pounding.

"Quit it," I called through the door. "I'm coming."

"Good afternoon," my mother joked as I entered the kitchen a little while later.

My eyebrows drew together in a frown. "What time is it?"

"Nearly lunchtime," she replied. "Better enjoy all this beauty sleep you're getting because school will be starting up again next month."

I groaned.

"By the way, you're supposed to have narrowed your college choices down to three. I haven't seen you take any of these information packets and look through them yet. How come?"

During the summer months, a rising senior was expected to research which Christian college they wished to attend. By the first week of school, the principal would ask for their top three picks. By Christmas, the final choice would be made so they could begin the application process. Of course, secular colleges were not permitted, and neither were Christian colleges not on the reverend's list.

"I don't like any of those," I said flatly.

My mother stopped organizing the pile of clutter on the counter and turned to look at me. I could tell the reels of her mind were flashing like images on a projector screen somewhere in her head. I imagined the snapshots she envisioned were reprimands by the reverend for not controlling me better.

"Why not?" she asked.

I stuck my chin out. "What if I wanted to go to a different college? One not on the reverend's list? Maybe I'd rather go to music school instead of Bible college?"

Mom resumed putting things in their proper place. She did pause long enough to hand me the small stack of envelopes from the approved colleges. "Look them over later. By the way, your friend Karina called for you this morning."

"She did?" I hadn't seen much of Karina during the summer. She had gotten a part-time job helping her mom who was a nurse at an assisted living facility.

"I told her you'd call her back later." And with that, my mom left the room.

UNDER AUTHORITY

Half an hour later, I called Karina. "Hey, it's Katie," I said, surprised she answered on the first ring.

"Katie," Karina was talking fast. "What are you doing?"

"Nothing much, just helping my mom. Why?"

"Listen, come over. Something you need to hear." Karina sounded cryptic.

"What's up?" I asked. "Tell me now?"

"Just come, okay? Soon." Karina didn't wait for an answer before she hung up.

I was a bit puzzled as to why Karina was being mysterious. What was so important she couldn't tell me right then? At least, we didn't live far from one another. After a hot shower, I was granted permission to use the car for a few hours to go visit my friend.

As I pulled into the driveway of Karina's house, I noticed an unfamiliar truck parked in front of the garage.

A minute later, Karina practically yanked me into the house. "Hey, what's gotten into you?" I grumbled. Then, I realized her brother Victor was there. "Oh. Hey, Vic. Haven't seen you in a while."

Karina's oldest brother by several years, Vic was in and out of town working as a supervisor for a truck-driving business. He was one of the few graduates of Cross who had not gone to a Christian college but had somehow managed to stay under the reverend's radar. I thought he was quite clever to go to truck-driving school and then end up traveling the entire country.

"How's the haulin' business going?" I asked.

"Going great. Can't complain." He glanced at Karina.

"All right, I give. Why am I here?"

Karina motioned for me to sit at the table. Vic sat on the other side. She nodded to her brother.

"I'm the one who wanted to talk to you," Vic said.

I sat up straighter.

"It's about Jolee." Karina's voice was hushed.

"What about her? Have you heard from her? She's been in a funk or something all summer. She hasn't called me or—"

"She's in trouble," Vic said.

"So, what else is new?"

Vic leaned forward and clasped his hands in front of him. "What I'm about to tell you, you can't say a word to anyone. Okay?"

"How do you know anything about Jolee?"

"I've gotten to know a lot of people in this town for my business. Piedmont Freight manages a lot of the shipping for the college downtown."

"So?"

"Like I said, I've gotten to know a lot of people. One is a landlady at a frat house off Main Street. Ever hear Jolee mention the name Veronica Dearden?"

"No." I shrugged.

"Well, her boyfriend is Jake Benter. He's one of my drivers." Vic rubbed the stubble on his chin. "I've been to their house a few times and met some of her student tenants that are in and out of there. Including a guy named Robbie Suthers."

That got my attention. "The same Robbie Jolee has been dating?"

"One and the same. Did you know he's twenty-one?"

I threw my hands in the air. "I don't know anything about him at all."

"Well, you're not going to like what you hear."

"Just tell me. She's been acting odd all year and won't even talk to me."

"Robbie got Jolee pregnant," he said.

I gasped. No way. That couldn't be true. Fornication, as the reverend called it, was one of the gravest sins. He spent a lot of time preaching against it and imposed a long list of rules about dating or even fraternizing with the opposite sex. A teenage pregnancy at Cross? Such vile acts of sin were unheard of.

"And that's not all." Vic lowered his voice to a near whisper. A troubled look came into his face, which made my heart beat faster.

"Tell me," I urged.

"She was confused, and I think scared of what Reverend Abbott would do if he found out that she—"

"She what?"

"She got an abortion. And Veronica is the one who paid for it."

I pushed away from Vic like he was a convicted criminal. "It can't be true." I glared at him, horrified.

Karina pulled me back into the chair. "Katie, think about it. This fits the timeline of when she started her strange behavior."

"Jolee first met Veronica at work," Vic said.

"That part-time job she told us she had," Karina reminded me. "She invited Jolee over to her place, and that's how she met Robbie. They began hanging out and then before long, dating."

"But why would a twenty-one-year-old date a sixteen-year-old?"

Vic shook his head. "Opportunity, maybe. Who knows? But she did get pregnant and then had the abortion."

"When?"

"Sometime in June."

I almost choked. "She had it done in June? When in June?"

Vic thought for a minute. "Late June, I think."

"Graduation." I supplied.

"She wasn't sick that night. She was recovering from—" Karina could not finish.

"Hey," Vic said. "I know this is all a shock, but there's more."

"I'm listening."

"Veronica said at first, Jolee didn't want the abortion. But Robbie told Jolee he would dump her if she didn't get it. Veronica said Jolee was head over heels with this loser. So, she did what he wanted, and he dumped her anyway."

"What?" I couldn't believe what I was hearing.

"Well, he's gone. Left town." Vic paused. "There's one more thing."

My mind was spinning. "How on earth could there be anything else?"

"Sadly, there is. And it's important. Robbie got Jolee hooked on drugs. Even before she got pregnant."

I hugged myself around the middle while Karina cried, her soft heart not taking any of this well. I was too stunned to have a reaction other than disbelief.

"I need to go." I needed air. Just as I was about to open the car door, Vic appeared next to me.

"Wait a sec," he said. "You need to realize something."

"What?" I spat the word.

"I know you're upset, and I'm sorry about that. But Karina mentioned you and Jolee were close. That's why I felt you needed to know. I found all this out just a few days ago. But remember"—he paused to make sure he had my attention—"if I found out, it's only a matter of time before Reverend Abbott learns about it too."

Another blow. Vic might as well have slapped me across the face. The sting of his words made my head throb.

"I'm sorry," he offered again.

"Thanks, Vic," I mumbled. "I appreciate you letting me know."

With a nod, he turned and went back into the house. I sat in my dad's Volkswagen for a few minutes as disbelief turned into heartbreak.

UNDER AUTHORITY

An unexpected baby. A terminated pregnancy. Drugs. All right around her seventeenth birthday.

I had to find Jolee. I would find her and make her talk to me. Decision made, I headed home to begin a list of people to call, starting with her mother.

My grief for my friend would have to wait until later.

CHAPTER 17

DARE TO QUESTION

I pondered what being in a coma would be like. Was it peaceful? Did one feel pain? Experience happiness? Sadness? Fear?

Does a person dream while in a coma? I imagined they did because of stories I'd heard of someone being in a near fatal car crash, sinking into a coma, then waking up weeks or months later with a lot to say about what they saw and heard. After their recovery, did they laugh at the preposterous visions they saw during deep slumber and then brush them aside, knowing they were illusions of the imagination?

Except for me. I wanted to fall into a coma to escape what I currently knew was real.

Numbness followed me all the way home from Karina's house that afternoon. Like a phantom drifting behind the puttering Volkswagen, I could not hear or see it, but it engulfed me. I tried to pull myself together before I arrived home.

"Oh good, you're back," my mom said as I entered the house. "You can help me unpack these boxes."

I turned my attention to moving boxes from the kitchen into the living room near her writing desk. At least this small task would chase away a portion of the emptiness inside.

"All right," she said. "Let's open these up. I need Mark's books stacked up over here on his desk and Kyla's on hers."

"Oh, you got their textbooks already?" I hoped my voice sounded normal.

My mom's eyes darted from her packing slip to the books I was stacking on each desk. Deep in concentration, she made tiny black checkmarks on each line as I placed an item. She seemed oblivious something was amiss.

"Yes, they came while you were out, which is perfect because I need to plan out their year and lessons in advance so we can schedule testing in April. All that good stuff."

"Oh, right. How did their last test scores come out?"

"Excellent." She glanced at me then, beaming. "Mark tested out a grade level ahead in math and science. Kyla was right on her grade level, except for reading, where she was also above grade level."

"That's great," I responded.

She set her clipboard aside and studied me. "You okay? You seem upset."

My efforts at concealing my sorrow were in vain. She had noticed after all. Before I knew what was happening, my hands were covering my face.

"What's wrong, Katie?" Mom pulled me over to the couch to sit.

"It's Jolee," I whispered, my throat tight. "I don't know what to do. I need to help her, but I'm afraid it might be too late."

"Help her how? Is she okay?"

"No." I shook my head. "She is not okay. She hasn't been in a long time."

And the words spilled out. When I finished, we were both wiping our eyes. In our troubled silence, we sat alone together and stared at the open boxes on the floor. The old clock on the mantel chimed, startling us.

"I'm afraid," Mom surprised me by saying. "I'm afraid for Jolee but ..." Her face looked gray, her eyes distant.

"What is it?" I asked.

"Reverend Abbott will make an example of her."

She did not need to elaborate. "Then I have to find her first."

As I rose to leave, she stopped me. "Don't be angry with her. She's been through enough. She needs compassion right now, okay?"

I nodded and swallowed hard. I was proud of my mom at that moment. She could have reacted like other Cross members who would have picked up the phone to report Jolee's unspeakable wickedness. She could have forbidden me to ever speak to her again. She could have called Jolee's mother to rebuke her despicable child-rearing skills. But she did none of those things. She showed heart. Something not encouraged at Cross.

Exposing one's heart under Reverend Abbott's rule was a luxury a member of the congregation did not risk. Such an indulgence of one's own sin nature was interpreted not only as weakness but also lent gratification to iniquity.

The reverend preached that emotions were flaws. Lowly church attendees were all sinful sheep that had gone astray. The reverend was placed by God in the church to shepherd a disobedient flock. Laws were created. Rules were to be obeyed. Swift discipline was administered to those who did not submit. The pastor of the church was the perfecter of saints. No one could be permitted to think or feel for themselves. This was considered divisive and destructive to the unity of the brethren. Exhibiting free will was a sin of the flesh worthy of repentance.

And yet my own mother had enough mercy in her heart that not even the reverend's supreme power could exterminate it.

I hurried to the phone to call Jolee's house. I knew the chances of her being at home were slim. She had not been at home most of the summer as far as I knew. But I had to start somewhere.

I let it ring. Finally, after the sixth ring, a voice said hello.

"Mrs. Tisdale?" I squeaked, excited that she answered. "It's Katie. Is Jolee there? I need to speak with her."

An unmistakable gloom closed its ugly clutches over the telephone wires. The familiar hum of the phone line had turned into a strained echo. An old song I'd heard playing in the grocery store found its way back into my head. *Hello darkness, my old friend ... and no one dared disturb the sound of silence.* I was not sure who had penned such a piece but wondered if their own trouble had been so great that they found music as a solace for their sadness.

Focus, Katie.

"Mrs. Tisdale?" I prompted.

"She's not here." She did not offer anything else.

"Can you tell me where to find her?"

"I really can't talk right now."

"Wait," I pleaded. "I know something is wrong. I can help her. Just tell me where to find her."

"It's best for you if you don't get involved. And don't bother coming here because Jolee moved out."

"What?"

"I really must go now. Goodbye, Katie."

I placed the receiver back into its cradle and closed my eyes.

Think, Katie.

The wall, the voice reminded.

I shoved the curtain out of the way, revealing the tiny square box mounted on the wall. I hit the left arrow several times on the caller ID hoping this thing had enough memory. I slowed down my button-pushing as I got closer to the month of June. I stopped when I got to graduation day.

There it was. The number Jolee had called from that night after we had all returned from the graduation ceremony. The night when the entire junior-senior class was angry with her for ditching them.

If only they knew why.

I redialed the number, thankful I was able to find it. But my hopes plummeted when a computer-generated voice informed me the number I was trying to reach had been disconnected. It must've been Robbie's number. And Vic said he was gone.

Vic. Maybe I could track down Jolee through his driver's girlfriend, Veronica something or other. Since I forgot her last name, the fastest thing to do was call Karina.

"He went to check on some loads," Karina said a few minutes later. "I can have him call you when he gets back?"

Frustrated, I set the phone down, hard.

Why didn't you tell me, Jo? I would have tried to help. Did you think I wouldn't have?

It's only a matter of time before the reverend finds out, Vic had said.

I prayed that nothing would be discovered by this upcoming Sunday. I needed more time to locate my friend.

My bad attitude followed me all the way to church that Sunday evening. At the morning service, I found Karina and asked about Vic. She said he had to cut his trip to Twin Rivers short because one of his drivers had a family emergency. I now had to wait two days for him to return so I could get the phone number of his driver. I still hadn't located Jolee and being present at church only made my mood worse.

I glanced over at my mother as she removed her notebook and Bible from her purse. Though I never understood why she kept doing it, I marveled at her faithfulness to continue taking sermon notes.

After special music from the Abbott sisters, the reverend stood and buttoned the top button of his dark suit jacket. "Turn in your Bibles to Hebrews 13," he instructed after settling himself behind the pulpit.

I decided I would not be opening my Bible tonight.

"Verse seventeen says, 'Obey them that have the rule over you, and submit yourselves ...' I want to stop right there for a minute. Tonight, I'm going to speak about the role of the preacher, the role of the church, and the role of the Christian school."

I breathed a sigh of relief it was not a sermon against Jolee. But her parents had been absent for a few weeks now. I'm sure this did not go unnoticed by the reverend.

"The role of your pastor is to lead the church. To rule over the membership. Why? Because I must give an account of you. Submit and follow is your command."

I closed my eyes so he would not notice me rolling them.

"And then the role of the church. First Corinthians 11:1 says, 'be ye followers of me, even as I am also of Christ.' This goes hand in hand with the verse I just read about 'whose faith follow.' Follow does not mean lead, nor does it mean question. It means follow the leadership that God placed in the church, which is your pastor."

Out of sheer disinterest—plus having heard all this before—I chose to resume an old favorite pastime of people watching. Toward the left, I saw my mom's close friend

Renata Tyner. Her husband Burt was back in town from one of his frequent business trips. Their oldest son Kyle sat at the end of the pew next to his brothers. Behind them sat the Kittridge family, minus Jack, whose six-month church discipline was not yet complete. On the second row, not too far in front of us, sat Ross Kelley and his clan, which included the Brayton family, his own daughter and son-in-law.

A newly ordained minister and recent graduate from Christian seminary, Kevin was being trained for church leadership roles by the reverend. I imagined he considered Kevin his apprentice as he shaped him to be a *real* man of God.

Beyond them was a dejected-looking June Britton sitting alone, the music and joy she once possessed having been long since snuffed out. I wondered what had become of her husband now they had separated.

Stealing a glance behind me, I saw the Cobb family had come in late again. Next to them sat Diana Holtz, the daughter-in-law of Floyd and Velma Holtz, gazing at the reverend. At one time, I thought I could call Diana a friend, but any mention of the reverend's name and she almost became starstruck. Her young daughter had teased my little sister in Sunday school because Kyla was homeschooled. I knew Diana could not be trusted.

The sanctuary was full, and I seemed to be the only one not paying attention. I sighed and turned forward again hoping this would be over soon.

"And as a vision ordained by God," Reverend Abbott was saying, "the Christian school is a ministry of the local church. Therefore, anything against this ministry would be in clear disobedience of his command." He paused and glanced at his notes. "It has come to my attention there has been some division in the church body regarding those who choose to homeschool and those who support our Christian school."

My head snapped up. Homeschoolers?

"We have attached great importance to this ministry. Much work and sacrifice has gone into making our school a ministry that has produced good fruit in the children of our people. Hours of labor and much sacrificial money have gone into the school. We have done everything we can to make it a great educational facility to give youngsters every possible educational advantage. Our teachers are dedicated to your children."

I tried not to croak out loud at that remark, placing my hand over my mouth and faking a cough to cover it.

"The Bible illustrates Jesus taught in groups. The book of Matthew reveals his twelve disciples were taught in a group situation, and this set an early standard for education. The Bible says the law was our schoolmaster. They had schools with schoolmasters and not mothers educating boys and girls."

Heat circled its way up my neck and into my face. I turned to my left to look at my mother and found her writing in her notebook, but what an angry pen she held in her hand. Her face looked flushed. She kept her head down and that ink moving. My father sat unmoving, but there was no mistaking a troubled look on his face.

"I have seen no good fruit from homeschooling," Reverend Abbott said boldly. "In my experience, homeschooled children don't learn everything they need to be taught. It is a way to depart from the authority of the church. The church's ministry is the Christian school. We have a biblical and financial obligation to support this as God has called us all to do. Homeschool is an easy way out for those who say they can't afford it. There could be many reasons for the interest in home education. Saving money could spark that interest. Some students might desire to be homeschooled thinking they could have a much easier time manipulating their mother rather than having to pay fines in school. If parents were courageous and obedient to the Scriptures, they would make sacrifices, and God would reward them for their obedience. Those who want to home educate have a pride problem, and it's been influencing the unification of the brethren. I have been made aware of comments some students have been doing better with home education than in Christian school. Bragging only causes disruption. Proverbs 13:10 says, 'Only by pride cometh contention; but with the well advised is wisdom.'"

I sat rooted to the pew. My parents' faces were crestfallen. I felt a stab of anger at what this was doing to them.

Homeschooling was unbiblical? No good fruit?

I dared steal a glance at the Cobbs, also homeschoolers, behind me. Mrs. Cobb's nose was red, and tears streamed down her face. I felt terrible for her. Craning my head over toward the Tyner's, I tried to see Renata's face but her head was bent toward her lap. Renata homeschooled her youngest child Bryce because of some health challenges and her middle son because he thrived being at home. Kyle attended school every day. I knew there were a few other families within the church who preferred to homeschool their kids. I wondered what was going through their minds right now.

After the reverend read the entire chapters of Acts 1 and Matthew 24, he went on to state the passages were proof that Jesus taught in groups, therefore the Christian school was to be supported as a ministry of the church. He also said that legally, homeschoolers had the right to educate their children at home, but it was God's will for all children to be educated in the Christian school.

"In conclusion"—the reverend closed his Bible and placed his hands on either side of the podium—"the Bible teaches there is one way to have peace. That way is humble repentance. Follow the guidelines set forth in the Bible. Trust in the preaching of God's Word. God has given me the oversight of this church. Therefore, it is my responsibility to do what I can to bring about the joyous restoration of unity within the brethren."

After a prayer and invitation—to which no one responded—the reverend motioned for Kevin Brayton to say the closing prayer. Mrs. Abbott played the piano as people gathered their things to head home for the night. Most services concluded with chatter and fellowship. Tonight, however, there was an awkward hush. Condescending glares were sent in the direction of the known homeschoolers, who had been reduced to mere dogs with their tails tucked between their legs.

The long hallway out to the front door of the church filled with people and subdued conversations. Mothers lined up in front of the door to the nursery to collect their young children. Men stood nearby talking in quiet tones. Kids chased each other down the hallway. Groups stood together staring at my family as we headed for the door.

But to get outside, we had to pass by Reverend Abbott first.

I knew it was going to be a long night for all of us when we got home. I wanted to make sure we got Kyla out of children's church so we could leave right away.

"Meet you outside?" I said to my dad. "I'll get Kyla."

He nodded and proceeded to gently guide my mother's arm and keep her moving. She looked like she was going to be sick.

A moment later, with Kyla in hand, I rounded the corner to see everyone frozen in place with horrified looks on their faces. I stopped in my tracks at the scene emerging in front of me.

No, Mom!

I watched as my mother broke away from my dad and marched right up to Reverend Abbott. With a clenched jaw and a blaze in her eyes, she stopped in front of him, cutting off his dialogue with Ross Kelley.

"Jan!" my dad called her.

She ignored him.

Brynn showed up beside me and placed her arm around me. Del also came by and stood on the other side of Kyla. I hardly noticed them. There could have been a thousand naked people in the room, and I wouldn't have known it. I was like a champion racehorse with blinders on, focused on one thing. The finish line. And I was terrified that whatever my mother was choosing to do was going to place her at her own finish line.

Reverend Abbott turned his head. Using his tall stature to his full advantage, he looked down at my mother in a way meant to make her feel as small as possible. His stony eyes stared hard at the flames in hers.

If a cargo plane had crashed through the ceiling, any survivors of that wreckage would have been treated with care. The wreck my mother was about to initiate was not survivable, and she would not be treated with care.

Mom, what are you doing?

The reverend continued to regard my mother coldly, his eyes challenging her to say something. A mastermind at intimidation, superiority and arrogance were his clothing. Most people did not want to sustain eye contact with his piercing eyes. Some believed he even had the ability to see into one's soul, another gift the man believed God had blessed him with.

"Why?" she demanded.

Gasps from the crowd.

The reverend said nothing, just continued his icy gaze.

"How can you be prejudiced against homeschooling? Do you really think we choose to homeschool because we are cowards? It takes a lot of courage and hard work to home educate my kids every day. You know Kyla can't focus in a big classroom."

Women nearby watched with their hands over their mouth. Men stared at the display in front of them. I could almost hear their thoughts. *Has a member of the congregation dared to defy the reverend and question his authority? To question God himself?* The fact that a woman had the audacity to perform such an act was viewed as scornful and reprehensible.

With tightly closed lips, Reverend Abbott turned to his left and nodded at Ross Kelley. He immediately darted forward, ushering my now sobbing mother out the door. I managed to put one foot in front of the other and follow them out, dragging my little sister behind me.

My phantom of numbness returned to say hello and brought along a friend—the spirit of fear. Invisible as they were, they could be felt with the intensity of a genuine physical presence. The two forces united, twisting and squeezing my heart like a wet, wrung-out rag.

Such an exhibition as my mother had demonstrated in front of everyone would result in immediate punishment handed down from the reverend. All we could do was wait to see how long it would take to discover what it would be.

The short car ride home seemed to take an eternity. My dad drove, saying nothing. My mother rested her arm across her forehead. I knew whenever she cried her head would ache soon after. My siblings seemed to have taken their cue and were quiet for once. They knew something was wrong.

As for me, the only sounds I heard were the soft puttering of the Volkswagen and with it the tune that had been playing in my head from a few days ago.

The sound of ... silence.

CHAPTER 18

CHURCH DISCIPLINE

"What else do you need?" my mother asked.

School would begin next week, so it was time to get the supplies Marty and I needed before the big rush.

"Marty? Did you say you need a new backpack?"

"Yep. Old one's busted." Marty snagged a black backpack off the store shelf and handed it to her. "This okay?"

After checking the price, she nodded. "Let's finish up. I don't want to be here all—"

I followed her gaze to the end of the school supply aisle. Sally Gordon veered her cart toward us.

Oh boy. I cringed, half expecting to see Pam Kelley on her heels.

"Hi, kids," Sally chirped. "Katie, can I talk to your mom a quick second?"

Any moron at Cross knew Sally was one of the biggest snitches to the reverend, even if for no good reason. I was curious if even he became weary of her obnoxious high-pitched voice and pathetic overkill on her devotion. Sally presumed I would obey her and walk away. She was mistaken.

"Sure." I stood still.

Surprised mirrored off her face, but I stayed right where I was, enjoying her bewilderment.

"What's up, Sally?" My mother attempted to be cheerful, but I knew better.

"Jan," she began in earnest, "I am glad I ran into you. I want you to know I'm praying for you and hoping the Lord will convict you and Sam about putting your younger kids in the Christian school where they belong. To deprive your children of ... Jan? Jan?"

My mother laughed with contempt, calling a solid goodbye over her shoulder. I rejoiced when she left Sally standing there looking quite stupefied.

Back in the car a few minutes later—without all our school supplies—Mom slammed the door and started the car. She slapped her hand hard on the steering wheel.

"Hey," I said. "Want me to drive?"

"No, I'm okay. I just didn't need ... *that*. It's none of her business. Besides, we do have you and Marty in the Christian school."

"I know, Mom. Just ignore it. Sally always sticks her foot in her mouth."

"Bet her feet taste gross!" Marty chimed in from the backseat.

My mom smiled for the first time in two days. The past forty-eight hours had been tough. We knew there would be some consequence delivered by the reverend but, so far, nothing. Waiting for the verdict just added to the emotional torture of the inevitable.

After the disaster of Sunday evening, we all went to bed out of sheer exhaustion. I tried to be helpful with my younger siblings by keeping them quiet and in bed to give my mom space. My dad made her a cup of chamomile tea and held her hand while she cried. A man of little emotion, my dad bore and buried things well. I wondered if there would ever come a day when his strength would run out. Or be crushed.

UNDER AUTHORITY

My dad was waiting for us when we arrived home a few minutes later. Still in his work clothes, he had come inside for a coffee break after retrieving the late afternoon mail. He didn't look happy. "I waited for you," he told my mother, then handed her an envelope.

My mother took a deep breath as she pulled the single piece of paper out of the envelope and began to read silently from the Cross Independent Baptist Church letterhead.

To: Janet DeConner
RE: Church discipline

In direct disobedience to Hebrews 13:7, which states that your pastor has command over you and he is to be obeyed, you shall receive the following disciplinary action for the rebellious violation of disrespectfully questioning the wisdom and authority of your pastor:

1. A period of silence in the church for two months. You will arrive for services, sit in the back, and speak to no one. No one is to speak to you.

2. A letter of repentance and an apology to me for your outburst which will be read in front of the church at the end of two months.

—Rev. Rhuttland Abbott
Approved by:
Ross Kelley, Elder
Pastor-in-training, Kevin Brayton

My mother handed her doom back over to my father. "Jan?" Concern filled his voice.

"Not now." She held up a shaky hand. "I can't."

"Keep an eye on the kids," my father told me after he read the letter himself. He followed Mom into the den and closed the door behind him.

I lunged at the letter he'd dropped on the counter. Within seconds, I was fuming. How cruel could one man be? How could he treat his own people like they were convicted felons?

I needed to get busy doing something. I couldn't just stand there and seethe, and I knew it wasn't a good idea to bother my parents. My siblings seemed delighted when I told them to go upstairs and play instead of assigning them a chore. I washed the dishes and rummaged around the kitchen to come up with a simple dinner plan.

Making myself useful was the least I could do for my mom since I was not at liberty to help her escape the hurt and grief she had to bear.

It was going to be a long two months.

Late Friday afternoon, Floyd and Velma Holtz came over. At the end of every summer, they came by to have my dad give their car a thorough check for their drive back down to Florida for the winter. How I envied them. They got to leave.

Velma and my mom would spend a few hours having tea before they said their goodbyes for the season. Thank goodness the reverend had not forbidden any members of the church to be on my parents' property, knowing full well my dad's business was here too.

Not long after they arrived, we noticed Velma wasn't coming in. By now, Cross members had been made aware of my mother's church discipline, and no one was to speak to her. I had hoped Velma would at least say a hasty goodbye as they would not see each other again until late spring.

"She's not coming in."

I was startled to see my mom standing behind me. She looked tired, and I knew she had not slept well that week. She had also begun sleeping downstairs again, preferring that bed over the one upstairs.

"What's that?" I nodded to the book she was holding.

"Can you do something for me?"

"Of course."

"See if you can slip this to Velma. I know she's out there, but if Floyd is with her, that's probably why she isn't coming in to see me."

Ah. That made sense. Floyd, along with his son Barton and daughter-in-law Diana Holtz, were loyal to Reverend Abbott. Even though Velma had more of a sensitive spot for my mom, she didn't dare go against her husband.

"No problem." I slipped on a pair of flip flops by the front door.

These last few days of August gave us the gift of flawless blue skies, zero humidity, and unlimited sunshine. The air smelled clean, the dogs bounced in the pen, and my Siamese washed himself in the sunshine of my open window. Any other time, we would all be outdoors enjoying such a beautiful day, but my mother was not feeling up to it.

I entered my dad's shop to see his back bent over the open hood of Mr. Holtz's car. I walked around to the open window where Velma sat alone in the front seat.

"Hi, Mrs. Holtz," I rested my arms on the open window.

"Oh, Katie," she faltered. "I ... I didn't see you there."

Mr. Holtz poked his head around the car with a frown, then turned back to something my dad was pointing out. I knew he was making sure his wife wasn't violating the reverend's order by talking to my mother. Once he saw it was me, I was dismissed.

"How is she?" Velma asked, her voice a whisper.

"Hurt."

Velma bit her lip and looked down at her lap. When she looked up, tears shimmered in her eyes. I forgave her for not coming in to say goodbye.

"Mom asked me to give you this." I slid the book to her.

She took it and turned it over. She echoed the title, *"Liberty of Conscience?"*

"Keep it to yourself, okay?"

With a nod, she thrust the book into her bulky purse and zipped it.

I returned to the house pleased I had been able to help my mom with that small task.

School began the following week, the day after Labor Day. I was unhappy to be there, torn between my oppression by Cross and my mother's church discipline.

Nervous about church that Sunday, we prepared ourselves for the worst. To our surprise, the service came and went with ease. We sat where we had been instructed. Since my mother was under disciplinary action, my father was not permitted to handle the offering, which I think he was relieved about. Being in the back of the church, we were ignored. We left right after the service, so it would not be awkward for my mom. At least, not any more than it already was.

My first week as a senior was complete, and I was glad to learn the year would not be an academically challenging one. Brynn, Karina, and I exchanged sad glances with one another as Jolee's absence remained a daily reminder of what could have been. We had big dreams, the four of us. We were all going to attend the same Christian college. Jolee and I were going to study music. She would play the piano, and I would sing. Brynn also played piano but wanted to pursue an elementary education major. Loving sports, Karina thought about studying physical education in hopes of returning to teach PE to kids at Cross because the current teacher was terrible.

But things change. Plans change. People change.

Karina's brother Vic was starting to frustrate me. I had left countless messages for him to call me, but he never did. My one lead on Jolee, Vic knew how to get in touch with Veronica and still hadn't called. I had no other choice than to place my hope in Karina, who promised she would try to light a fire under Vic and get me that phone number.

Happy it was Friday, Marty and I looked for my dad's Volkswagen in the parking lot. Instead, we saw Renata Tyner motioning for us to come over to her car.

"I'm taking you home today," she told us.

"Where's my dad?" I asked.

"Home with your mom."

I was instantly suspicious. Why hadn't he picked us up? My mom had chosen to continue her plans to homeschool Kyla and Mark, despite the reverend's attack on homeschoolers. We all began school the same day, and my Mom seemed eager to be busy again with her routine. But now, something was off.

"What's wrong?" I asked Mrs. Tyner.

"You can ask when you get home." I could tell she didn't want to talk or maybe felt she shouldn't.

Several minutes later, I dropped my backpack and saw my parents sitting together at the kitchen table. I saw my mom had been crying again. With an elbow on the table, her head rested in the palm of her hand.

"Come on, kids." My dad stood. "Let's go outside and see the new scooter a customer gave me today."

Shrieks of delight chased him out the door. Mrs. Tyner put some tea on for my mom, then seeing I had not gone outside, motioned for me to follow them.

I frowned and shook my head. "I want to stay."

"Let her stay, Renata," my mom mumbled.

"Mom, what's going on?"

"Sit with me," she pushed an envelope across the table.

"Do you think it's a good idea for her to read that?" Renata asked.

Mom's shoulders sagged. "She knows everything anyway."

"I just realized something," I said, looking at Mrs. Tyner. "You're here. You might get in trouble with Reverend Abbott for talking to my mom."

"Read the letter," Mrs. Tyner said. "Then you'll see why I came."

To: Janet DeConner
RE: Letter of rebuke to disobedience

I believe it is appropriate I address you forthwith. Your letter of apology has been received but I have doubts as to its merit. You asked for forgiveness for your outburst, yet you deliberately went behind my back and gave Velma Holtz a book which can only be regarded as a premeditated act of intent to undermine my biblical position of authority as pastor of the local church.

Not only have you chosen to go against the ministry of our church by choosing to home educate rather than fully support the Christian school, but you are also in violation of your period of silence in the church. I would have thought an intelligent person such as yourself would have understood this also meant not covertly giving a book to another believer in efforts to make her stumble and undermine me. Faithful followers of Christ like Floyd Holtz discovered the book and reported back to me.

I have also had the distinct impression that Burt and Renata Tyner are rumored to be seeking to find inconsistency with my preaching. Not only that, but I also have it on good report that both your families have sought to diminish the biblical truth of pastoral authority and have tried to elevate individual freedoms beyond what the Bible has taught. I would be glad to hear from you, to get your assurances what I suspect is not true, that you are keeping the verse that states that I am to be highly esteemed as your pastor.

You may not like this assessment, but there is no other way to solve your problem but to see the root of it, face it, and repent. The solution is not to gloss over the error. You may dispute what I assert, but these recent events demonstrate how far from the Lord you have been. Godly people, people who fear the Lord, do not proceed as you did. It was sin. It must be admitted and repented of. Until you admit your rebellion toward me and the resulting behavior, you will not be content in your life.

You need to take this as a serious matter. Your actions do not give you the right to contend with preachers. You need to take a good long look at yourself before you become a castaway. What you need in your life right now is repentance.

The choice is clear. You can either accept my authority and wisdom or reject it and elevate your own wisdom above mine. I hope you will give this thorough consideration, do the right thing, and avoid any further discipline.

—Rhuttland Abbott
Read and approved by:
Ross Kelley, Elder
Kevin Brayton, Pastor-in-training
Kenton Hearn, deacon

I dropped the letter on the table, astounded. Blood raced through my veins. Placing my hands on the sides of my head, I forced the whizzing sound in my ears to stop.

"We shouldn't have let her see that," Renata said.

I looked up, willing my pulse to slow down. "I'm fine. Just shocked."

I stared at my mom's face, swollen from tears which brought out the pink scar from her boating accident. The faint *S*, left by the bungee cord when it broke, was now visible. Just as if Reverend Abbott had come by to paint the *S* on her face so all the world would know of her sin. A reminder of Hester Prynne in Hawthorne's novel *The Scarlett Letter* who had to wear the letter *A* for her adultery. The similarities of their hierarchal church circumstances struck me.

Renata came to sit by me. "I'm not sure if I agree with your mom letting you see that, but now that you have, you need to be discreet about it."

"I know," I nodded. "Why were you mentioned?"

She surprised me by smiling. "Your mom and I have supported one another in recent weeks. We both choose to homeschool and try our best to live the way God intends us to live. Mr. Tyner and I have tried talking with others about God's love for us and his desire to be in a relationship with us, rather than the reverend's focus on obedience and punishment. This was poorly perceived in the eyes of the reverend once it got back to him. We meant no disrespect toward him. We just hoped to fellowship with other believers and explore the concept. We are working with the reverend to iron it all out."

"So, he knows you're here?" I asked.

"Of course not. I'm here for your mom."

My heart swelled with gratitude. Her choice to continue to befriend my mother, even at her own risk, was something I would never forget or take for granted.

"So, you're homeschooling this year too?" I asked.

"We made an arrangement with the reverend," she explained. "To show our love and support for him, we are paying the tuition at the school for Rayne even though he will not be in attendance. Bryce, of course, can't be in a classroom setting because of his health. I think the Reverend is satisfied with this agreement."

"You're paying Rayne's tuition, and he's not even going there? That's not right at all," I was incredulous.

"I don't do it for the man," Renata said. "I do it for the Lord."

"How so? The reverend gets his money. And what do you get?"

"I get my reward in heaven." She smiled again.

I couldn't take it, her grinning like that. "Why are you so happy about this?"

"I'm not at all pleased with the things that have occurred. But I'm happy in the knowledge my relationship with the Lord is such he has called me to minister to others right where I am. And right now, that's being here to support your mom."

"But what if the reverend finds out?" My question sounded more like a challenge.

"I imagine he will ask me to answer for that. But I feel God has asked me to be here, so I am." She leaned toward me as if to say something important. "If God calls me to do something, it's my duty to him to do it."

"But Reverend Abbott always says—"

"I know, Katie. Just remember, we answer to God, not a man."

I let that sink in and experienced something I hadn't felt in a while. Hope. It had been there all along, just buried deep within so it couldn't be stomped out at first sprout. Even though it couldn't be seen, its tiny bud had risen with enough bravery to want to grow and blossom.

I prayed this hope would one day flourish enough for all of us to gather the courage to confront the reverend. That one day we'd be free.

CHAPTER 19

JOLEE

After many weeks of waiting, I finally had it. Veronica's number.

I held the piece of paper in my hand, staring at the number like a map to a coveted pirate treasure.

"Sorry," Vic had said minutes ago on the phone. "I got your message from Karina and just now had time to get back to you."

I told him how grateful I was.

"About Veronica"—he said before I could hang up—"Don't let her appearance intimidate you if you decide to meet her. She's a nice lady."

"Um ... okay." I hung up and dialed the number he gave me, letting it ring while thinking about what he could have meant.

"Hello?"

I was surprised somebody answered so fast I almost forgot who to ask for. "Hi." I cleared my throat. "Is Veronica there?"

"Speaking. Who's this?"

"My name is Katie. You know Jolee Tisdale, right?"

There was hesitation on the other end of the line. "Yes."

"Uh, would it be okay if I came by to meet you? I'm Jolee's friend."

"I'm about to head to work. Later tonight?"

"Yes." I tried not to sound too excited. After jotting down a time and location, I was glad to see that Veronica lived downtown, not far from the state college. Had Jolee been right here in town the whole time?

Veronica wants to talk.

Later, when I told my parents where I was going, they asked me to be cautious of my surroundings. Happy I was finally going to be able to find my friend, they gave me the keys to the Volkswagen and asked me to be home at a reasonable time.

As I pulled out of the driveway to head downtown, I thought about the Tisdale family. A rush of sorrow overcame me. The reverend had preached a sermon against the family that past Sunday.

I knew it was coming at some point, even if Vic hadn't warned me. Jolee's parents had been absent from church for months now. They left without saying a word to anyone, their small section of the fourth pew on the right empty. Leaving the church without the reverend's prior consent was considered departing from the local church for unbiblical reasons.

"They must be backslidden," I overheard Diana Holtz tell Earl Simpson's wife Joan during prayer group that past Wednesday evening. It took every ounce of strength I had to keep my lips pressed together. Had I once considered Diana a friend? She came to see me a few times when I had my wisdom teeth out. But it wasn't long before she became infected with the Rhuttland Abbott disease just like the rest of the folks at Cross.

"The headstrong rebellion of the young teenage Tisdale girl will not be accepted here at our church!" the reverend shouted.

My hands gripped the metal chair until my fingers turned numb. Those who were relinquished to the back row were not given the privilege of a cushy, padded pew.

Somehow, the reverend did not seem to be aware of all the details about Jolee's actions. What a relief that besides me, only Vic, Karina, and my mom knew. I was relieved his spies had not discovered the abortion.

"God hates fornication!" he bellowed. "What does the Bible say about evil doers? It says they will surely die in their iniquity. Look at Ezekiel 3:18. Now, flip your Bibles over to Proverbs 11:21."

I nearly wore a hole in the dark blue carpet with the toe of my shoe. I looked over at my parents. My dad stared into his lap. My mother no longer took notes. My brothers doodled in a notebook. Kyla colored a picture. We were just present, so Mr. Kelley could check us off his attendance sheet.

"Some people like to depart from the church rather than answer for their transgressions," the reverend continued. "They'd rather slither away and pretend we don't have to give an account for our sin. The parents in this family will surely have to give an account for the sins of their daughter."

I squinted at the floor, counting tiny dots on the patterned carpet. How long until this tirade came to an end?

"Until the Tisdale family returns to church to confess their sin, they will be out of the fellowship and separated from any contact."

"And now they're all outcasts," I muttered as I made a turn from Main Street onto Maple View Road. As I neared Veronica's, my pulse quickened.

Several minutes later, I took a deep breath and knocked on the large apartment home before me. When no one appeared, I spotted a doorbell to the far right and pushed the button. Just as I wondered if I had the right house, the door opened.

"Hi." The woman standing in front of me was covered from the neck down in tattoos. I couldn't take my eyes off her. A walking museum of art with numerous piercings, including one in the nose, eyebrow, and upper lip.

"Katie, right?" she asked.

I nodded.

She invited me in. I was taken aback by how clean and neat her apartment was.

"Please." She gestured to the couch.

Her dark eyes flashed. I could tell right away she was an intelligent person, not at all how I had pictured the crowd Jolee chose to hang out with.

Veronica came straight to the point. "She's here."

"Now? Where?"

"Hang on a second. A few things you need to know."

"I talked to Vic already," I told her.

"Right, he mentioned that." She looked me over with a curious expression. "Why do you want to talk to her?"

"She's my friend. I've been worried about her for months."

Veronica angled her head as if trying to measure me up. Or maybe she was trying to decide whether I could be trusted. "She may have been your friend before, but you need to know that Jolee is different now."

"Different how?"

"You know what happened," she said. "But you can't know what it did to her."

"And you helped her do it." The words were out faster than I could stop them.

Veronica looked down at the floor. "Yes, I did. And I wish I could take it back. She was desperate. I had no idea it would break her."

To my amazement, Veronica began to cry. Tears pushed her heavy, dark eyeliner into black lagoons down her cheeks.

"I thought I was helping her get out of a bad situation," she murmured. "I've even tried to help her since then."

"Can I see her now? You said she was here." I could tell Veronica was a kind person and never meant for anything bad to happen.

"Yes, but she doesn't know you're here. She came back to pack up her things because she's moving out. She's been staying in the apartment upstairs that Robbie had but he split after ... well, you know." She sniffed and wiped her eyes with the tips of her fingers. "She's upstairs in unit D."

I jumped to my feet, and Veronica touched my arm. "Just remember what I said," she urged. "She's not the same person."

I nodded and started up the stairs. A door closed at the end of the hallway. A couple stumbled out, laughing. I froze upon seeing a spark of red hair, but it was not Jolee. The pair did not pay any attention to me and hurried out the front door. I kept my hand on the railing and kept going on what seemed like the longest staircase ever built.

Once at the top, I looked around and spotted a gold D on the outside of the door to my left. I realized my hands were shaking. Could I be about to see my friend after all this time? Was she all right? What had she been doing all these months? Going to school? Would she be happy to see me?

I knocked on the door and waited. Footsteps got louder as someone approached.

"Yeah?" A gruff-looking man stood in the open doorway, massive and muscular. He was tall with a full head of shaggy hair. His goatee covered a harsh, unsmiling face. "Better move on," he boomed. "You got the wrong place."

"Is Jolee here?"

His eyes narrowed. I knew with one blow this guy could knock me to the ground. But I refused to leave until I saw her.

"Yeah." He turned, leaving the door open. Taking that as an invitation to enter, I walked into a living area cluttered with boxes.

"Jo," the goatee called, "somebody here for you."

When the door beyond the kitchen opened, my heart dropped to my feet at first sight of my friend.

As our eyes met across the room, a thousand blurred images levitated between us. The church and its members. School. Trips to the country store. Volleyball games. Hanging out. Making music. Doing homework. School fundraisers. Camps. All of it. But the one vision that towered above the others was the reverend, his shadow attempting to obliterate as many of our childhood memories as he could.

A mere shell of her former self, Jolee stared at me, expressionless. She had lost a horrible amount of weight. I guessed she weighed barely a hundred pounds. Her cheekbones were more pronounced, making her look ten years older. She wore a long silky bathrobe, and her hair had been hacked above her shoulders with purple streaks running through it. Piercings on her nose and eyebrow startled me.

I closed my eyes to push away the pain at the stranger standing before me and focus on why I came.

"What are you doing here, Katie?" She was not happy to see me.

"Can we talk?"

"Good idea," the goatee said. He collected a set of keys on the counter and headed for the door. "I'll grab the beer."

"Who was that?" I asked, my eyes darting to the door the minute he left.

"My boyfriend," she said in a tight voice. "Shawn and I have been going out for a month now. I'm moving in with him."

I opened my mouth to protest, but quickly shut it. Jolee did not hide the fact she was not pleased to see me, and the last thing I wanted her to do was toss me out before we even got to talk. She began shuffling some boxes in the kitchen.

"So, can we talk?" I asked again.

"How'd you find me?"

"Does it matter?"

"There's nothing to say, Katie." She sighed and looked away.

I shook my head. "You know that's not true. We have a lot to talk about."

"Fine." She sighed again and flung a roll of packing tape onto the counter. She folded her hands across her chest and leaned against the refrigerator, waiting.

I could tell it was up to me to begin. Closing the distance between us, I walked over to her. Now that we stood only a few feet away from each other, I could see her face better. Jolee's beautiful eyes had once glittered with a mixture of mischief and glee. Now they appeared vacant and hollow.

"Well?" Jolee snapped. "You said you wanted to talk. So, talk."

"What's happened to you?" I whispered.

"What do you care?"

"How can you say that? What did I ever do to make you think I didn't care? You disappeared. I've been looking for you for months."

"There's things you don't know."

"I know Robbie got you pregnant. And the choice you made."

Her face took on an even darker look than I thought possible. "Get out!"

"No. I'm not leaving yet. Can't you understand how worried I've been about you? And Brynn? And Karina? How could you just leave us like that without any explanation?"

"Since you know what happened, you know why I couldn't come back."

"Look," I said, "I get why you didn't come back to Cross. Trust me, my family is going through our own share of problems." I paused to see if she would ask what they were, but she didn't. She just continued to stare at me with those lifeless eyes. I pushed on. "I guess what I really want to know is why you didn't tell me you were in trouble. Why didn't you trust me?"

She shrugged. "No reason. You were still at Cross. Look at it like this. I protected you so you could deny you knew anything."

I scowled at her. "That's the reason you cut all ties with me?"

Another shrug.

"I don't buy that."

No response.

"I understand about leaving the school and church, but why me? You know how I feel about that place. We've been best friends since we were little. If you don't want to hang out anymore and forget our friendship ever existed, then fine. But I think you owe me an explanation."

She just continued to stare at me. "I really thought it better you didn't know."

"Why?" I demanded. "You were in trouble. That wasn't your fault. Then you chose Veronica over me? I would've helped you figure this out."

"So, you've been buddying up to Veronica now, huh?"

"What? No. I only met her tonight. She told me you were up here. I want to know why you chose Robbie, Veronica, and ..."

"Shawn," she supplied.

"I was going to say this life. What happened to finishing school? Are you going to do that? Are you going to study piano like we've talked about for years? I'm guessing you're no longer interested in going to college with me. I'm not even sure if I'm going to go to a Christian—"

"Do me a favor," she snarled. "Don't mention the word *Christian* around me again. I've had my fill of Christians, and I'm surprised you haven't."

"What makes you think I haven't?" I tried hard not to raise my voice. "You have no idea what my family has been going through. Everything has gotten a lot worse there, Jolee. A few families have left, and I'm not sure how much more my own family can take."

That seemed to have a slight effect on her. "Sorry it's been rough," she mumbled.

"What I need to know is what changed? Did something happen to make you choose this life over the one you had? Your parents loved you, didn't they? Would they not have allowed you to go to another school?"

"They wanted me to stay this year, so they could leave Cross." Her ice thawed a bit. "I asked if I could transfer to Twin Rivers High, but they said they wanted me to finish at Cross since I'd been a student there since kindergarten. We got in a big fight about it. So, if anything changed, I guess it was that. They got mad. I got mad. I left."

"So why didn't you tell me?" I pleaded.

"What could you have done about it? I started hanging out with Veronica, then Robbie rented this apartment from her, and I met him. I fell in love with him you know."

I nodded, knowing that must be true.

"He promised me a lot of things." There was no empathy or feeling in her tone. "He packed up and left me after I told him about the pregnancy."

"I'm sorry he did that to you."

She pushed away from the wall. "I need a smoke."

"You smoke?"

She motioned me to follow her out onto the small balcony, pausing just long enough to pull a jacket over her shoulders. Nauseated by the smell, I stood back from her as much as I dared without offending her.

"I know." She waved her free hand at me. "You hate it. It stinks."

"Whatever." I turned my nose to the side.

"I can thank Robbie for introducing me to these." She held up her glowing cigarette. "Among other things." She mumbled the last part so quietly I almost didn't catch it.

Almost.

"What other things, Jolee?"

"Nothing," She popped the cigarette in her mouth.

"Drugs?"

She exhaled. "Look who's been a nosy little bee."

"Since when is being concerned about my friend considered nosy? What kind of friend would I be if didn't ask questions? If I hadn't tried to find you? If I hadn't bothered to show up here tonight?" I couldn't stop the frustration creeping into my voice.

She flicked the finished cigarette butt over the railing and turned to me. "Little miss perfect." She sneered, and I saw her teeth in the lamplight above her. They appeared to have yellowed, and I saw a blackened area over her upper gums.

"I never said I was perfect. You know me better than that," I shot back.

The goatee had returned with beer and called us inside. I was glad to be back indoors where it was warm, but the chill on the balcony had nothing to do with the weather.

"Thanks, babe." Jolee popped the metal cap off the glass bottle and took a long swig.

"No thanks," I said to her boyfriend who offered me one too.

He secured another before walking into the bedroom and closing the door. I was relieved he left the room as his presence made me uncomfortable.

"You drink too? You're seventeen."

"I do a lot of things now," she announced with a grin, revealing her teeth again. I had not been mistaken about the blackened area above her gumline.

Drug use.

"I'm not here to judge you," I told her.

She laughed out loud at that. "Oh, wait a minute." She pushed a section of purple hair away from her face. "I get it now."

"What?" I drew a blank.

She saluted me with her half-full bottle. "You're here to save me, aren't you?" Her bitter laugh was empty of any joy.

"Well," I mused, defensive. "That's not a bad idea."

"Aw, little churchy Katie here to rescue me." She swallowed another gulp of beer.

"Why are you calling me that?"

"So, did the reverend send you? Or did you just drop by to see if there was anything left to salvage?"

"You know he doesn't know I'm here." Exasperated now, I knew she was trying to bait me.

She regarded me over the mouth of the glass bottle with a wary expression. An uncomfortable silence passed. "Well?"

"Come with me," I urged. "You can stay at my house. No one from Cross must know. You can go to Twin Rivers High and—"

"And give all this up?" She waved her arms around.

"This isn't you, Jolee. Please."

"You're right," she said. And out of nowhere, a sad, bitter tone crept into her voice. "This is all that's left of her."

"It's enough!" I cried. Didn't she know she was crushing my heart?

"Okay. Therapy time's up," Jolee glanced at a clock on the wall. Her body shook, and she seemed eager for me to leave.

"Are you sick?"

"A savior *and* a healer!" She pretended to be triumphant. "Who knew?"

"Please, let me help you. I can get you out of here tonight." I was desperate.

"Goodbye, Katie."

For a moment, Jolee's countenance took on an almost mournful look, but it vanished before I could read it further.

"Please call me. Anytime. Night or day."

She nodded and opened the door to the apartment.

I crossed the threshold and turned to her one last time. "Please take care of yourself, okay?"

Another nod, and the door closed.

The door might as well have hit me full force in the chest, and the pain made me stagger. I managed to flounder my way down those endless stairs and back to the car. The magnitude of my failure in not being able to convince Jolee to leave overtook me. Tears blurred my vision as I drove home.

My adolescence perished that night. My friend of eleven years had chosen a different road with no wish to retreat.

Were we both lost now?

CHAPTER 20

WELCOME BUT UNINVITED

Ever since the night I'd seen Jolee, I'd been pondering the cliché life is a journey.

If my life were a journey, where would it take me? As I crept closer to eighteen, I was not one of those kids who had to run off with unrestrained recklessness at the prospect of turning into a legal adult. Quite the opposite. Stuck in an abyss, I contemplated my next move. Stay? Flee? Follow? Fight?

Sure, I could stay. Obey every single rule at Cross. Follow the commandments of the reverend—including attendance at an *approved* Christian college. I could be at church every week, prayer group on Wednesday nights, and even help with special music from time to time. With little effort, I could follow the course already set in place for us by the reverend. Was he not the man of God called to lead the congregation? Was he not placed behind the pulpit by God himself? I could submit and surrender, thus earning my crown in heaven. That would be easy, right?

Sure. As long as I never questioned the reverend's supreme authority.

I began to understand some things from my encounter with Jolee. Her own torment was so great she felt if she stayed, she would not make it. She fell into the arms of a stranger, who for a short time, showed her love and acceptance. And from what I could tell, she still searched for it any way she could, knowing full well she wasn't going to receive what she needed at Cross Independent Baptist Church.

Jolee was trying to escape all that plagued her. In some ways, maybe she was keener than any of the rest of us, despite her poor choices.

My own expedition of life up until now had been one of rules, regulations, and obedience to the pastor. I began to question this kind of life. Seeing what the reverend's tyranny had done to Jolee, my own mother, and many others at Cross gave me a lot to reflect on. I'd sat through more sermons than I cared to remember, each one as oppressive as the last. I wanted to be free of Reverend Abbott's dictatorship.

And so, I made my decision.

I just hoped my parents would support what I was about to reveal to them.

"Please say something." Nervousness trickled up and down my spine. It was almost ten o'clock by the time my siblings were asleep and I felt comfortable asking my parents if we could talk.

One thing was certain. The events concerning Cross and the reverend had brought us closer together. Despite my apprehension, I felt an indescribable peace. I knew I was doing the right thing.

My mother began wiping her eyes, which made me feel terrible. I knew this would cause a lot more problems for my parents, and that was the last thing I wanted.

"I'm sorry I mentioned it—"

"Don't be." My mom sniffed and surprised me with a huge smile, something I hadn't seen from her in ages. She looked over at my dad who appeared to be beaming.

"Wait ... you approve of this? All of it?"

"We sure do," my dad affirmed. "You just told us you have chosen your own pathway toward reaching your dreams. How could we be anything but happy for you?"

"But I'm leaving Cross to do it," I reminded him. "I'll finish the rest of this year at Twin Rivers High and then, I hope, be accepted into Juilliard."

"New York City?" my mother exclaimed. "Our daughter wants to sing opera. Who are we to stand in her way?"

"But it's not an approved college." I felt that was worth mentioning.

"Juilliard is a great school," my dad said. "And *we* approve. We'd be honored for them to accept you into their music program."

"I'm aware there will be consequences because I'm leaving Cross," I told them. "But I'm willing to take them as they come and work hard at making the best of it. I really want this, and I'm going to put in my application for the Juilliard School as soon as I can."

"You won't be doing it alone," they both assured me.

The next day, my parents allowed me to stay home from school so they could help me put into motion the beginning steps of change. While my mom stayed home teaching Kyla and Mark, my dad drove me downtown to the high school to get registered. We were told there would be no problem transferring even though I was almost halfway through the school year. I was surprised at the kindness the faculty at Twin Rivers High showed us. I hadn't expected that. I was also relieved the rules and dress code were less severe. Excited for my future for the first time, I dreamed about a more relaxed school environment and teachers who did not detest my existence.

But my elation screeched to a halt as I thought of the friends I'd be leaving in my wake. No doubt, after church discipline for my departure, I'd be an outcast. The peers I'd known most of my life would not be permitted to speak to me. That knowledge filled me with sadness but did not overwhelm me. I still felt I was making the right decision for my future.

I had been dreading the final task on my to-do list that day. I needed to compose a letter to the reverend resigning my church membership and withdrawing from the school. I decided not to say why. How was it any of his business? What gave him the right to dictate to me what I did with my future? Where I wanted to finish high school and attend college? Every time I thought about college, I felt immense relief I no longer had to choose one of the stringent Bible colleges. I knew the sooner I finished and delivered my letter, the faster I could look forward to a promising future.

I kept the letter short and straightforward. I told the reverend in a very businesslike manner I had chosen on my own accord to no longer be a member at Cross, I would finish school elsewhere, and I would attend college in the fall. I did not divulge where, why, how, or when. After my parents approved the letter, I took a deep breath and dropped it in the mailbox.

I had a few days at most to prepare myself for the aftermath of my decisions.

"Katie, come out to the shop with me," my dad said. "I want to show you something."

Three days had passed since I mailed my letter to the reverend, and I heard nothing in response. In a small town like Twin Rivers, the postal service moved fast. I knew by now Reverend Abbott had the letter in his possession. I imagined he was drumming up all kinds of ways he could discipline me.

My last few days at Cross Christian Academy were hard. I told my close friends what I'd decided but asked them to keep it quiet. Brynn's face turned white. Karina cried. Del said very little, but I think deep down he understood the time had come for us to admit we were going in different directions. I said goodbye and began planning for my new schedule at Twin Rivers High. My first time in a public school. I wasn't sure what to expect.

"What's up?" I asked as I followed Dad outside.

"Come see." He opened the door to the garage, and the first thing I saw was a midsize sedan in the middle of his main work area.

I raised my eyebrows. "What's this?"

"Call it an early graduation present." He grinned.

"You're giving me a *car*?"

"Well, I can't keep trekking you everywhere you need to go. Marty isn't ready to leave Cross yet, so you'll get to drive yourself downtown to school, and then you'll have something for when you go to college."

"Do you think you'll be ready to leave Cross at some point if Marty decides he doesn't want to attend school there?"

"We are discussing things," he said, then pointed to the car. "So, do you recognize this or what?"

"Hey, is this ..."

He laughed and smacked his hand on his leg. "Sure is. This Buick has been sitting here in the corner of my garage for years now. A customer couldn't pay for the new transmission it needed, so he signed it over to me. I thought I'd get it running again for you."

"You had to put in a whole new transmission?"

"I rebuilt one. Took a few days, but it's in and ready to go. This is a good first car and should last you a while. Not too heavy on the mileage and no rust."

I ran my hand over the dark gray hood of the car and took it in. It wasn't the prettiest car out there and already ten years old. But to me, it was perfect.

"Well?" he asked. "What do you think?"

"It's amazing. I can't believe it."

"I'm going to make a deal with you, Katie. This car didn't cost me anything except a few parts and my time. If you make honor roll in school and get good marks at college, I will put you on my insurance and pay it."

My mouth dropped open. "Really?"

"Just pay for your own gas. And," he warned, "deal's over if you slack off."

"I won't. I promise."

The next Sunday morning, an uneasiness filled the air as everyone got ready for church. Everyone except me. My siblings eyed me as I stayed in my pajamas, lingering at the kitchen table.

"Why aren't you ready?" Marty asked. "You sick?"

"No. I'm not going."

My parents escorted my inquisitive brother out the door, calling goodbye as they left. I said a quick prayer they would not be grilled as to my whereabouts that morning.

A few hours later, five very somber faces reentered the kitchen. My mother slammed her Bible and purse down on the counter. Her long skirt swished past me as she went into the den.

I felt sick when I heard her crying. I leaped to my feet and turned to my dad. "What happened?"

He told the other kids to go upstairs and change out of their church clothes. "I didn't realize it would happen so fast," he muttered.

"The preaching was about me today, wasn't it?"

"You were cleverly woven into today's sermon on insubordination, yes." He sighed.

"How bad?" I felt awful that he had to sit through a message in which his own daughter was banished.

"Well." He rubbed his chin. "We knew this was coming, so it wasn't any worse than the sermon against Jolee."

"Great." I rolled my eyes. "I'll bet he thinks I'm following in her footsteps, and that's why I left."

"Well, it doesn't matter what he thinks," he reminded me. "Do you still feel like you made the right choice?"

"One hundred percent."

"Then stay the course. Now, go comfort your mother."

Over the next several months, I woke up every morning looking forward to my new routine. I enjoyed the casual pace of life at my new school and making new acquaintances. My teachers were knowledgeable and helped me catch up with their curriculum. As my dad continued to drive Marty to Cross, I drove myself to school each day and remained focused on finishing the year strong. What an incredulous moment for me when my application from Juilliard arrived in the mail. I couldn't wait to select the piece I would send in for my vocal audition.

But I had other problems to deal with first.

Being cast out of the fellowship spread throughout the church quickly, like most viruses do. Brynn remained my friend and promised to play the accompaniment to my piece when I was ready to send it to Juilliard. Karina kept in touch as she did not live far away, but she was also preparing for her own future at a Christian college further south.

As much as the loss of some of my companions hurt, I was worried about Marty. He had been moody, which was unlike him. I decided to corner him into talking.

"Yo," I called to him, poking my head inside his room

one evening after dinner.

He sat crosslegged on the floor of his room working on his homework. "Yeah?" he said without looking up.

"Hey." I sat down in front of him. "What's going on?"

He frowned. "What do you mean?"

"Well ..." I offered. "You seem distracted lately."

"So? I'm studying." He continued to act as if deep in concentration over his science book, which I knew for a fact bored him.

"Yeah, I can see that. Can you stop for a sec?"

He dropped his pencil with a flick of his wrist which I took to be a little sarcastic.

"What's with you?" I asked. "Are you upset with me about something?"

"School blows, is all."

"Okay. In what way?"

"People are just mean," he muttered, looking unhappy.

Like the switch on the wall above his head, it was as if it had turned on all by itself. The room grew brighter as comprehension of what was really taking place sank in.

"It's me. You're hearing people talk about me, is that right?"

"Yeah."

"And?" I coaxed, sensing there was more to it.

"And they razz me a lot."

"Who?"

He shrugged. "Kids. Teachers don't like me much anymore either."

"Who?" I demanded, my anger rising.

"Mrs. Miller said you are a bad example to me."

I grunted. "That woman needs to mind her own business. She likes to say things before finding out if they're true or not. Remember what she said about your old friend Preston Terrell? She didn't know the full story then, and she doesn't know it now. She has some bad habits, that's it."

He nodded and picked up his pencil. "Yeah, she's just an old hag."

"Hang in there for me, will you?"

"Yeah, I guess."

After a quick noogie to the top of his head, I left him to finish his homework.

"Katie?" My mom was busy stacking homeschool materials in a neat pile on the right side of her desk when I got downstairs. "Can you go out and grab the mail? I'm expecting a refund for that defective crock pot I bought a few weeks ago. I'd like to see if it arrived."

"Be right back," I called over my shoulder, zipping up my warm jacket.

As usual, the mailbox was stuffed full. My dad often received solicitations or payments. He tossed aside what he didn't want and opened the more important-looking items. "More bills," was his customary reply to the daily mail.

I dropped the mail on the counter, then draped my coat around the back of the dining room chair. I plopped down after opening a thick Sears catalog from the bottom of the pile. "Hey, Mom," I joked. "At least we won't have to shop for long skirts anymore."

"Mmmm," she replied. She pulled out a white envelope and handed it to me. "Did you see this?"

Surprised, I reached for the letter. "From Diana Holtz to me," I told my mom. Her eyes grew cold as I tore open the envelope. I pulled out a pink piece of stationery with a short, handwritten note on the front.

Katie,

By now, you know we have all been made aware of your disobedience and rebellion toward Reverend Abbott and the church here at Cross.

How can you deny the reverend his right and

privilege to graduate you from Cross Christian Academy and give you his blessing as you attend Bible college? After all the reverend has done for us in the church and for your own family as well, the lack of appreciation for the loyalty that belongs to him is a great disappointment to me.

You walked into my life welcome, but uninvited. I thought I could become a friend to you, but I see now my only choice is to separate from you until you make a full confession of your sins of ungratefulness and defiance to your pastor.

Because you have left the church unity for unbiblical reasons, I will close this letter as a goodbye to you and a hope that one day you will repent.

—Diana

Furious, I crumpled the letter into a tight ball. I jumped out of my chair, then caught it before it toppled to the floor.

"Katie?" my mom said. "What did—"

I slammed the bathroom door without answering her and shredded the letter into a hundred tiny pieces. One flush and the pink confetti disappeared.

You walked into my life welcome, but uninvited.

How dare she judge me like that. Anger crept up into my face, warming my cheeks. I reflected on the time she came to visit me when I did not feel well from my oral surgery. Even though it was a routine procedure, I had some difficulties, developing painful phlebitis in my arm from the IV sedation, which required antibiotics.

At the time, Diana and her husband had not been attending the church long. They moved to Twin Rivers from another state at her father-in-law Floyd's request. She was beautiful and had a quick smile for others. When I had my wisdom teeth removed, she arrived that day with a pleasant-smelling lilac candle to cheer me up. Her kindness touched me. And though she was older, I started looking up to her. She was gentle. Intelligent. The kind of person I wanted to be one day.

You walked into my life welcome, but uninvited.

I fumed at her words. *I never walked into her life. I was here first. She's the one who walked into mine.*

I left the bathroom in a huff and almost ran into Mrs. Tyner.

"Oh, hi," I muttered. I had forgotten she was coming to give Kyla her piano lesson.

"I heard you got a letter."

"I don't want to talk about it," I was still seething. How could she? What kind of person tells a friend they were not invited into their life?

"I don't know what the letter said," Renata's tone was kind. "But remember, we are not here to please man. We answer to God. You are not responsible for her actions, only yours."

"Thanks," I mumbled. I did not want to engage with Renata about this or anything else for that matter. I just wanted to be alone.

Once upstairs in my room, I was able to breathe. Part of me mourned the loss of my short friendship with Diana. Part of me understood that maybe it wasn't all her fault. She was under the reverend's spell. How else could a warm human being like Diana morph into such a cold-blooded creature?

I could not deny how much her letter hurt. But with this fresh wound came the reminder I would rise above this. I would find new friends along my journey. I would make new memories at every stop along the way. I would learn new things. I would laugh, dance, and sing.

And I would bury each member of Cross Independent Baptist Church deep in a locked room within my soul and never hear from them again.

CHAPTER 21

ANOTHER SUICIDE

I was about to step into the kitchen when I heard Mom and Renata talking. Kyla's piano lesson was finished, and since it was early on a Friday night, Renata was in no rush to go home.

"You know me, Renata." The strain could be heard in my mother's voice. "You know I can't take this anymore."

"Yes, Jan, I do know you. And I know you're hurting, but—"

"It's bad enough I had to sit through a sermon where my own daughter's name was withdrawn from the fellowship. But it doesn't end. Now the Lesters and the Griffiths are out too. All because they wanted to homeschool their kids."

"They were cast out because the reverend felt they left for unbiblical reasons," Renata said.

"Oh, right," my mother mocked. "Homeschooling is *unbiblical*. I forgot."

"You know it isn't." Renata soothed. "Remember, it's not about homeschooling. For Reverend Abbott, it's about the money going into the Christian school to support it."

My mother scoffed. "You know, you'd think the reverend would be more concerned about losing families. You'd think he'd want to keep them around, right? Did you know Barry and Darlene Cobb are leaving too?"

"No, I didn't know that."

"Barry came by yesterday, so Sam could change the oil in his car. He told us Darlene has been very unhappy here in Twin Rivers. Their camp isn't doing well either. They're putting it up for sale and moving north. Darlene has family there."

"I'm glad for them," Renata said. "They're such a sweet family. I'll try to give them a call later to see if they're okay or if there's anything I can help them with."

"Keep that attitude up, and you'll be next on the reverend's excommunicated list."

Stifling a laugh at my mother's comment, I huddled in the corner of the mudroom near the doorway. I knew I shouldn't be eavesdropping but decided to linger a moment longer.

"Unfortunately, I think Burt and I are on our way there," Renata sighed. "Remember I told you we have been exchanging faxes and letters with the reverend? It's not going well."

"How so?"

"We wrote a letter full of love and respect, pleading with him to stop driving out more people over the homeschooling issue. We told him while he may not have intended to touch off this firestorm of dissent and hatred within the brethren, he had fertilized it, creating a big problem."

"That was no accident."

"We're giving him every benefit of the doubt," Renata explained. "Our latest issue is that we talked to Kevin and Gwen Brayton about these things, which turned out to be a mistake. Pastor Kevin took what we thought was a confidential conversation straight to the reverend."

"Didn't you know he would?"

Renata shook her head. "No. I thought we were just chatting with other believers. Since Kevin is a new pastor, we thought he would do a little reflection on the matter and keep it confidential."

"But he's being trained by Reverend Abbott. You had to know that wouldn't go well." I could hear the exasperation in Mom's voice.

"Well, I do now. We got a letter."

"And?"

"Pastor Kevin had his older brother Kory write to us, and it was rough."

"Isn't he a pastor too? Out west somewhere?"

"Yes, and quite the fire-and-brimstone preacher. His letter came across brutal, to be honest. He began by insulting Burt. Said his MIT education did not make him a genius with Bible scholars, and he had concerns with Burt traveling for work and not staying home taking care of his family and serving in the local church. He even accused Burt of being covetous with money by choosing to travel for work over being in the Lord's house each Sunday. The letter went on to say the Bible does not teach us to think for ourselves or independently of a church. According to him, all our thinking needs to be under the local church authority and accountability."

"What? That's ridiculous."

"It was a long and harsh letter. He ended it by saying Reverend Abbott was not a dictatorial and despotic pastor. He does not tell us what kind of car to drive, what house to buy, the color of clothes to wear, or the kind of peanut butter to eat. He went on to say what he saw in us was that we were the type of people who do not like to do what we are told, confusing the man of God with a godless national government. We need to repent and submit to the pastoral leadership in the church."

"And stop asking questions," my mom finished.

"Yes, but we're not done yet. I think we need to explore this further. I was not interested in getting Kory Brayton involved, but his younger brother Kevin does seem to listen better. Maybe we can get him to reflect on some things and open a line of discussion with the reverend."

"How's that working so far?"

Renata chuckled. "Well, let's just say I'm not ready to give up quite yet. We want to show the reverend our love by staying and supporting him. We think we can get him to soften up a bit about homeschooling and even see the light on some other things."

"I'd love to see the two of you having coffee and doughnuts with the reverend," my mom quipped.

"In one of our letters to him, we offered just that."

Things got quiet for a long moment, then I heard Renata say, "Are you really going to do it?"

"Yes," my mother replied. "I'm ready to say goodbye to Cross."

I knew what my mother had chosen to do. We talked about it as a family. Even though my dad decided to stay until after Marty finished the school year at Cross, my mom shared with us she could not sit through one more of Reverend Abbott's ruthless sermons. She knew full well she would be excommunicated, but she accepted that. I think my father held out hope the Tyners' communications with the reverend would produce results, so he was not ready to leave yet. I worried that things would become too complicated for him with only a partial family in attendance.

Two Sundays later, my father looked upset upon arriving home from church. Usually, he changed out of his suit and tie and entered the kitchen in search of lunch, chattering as he went.

Not today.

Sitting by the old wood stove, he leaned his head on the back of the sofa. "I'm no longer a deacon," he told us.

My mother set her book down and frowned. "What do you mean?"

"Ross Kelley informed me that since I have an insubordinate wife and rebellious daughter, I am no longer qualified to be a deacon. I was advised to get my household in order."

"We *are* in order," Mom snapped. "And he doesn't get to say we're not."

"I know. I guess it's my turn now. I'm getting the looks and stares. Like I committed some terrible crime."

"We have a plan," my mother reminded him. "We just need to wait for Marty to finish the year at Cross. Can you wait two months?"

"I guess," he said. "Maybe by then, things will change. Maybe Burt and Renata can get through to the reverend."

I admired my dad for his confidence in the Tyners, but I knew better. The problem wasn't that Burt and Renata couldn't produce a change. Reverend Abbott didn't *want* to change. He didn't want to compromise by admitting he had taken his position of pastoral authority too far. But most of all, he did not want to lose his power.

I hoped Burt and Renata would see the correspondence they had initiated with the Reverend and others in the church would not make any difference now or ever. One day, they would either be church disciplined for questioning the pastor, separated from, or cast out of the fellowship. Why would they be different from any other member at Cross who dared to question?

The Tyner family just wanted a genuine relationship— one of love and respect without tyranny and dictatorship. But the integrity in their hearts was not strong enough to withstand the reverend's power and would ultimately end up being their undoing. The reverend would see to that.

"Stop right there." Mr. Kelley marched straight toward my mother and me.

Lawn chairs in hand, we were ready to enjoy watching Marty kick a few goals in his spring soccer game on this cool but sunny Saturday morning while my dad finished up a transmission repair. We knew it would be uncomfortable to be around others from Cross, but we were there to support Marty, not them.

Holding up his hand, Mr. Kelley stopped us as we got out of our car. "You are not allowed to be here."

"Why not?" my mother asked, keeping her tone even.

"You are under church disciplinary action," he said. "You are not permitted to be in attendance at any church or school function."

Several heads turned in our direction. Chatter and laughter ceased. I could almost hear them saying, "Have the defiant DeConners risked showing up at a school event?"

"Wait just a minute," my mother shot back. "Who says I can't be here?"

"Well ..." Mr. Kelley cleared his throat. "Reverend Abbott said—"

"This property is in Roganfield, right? So, it's public property. This is a public field in the town of Roganfield. Correct?"

"Uh, well, I guess." Mr. Kelley's mustache twitched in irritation.

"As a taxpaying citizen in the town of Roganfield, I hereby declare I am permitted to be on this property. Come on kids, grab your chairs."

Strolling past a shocked Mr. Kelley, we entered the field and set our chairs down on the opposite side from where

Cross members were lined up. We felt there were more eyes on us than the actual game, but no one wanted to make a scene in front of the opposing team.

And no one could be prouder of their mom than I was that morning.

My mother and I stood on the front stoop of the Tyners' house and waited for them to answer the door.

"Come with me, Katie," my mother had asked earlier. "We need to bring lunch for Renata today. She's upset and needs cheering up."

"What's wrong?" I asked.

"It's a long story, but it does involve Reverend Abbott."

Kyle opened the door. "Hi, Katie. Mrs. DeConner. Mom's in the back." He motioned to his dad's office. A little ahead of me in school, Kyle had finished his freshman year at a Christian Bible college, but I could tell he was not enjoying it. As a natural born computer whiz—a gift he inherited from his father—I knew Kyle wanted to attend a college that had offered programming and information technology. Anytime something was amiss with our computer at home, Kyle would have it fixed and rebooted within minutes. And when he tried to explain what he did, we just stared at him. He might as well have been speaking a foreign language.

We followed him through the kitchen and into the large office where Mr. Tyner had several computers set up for his business. To my surprise, Mr. and Mrs. Tyner were both seated on the small couch against the wall. Tears rolled down Renata's cheeks.

Burt stood and took the bags of food. "Kyle and I can take these to the kitchen."

Kyle tossed a disappointed look over his shoulder before he left the room with his dad.

Renata adjusted her long skirt, then leaned back on the couch and dried her eyes with the tissue my mother handed her. With her red face and swollen eyes, she did not look well.

"I'm here now," my mother said. "Talk to me."

Renata cast a worried glance in my direction. "I'm not sure Katie needs to hear this."

"Katie knew things about June before the rest of us did," my mother reminded her.

June Britton?

I thought about June. I pictured her pretty face, long brown hair, and wide smile while she sang in church with the autoharp on her lap. The picture faded into another one of her seated alone in church, having been told to separate from her atheistic husband.

"I'm sorry, Katie." Renata sniffed and attempted a smile. "I'm just having a hard day."

"It's okay." I pulled one of the computer chairs over to the small couch.

"What happened?" my mother asked.

Renata stared at the floor. "It's about June's husband, Glen."

"I thought they were separated."

"They are," Renata said. "Thanks to the Kelley's. They're the ones who talked June into leaving him because he would not change his ways. He didn't believe in God, or so he told everyone. And he didn't want to come to church."

"I remember," my mom responded. "Has something changed?"

Renata looked up. "For all his faults, he loved June. And she loved him too." She grew quiet, and I could tell she was working up the courage to tell us something important. "He tried to get June to come back to him countless times," she went on. "Each time, Pam Kelley and Sally Gordon convinced her not to return to him because he was not a believer."

I made a disgusted throaty sound. I couldn't help it.

"But I found out just this morning ..." Renata covered her eyes and winced. "Glen has been in a deep depression and tried to commit suicide last night. He almost succeeded. Now he's in the hospital, in ICU. The doctors aren't sure if he's going to live, but if he does, he is expected to suffer permanent brain damage. He may never walk or speak again."

My mother's face turned white. Tears followed. My own eyes remained dry, as this news had me rooted to my seat in horror.

"Another suicide," I found myself mumbling. Stunning me even more was the realization it was not the first time I had said those words. I jumped to my feet. "Another one. How many does this make?"

My mother and Renata stared at me, startled at my outburst.

I glared back at them. "How can you be surprised this happened?"

"Katie, what—"

"The suicides. How many more will there be? And"—I leaned in close so they could hear the last part—"the reverend is responsible. He drives them to it. You know it, and I know it."

Mr. Tyner appeared in the doorway. "Everything okay in here?"

No one responded.

"Come in, Mr. Tyner," I said. "You might as well hear this too."

"I'm aware," he said grimly. "Katie, can you give us a moment? I want to talk to your mom and my wife."

Frustrated, I left the room in search of Kyle. I should've known he was hovering near the office doorway.

"I heard," he muttered.

I pulled out a kitchen chair and sat at the table. I gazed out the large window that overlooked their neighbor's apple orchard. The view was spectacular with countless rows of trees and mountains in the distance. Below the window and down a hill was a flat parcel of land in which rested the remains of an inground swimming pool.

"Think your parents will ever fix that pool?" I asked, calmer now.

"Maybe." He shrugged. "They've talked about it, but nothing ever came of it. One year, Dad needed a new car. My mom has been talking about replacing her piano for a grand. And now I'm in college. I guess the old pool gets put on the back burner again."

"It must've been amazing once—in its day."

"Well, this house was old before my mom and dad bought it, and it's always looked like that. I guess they don't really see the point in fixing it if we can only use it for the short summers here."

The long, empty pool spoke to me. I noticed the cracks along the cement and the thin ribbons of earth that pushed through them. Disintegrating blue paint and small sections of concrete were also chipping off the sides. I found myself comparing the Tyners' decrepit pool to Cross. How similar they were. Decaying from the inside out.

"One day, there will be nothing left," I told Kyle.

"Maybe." Another shrug. "So, after you're done at Twin Rivers, it's Juilliard, huh?"

I nodded with pleasure at hearing the name of the school I would be attending as soon as my senior year ended. It would prove to be an interesting summer, indeed, with Marty choosing not to return to Cross Christian Academy next year. He would be homeschooled along with Mark and Kyla. I knew my father wanted to leave, now that nearly everyone there looked at him with disdain. He even lost several customers from the church who no longer took their vehicles to him even for a routine oil change, including the reverend.

"You're lucky, you know," Kyle said.

"Because of Juilliard?"

"Because you got to have a choice."

"Maybe you can transfer," I suggested. "Talk to your parents. I think they'd listen."

Before he could reply, Mr. Tyner called us both into the office. "We want to have a little prayer meeting. If anyone is going to pray for Glen and June, it has to be us."

"You really think no one else will?" I asked him.

"I don't think they know how to pray. They will pray for superficial things like helping them repent of their sin and turning from their wicked ways, that sort of thing."

Together in a circle, we bowed our heads and began to pray in a different way than we ever had before. Mr. Tyner led a prayer of thankfulness for God's mercies toward us in all situations and ended with Renata's prayer for healing, not only for the Britton family but also for everyone at Cross. That moment became the best church service I'd ever experienced.

For the first time, I got a glimpse of what being in the presence of God felt like. As the five of us prayed together there in that moment, a true peace settled over the room, and we were all touched by it. No one was struck down by an angry God. Not a single one of us felt burdened by some imaginary sin we were told we had committed and needed to be punished for. And no one had to answer to the authority of the reverend.

Could our life with God be one where we really loved one another? Where we extended forgiveness? The little seed of hope deep inside me sprouted its first flower.

CHAPTER 22

THE LETTERS

After twelve tumultuous years of perseverance toward what we thought was godliness, we began to accept that all our efforts were worthless. Our strength was gone, and our hearts had run out of resilience.

Somehow, my father managed to make it through the next few months at Cross. The Sunday he had chosen to be his final church service, he came home with a sorrow that was hard to witness. Instead of being jubilant he would no longer have to attend services, he was subdued and went off into the woods to be by himself.

I later learned many people had said spiteful things to him at his departure.

"You will need to answer for your failures toward God," Mr. Kelley told him.

"You will give an account for your disruption of the church unity," Floyd Holtz warned.

Pastor Kevin Brayton said, "You would do well to fall on your knees in humble submission."

"The reverend is the man of God. You will pay for your sin of disobedience." This from the church music director, Mr. Hearn.

The reverend wouldn't even look in his direction.

No one said thank you for all the years of hard work in helping others there, whether for a churchwide workday, giving discounts or free auto repair, or extra deacon responsibilities. No one said goodbye. We had been wiped clean of the Cross registry and obliterated. To them, we were dead.

I was fearful the Tyners were now in range to be the next targets.

Amazed at Burt and Renata Tyner's endurance at the many months of letter writing, fax exchanges, and emails with the reverend, I couldn't help wondering at what point in time it would come crashing down around them. If not careful, they'd be buried under their own rubble of wasted endeavors and the irretrievable loss of time.

The downward spiral had already begun.

Right after one of our weekly prayer circle meetings with the Tyner's, they told us about the letter they received from the reverend.

"He began with a rebuke," Burt explained. "He believes our letters and faxes are unbiblical because they are disrupting the unity of the brethren as well as placing our wisdom above God's."

"But how?" my dad interjected. "This isn't about the brethren. You've communicated not only your support for Reverend Abbott but also ways to reconcile."

"We have apologized for any misrepresentation he said we portrayed regarding preaching or church leadership." Renata said. "But he viewed our approach as disobedience to his authority."

I listened with a heavy heart as the Tyner's revealed they were now under a two-month church discipline in which they could not attend services or be in communication with any members.

"We need to let him know we still support him and his ministry. We think there is a way to rectify things," Burt stated.

I marveled at their determination but had my doubts they would succeed. Regardless of Burt and Renata's personal sacrifices to reach the reverend's heart, they did not give up hope even while under the discipline period. They prayed in earnest. They believed change to be possible. They composed more letters with faith they would be read and considered. With each letter, they approached the reverend in love and with respect.

"Mom," I began as we cleaned up the kitchen together after dinner, "how long do you think the letters and faxes will go on with the Tyner's and Reverend Abbott?"

"I'm not sure," she replied. "But I worry for my friend."

More painful responses were received from the reverend. Try as they might, he would not budge with his view of them as anything but disruptive. His next letter to them was proof.

Over tea the following week, Mom expressed concern. "Renata, you look tired."

"I'm all right," she assured us. "Just troubled. We don't seem to be making any headway with Reverend Abbott."

"What about his wife?" I thought of Mrs. Abbott playing the piano each Sunday. She was a quiet, submissive, and obedient example to the ladies of the church. Everyone seemed to revere her. "Would she listen if you tried speaking to her?"

"She is not receptive." Roberta shook her head. "Probably not allowed to speak with us."

"Is it the most recent letter that's upsetting you?" Mom refilled Renata's mug.

She nodded, closing her hands around the warmth. "This one has us confused. He is telling us we need to repent of our disobedience, but we have yet to find in Scripture where we disobeyed him. And now because of this, he is saying we cannot return to church at all until we repent and ask for his forgiveness."

"Repent of what?" I was exasperated.

"We don't know for sure. We have been trying to get him to tell us how we sinned. But so far, he keeps repeating the Bible verse that tells us to obey them that have rule over us and to submit ourselves. We are happy to do this, but we feel this Scripture does not apply to this situation."

I was amazed that the Tyner's refused to give up. They believed in the reverend and thought they could get him to accept that they meant no harm by talking with the other church brethren. We were getting concerned for them that their fate had been sealed, and they refused to accept it. A swift response arrived for them upon their repeated request for the reverend to explain the sin they committed.

"It's getting personal." Renata slid the letter across the table.

I opened the letter and began to read out loud.

To: Burt and Renata Tyner:
You have been warned not to make statements that could be misinterpreted as undermining or divisive, and you did not heed. I was approached with accounts of undermining statements made against me. You continue to distort and cover up your words, passing them off as "bearing one another's burdens" and blaming others for their own misinterpretation. Because you would not repent of your divisive words, we felt that imposing church discipline might move your hearts to see your sin and repent. Rather than choosing to repent, you sought to be contentious with evading issues and spreading your own opinions on topics such as homeschooling, church attendance, and discipline.

Further, do you want true reconciliation, or is your

goal to discredit me? Knowledgeable Bible scholars understand there is a case for putting people out of church, which would exclude them from having the choice of assembling. God put Ananias and Sapphira out of the church for lying to the Holy Ghost. Therefore, to obey my authority does not contradict Scripture. If you spread your opinions to others, I will see it as a deliberate attack of slander against me.

You are consumed with pride. You seem to delight in instructing others in spiritual matters which is not your place. You can submit to the wisdom of the overseers of our church or continue under church discipline. You are to stop your continued efforts to discredit my wisdom and actions. The Bible is clear in 1 Thess. 5:12–13. I do not believe you can build a case for your obedience to these commands. And until you do, you shall have no fellowship with other Bible believers.

I dropped the letter on the table, dumbfounded.

"What divisive words is he referring to?" my mom asked.

"It all points back to when we were attempting to speak with other families in the church regarding the homeschooling debate. But we never undermined, criticized, or verbally assaulted him in any way. We explained this and continue to be baffled as to why this remains unresolved." Renata sighed.

"Why do you want to go back though?" I couldn't help but ask. "We are enjoying our prayer meetings each week. Maybe there is another church you could visit?"

"We have been members at Cross a long time and want to be reunited with our brothers and sisters in Christ. We have searched our hearts as well as our actions, and we do not believe we have sinned."

"I don't know what to say." I handed the letter back to Mrs. Tyner. We discussed the Tyners' next steps. My mother warned Renata there would be no winning for her or Burt in the end.

"But it's not a race," she insisted. "We're not trying to win something. We want him to believe our intent was not to slander him. We asked him to show us where in the Bible we violated God's commands. We feel we haven't done this and to be accused of it is frustrating."

"But you did talk to people in church about him, correct?" my mom pointed out.

"Yes, but not like he says we did. We were merely showing our support to other homeschoolers and trying to get those families to stay."

"Your intentions were good but imagine how the reverend perceived that." Mom set her empty mug on the table and reached for the butter cookies.

"I don't understand how this has all gotten so out of proportion."

"You were only trying to help others," I offered.

"Exactly," Renata agreed. "That's all we've ever wanted to do. Help others, edify fellow believers, share our burdens with one another, encourage those who are discouraged. How is any of that wrong?"

"It isn't," my mother said. "But the reverend doesn't see it that way."

"Then we must continue to persuade him to see the truth." She stood with a face full of new determination.

A full week had passed when we read this most recent response with eyes wide. Mrs. Tyner had just finished Kyla's piano lesson. My dad was out in the garage tinkering with their car, and the kids had gone outdoors to play.

> To: Burt and Renata Tyner,
>
> Many times, you have assured me of your love and support. However, I have not had your assurance that you will *esteem them highly* or *obey* them or *submit* or *whose faith follow.*

UNDER AUTHORITY

(Read: 1 Thess.5:13, Heb 13:7, Heb. 13:17)

It is obvious you do not honor those commands, for you would have done so. Are you ready to allow your pastor to do the *perfecting of the saints* with you? Or are you still of the opinion that you should be doing the perfecting of me?

(Read: Eph 4:11–13)

I once again remind you that until you are ready to deal with your actions and give assurances NOT of your love, but of your obedience to the verses listed above, we will not be able to come to reconciliation in the unity of faith.

PS: When you answer for your sin of divisiveness, I will correspond with you again. I will give you one simple answer at a time, so you will not be easily confused. To give you instruction as to what I mean, you can tell matters that need to be dealt with because if the sentence has been italicized, that is particularly important.

"He's getting more brazen with you now." My mother's voice was etched with concern as she folded the letter and handed it back to her friend.

Renata rubbed her eyes. "That one stung a bit more than the others."

I sat nearby, sorry for her, yet at the same time the sorrow was beginning to wear thin. Didn't she know she was not going to get through to the reverend like she believed she would? Did they hope a day would come when they would change his mind?

"They don't get it, do they?" I said to my mom after they had gone home.

"They just don't want to give up."

"But how far will all this go?"

"I think you know," Mom said with a long sigh. "It will be over when the Tyner's are cast out of the fellowship for good."

"You're kidding!" I was incredulous.

"I'm as shocked as you are," my mother said. "After several months of church discipline, the Tyner's showed up at Cross Sunday."

"But why?"

"For one thing, they missed being at church. Second, they had it in their heads the reverend didn't believe in their love and support for him. So, they decided that returning to church would show their devotion to him and loyalty to Cross."

"But they had to know their presence would upset him."

"You and I know that. But Burt and Renata are seeing this another way."

I couldn't even imagine how angry Reverend Abbott must've been upon seeing the Tyner's show up at church when he told them not to.

As predicted, they did receive a reply later that week. And no one was prepared for how cruel and savage it would be.

CHAPTER 23

THE REVEREND'S FURY

Weary from my incessant pacing, I dropped into a heap on the couch next to my youngest brother Mark.

He frowned. "What's your deal?"

"Nothing," I muttered.

"It's something." He rolled his eyes and continued fiddling with a contraption he was making.

"What's that?"

"My trap." He looked annoyed. "Dad told me I could have it. I'm trying to fix it."

"What's it for?"

"Squirrels. Maybe I'll catch a skunk instead and put it in your room."

Just as I opened my mouth to retort, the phone rang. I leaped to my feet—ignoring Mark's order to watch out—and nearly knocked the wooden snare out of his lap.

"Atlantic Transmission and Repair," I answered. At any given time during Monday through Saturday, we had been instructed to answer the phone with my dad's business name.

"Hi there," a voice responded. "Is Sam around? Gotta question about my old Chevy that's making a funny noise."

"Sorry, he's not available." I took a message and promised the man Dad would call back as soon as possible.

Not the person I expected. *Why won't they hurry up and call?* My mind reprocessed the afternoon events hoping to recover something I had missed.

"Katie!" When Dad called my name earlier that day, he didn't sound right. At two in the afternoon on a weekday, he should have been in his garage working. He usually came in the house for a morning coffee break for about fifteen minutes followed by a quick lunch. For my dad, being self-employed meant long hours in the garage and doing his best to keep up with vehicles awaiting repairs. Calling for us in the afternoon was not customary. But the urgency in his tone alarmed me more than his presence.

I rushed down the stairs, entered the kitchen, and saw my mother crying. She was gathering her purse and a few other things. My dad was fishing around in the junk drawer for his car keys. He slammed it shut just as I hurried over.

"Katie," he said. "I need to you stay here and watch the kids."

I shivered. "What's going on?"

"Don't have time to explain, but something's happened to Renata. She's in the hospital. We'll let you know when we find out more. We're heading there right now."

"But I want to come with you."

"Stay by the phone and watch the kids," he called before closing the door.

"Was that Dad on the phone?" Mark pulled me out of my thoughts.

I shook my head. "No. Just a customer."

"If you're worried about Mrs. Tyner," he said, "why don't you call Kyle?"

"He's at work right now." I thought about how glad Kyle was to be working at a small computer repair shop for the summer as well as his excitement at being accepted as a transfer student into the same college where his father received his own computer science and engineering degrees—the Massachusetts Institute of Technology.

"Maybe he isn't. Maybe he's home with his brothers."

I hadn't thought of that. But it made sense as someone would have had to stay behind and take care of Bryce, even though Rayne was closer to Marty's age and able to fend for himself.

Worth a shot, I decided.

"Hello?" a voice said into the phone a few minutes later.

"Rayne, it's Katie. Is Kyle there or at work?"

"Hang on." The receiver made a thumping sound as it hit the table.

"Yes?"

"Kyle," I exclaimed. "Can you tell me what's going on? Why didn't you call me?"

The line grew quiet except for the low hum in the wires. "Kyle?"

He moaned. "It's so horrible."

"Please tell me what's happening."

"Mom collapsed this afternoon. Thank God, Dad was here and not on a trip. I was at work. Dad called me to come home to be with Bryce. Mom was taken to the hospital by ambulance."

"Have you heard anything yet?" My heart pounded. I couldn't believe what I was hearing. Having just turned fifty, Mrs. Tyner was a happy and joyful person, in good health. She ate well and exercised often by either taking walks in the orchard or tending to her summer vegetable garden. "What would make her fall? Did she faint?"

"Hey, if the line beeps, I'm going to let you go, okay? It'll be my dad. It's been a few hours now, and I haven't heard anything but …"

"But what?" I prompted.

"I think Mom collapsed after she read the letter." His voice faltered. "Dad found it next to her on the floor near the refrigerator."

My blood stopped flowing, and my veins seemed to freeze in place. Suddenly, it felt like an icy winter day in the middle of July. Goosebumps the size of pebbles dotted my arms and legs.

"What letter?" I whispered.

"From the reverend." His voice broke, and he coughed to correct it.

"Read it to me," I commanded, swallowing hard.

"I'm not sure I can. It's bad."

"Please, Kyle. I need to hear it."

A moment later, Kyle cleared his throat and began to read the most vicious words I've ever heard come out of someone that called themselves a human being.

> To: Burt and Renata Tyner
>
> I see now that delaying my response between letters from you was a good thing to do. Now that I've received your latest fax, I can see much more of what you're really like.
>
> You have stated that you would accept my God-given authority as pastor and that you would follow me. However, you have now shown you would rather challenge my authority and disobey my instructions. The implications of your last letter have shown you are willing to disobey Scripture (1 Cor. 6) and that you would be willing to challenge our scriptural understanding. This shows me you are ready to be much more of a troublemaker than I originally thought. You have demonstrated you are willing to be a disruptive force against me and all this under the guise of love.
>
> You have been commanded in the Bible to obey your pastor (Heb 13:17).
>
> You are in disobedience to this command.

You come charging back into church in clear violation of your church discipline. Do you think you are able to self-terminate your discipline? No, you are not. More and more it looks to me as if you are inventing your own new peculiar doctrines, many of which come from a contentious spirit. Your doctrine is in grave error, and your empty words about love will not fly with intelligent people.

Ungodly defiance will never work with me. Your tactics have no basis in Scripture. The Bible teaches meekness. You are the opposite of meekness. You are the highest of the high maintenance Christians. You bombard your pastor with letters, faxes, and emails that are filled with twisted thinking that would take almost all the pastor's time to endeavor to straighten out.

You will no doubt continue your behavior of defying a pastor and appearing where you have no business to be. You do not come to church to be a blessing but rather to impose your will. You will take up valuable space. You will take up too much space because others will not want to be too close to such defiance.

Your words of love are phony. If you loved me as you say, you would not defy me. Your statements of love are just there to cover your intentions of undermining me and disobeying me like when you showed up for church Sunday to show me that I cannot stop you from being there. You are like Cain in the Bible who wanted his own way. Your love is more like rape. As a rapist violates the object of his lust and forces himself upon her, so I feel violated as you have forced yourself upon us. I see no recovery or reconciliation from this act.

I would be an unfaithful pastor if I permitted you to continue to defy me and my God-given authority within the church. You seek to break down this authority, which you demonstrated for all to see by self-terminating your church discipline. This showed us once again the barrenness of your Bible understanding.

It is now time to announce to you that I, Ross Kelley-Elder, and Kevin Brayton-Pastor-in-Training have taken a vote to permanently terminate your membership at Cross Independent Baptist Church. You have now been exposed as defiant and disobedient.

Read 2 Thess. 3:6.

You are not welcome at church services. You are no longer a part of the fellowship. Every time you appear would build up and heap up a level of repulsiveness that would be very hard to reverse. You will remain a heathen and publican and continue your repulsive behavior elsewhere.

Rev. Rhuttland Abbott

Special note: All correspondence now terminated.

Kyle read the last line with a hint of relief in his voice. As soon as he finished, we were both quiet. He then heard the beep he was waiting for and said he had to go.

The correspondence has been terminated. It's over.

Setting the phone back into place, I allowed tears to come. Disbelief over what the reverend had written consumed me. Did he really hate the Tyner's that much? Did he truly despise anyone who went against him? How could someone calling himself a man of God spew such hatred and disgust over another believer? How could any person treat another individual with such animosity?

You are like Cain in the Bible ...

Every time you appear, you will heap up repulsiveness ...

Your love is more like rape ....

Rape? I suddenly felt dirty. And sick. Running into the bathroom, I barely had the toilet lid lifted before I vomited.

Moments later, I stood at the bathroom sink breathing in big gulps of air. I grabbed a bar of soap and washed my face and hands. I scrubbed my skin until it turned bright pink and the bar of soap was only a small wedge. But soap would never wash away the poisonous words the reverend wrote nor the ache in my heart for the Tyner's.

Pulling myself together, I went to check on my siblings while I waited for my parents to come home. I made a quick meal of pancakes and eggs. The kids thought it great to have breakfast for dinner. But as for me, I didn't touch my food.

My parents returned after dinnertime. Upon hearing the front door open, we badgered them with a million questions.

"Come sit down in the living room," my dad instructed.

We listened as he shared what happened to Mrs. Tyner. Part of it I already knew, and for the benefit of my siblings, my father did not reveal what made her collapse. The doctors called it a ministroke. She would be hospitalized for a few days. Mr. Tyner canceled his business trips, saying he could work from his home office for a few weeks while Renata began her treatment plan.

"She's going to be all right," my mother said later, after my brothers and sister went upstairs to read before bed.

"How did she seem?" I asked.

"Tired." Mom stifled a yawn. "Sorry, it's been a long day. She had some weakness on her left side and couldn't lift her arm. When she tried to smile, she was not able to smile on that side either."

"That's awful. She'll recover all that though, right?"

"Yes. She begins occupational therapy in a few days and will be fine."

"I talked to Kyle."

She stared at me, waiting.

"I made him read the letter to me. It hurt him, but I had to know."

The dark cloud that had become a familiar element in our lives settled over my mother. "Burt told us what it said," she murmured. "You should have seen that poor man's face when he told us and what the shock of it did to his wife."

"She didn't deserve that."

"No one does," Mom affirmed. "What the reverend said in that letter was not only wrong, it was evil. God does not want his people treating others this way. We can learn from this."

"Learn what?"

She leaned toward me. "We need to be the light others cannot see. We can rise above this by choosing to be strong and showing others that God's will is not for Christians to hurt each other this way."

"But how?"

She surprised me by smiling. "We ask God for help first. We ask him to help us treat others with kindness and respect, whether they be Christians or heathens or anything else. God loves us all the same, even the reverend himself."

"No way."

"Yes. God's love finds all of us equally. We honor him by the example he wants us to be, and *this* is the light others will see in us."

"What example?"

"Grace," she replied. "I've been learning the true definition of grace. I believe God is showing me the real side of him that the reverend never wanted us to see."

"What do you mean?" I was confused.

"Grace is free," she explained. "Grace is not something we earn. Grace is something God gives us when we do nothing to earn it. I am going to continue exploring more about this wonderful grace, and I can help you discover it too."

Gliding in the rocking chair near the sliding glass door, I let the cool midnight air drift in. I loved summer nights in

Twin Rivers. Lightening bugs filled the yard near the trees with their magic, causing the evergreens to blink green and yellow. Mosquitos sensed my presence and rushed over to be punished by the large bug zapper my dad had hung outside. The continuous buzzing of the fluorescent bulb and light squeaking of my mother's antique rocker was comforting, breaking up the stillness of the night.

Unable to sleep, I'd come downstairs. The house was dark and silent, but my thoughts roared in my head. Images of Mrs. Tyner in the hospital and the reverend pounding the pulpit plagued me. And then that horrible letter—words that would haunt me for a long time.

What had become of us? What *would* become of us? We were outcasts now. No longer a part of the fellowship of believers. At least not at Cross Independent Baptist Church. Those we'd known for many years were now turned against us. They'd been informed about our church discipline, and we were now nothing more than nomads.

We belonged nowhere.

My thoughts then turned to all the others who had experienced the reverend's reign of terror and the subsequent pain of rejection. The Wendell family. The Raker family. Cal Iverson and his son Wesley. Mrs. McKenzie. Randy Sturbridge. Dana Terrell and her son Preston. The Kittridge family. The Cobb family. Other homeschooling families Renata Tyner had tried to save, only succeeding in adding her own name to the list. Velma Holtz. Jolee Tisdale and her parents. Glen and June Britton. My family. And what of those families I didn't know about? Did the reverend hate us all so much that he turned an entire church against us? How could he do that? How could he not see the way he made people suffer? Why did so many people blindly follow him?

The spark of another unfortunate victim of the bug zapper flashed outside the screen door, its lifeless body falling to the ground in a dusty grave of charred bodies below. How odd in that moment I equated our lives—and all the lives of those the reverend ruined—to the lifeless insects below the beam of light.

Wasn't the pastor of a church supposed to be the one to shine a light in the darkness and bring people to Christ instead of destroying them?

We honor God by being the example he wants us to be, and this is the light others will see in us. My mother's words came back to me now as I continued to watch the bug zapper resume its low purring. My eyes got heavy.

A light that others can see. And grace is free.

The rocking chair ceased moving, and I finally fell asleep to the rhythm of the bug zapper.

That night, I dreamed of lights flashing all around me. White horses flanked both sides of a golden pathway which led to a huge plateau above the entire area, illuminating everything. I shielded my eyes from the brilliance that dazzled me and at the same time frightened me.

Closer, said a voice.

Buzz. Zap.

I can't. I'm afraid, I cried out as I turned to run.

My feet hit the ground, and I did not stop.

CHAPTER 24

SEARCHING FOR SOMETHING

The golden pathway seemed to be disappearing underneath my feet. The white horses nodded farewell as I embarked on my journey past them. Behind me, the lights that shone from the vast plateau became smaller.

Running away again? the voice asked.

Buzz.

"I'm not," I murmured.

Buzz.

What was that noise? My eyes snapped open. My right hip seemed to be having a spasm. *Where am I?* I looked around, frantic, and realized I was shivering on a rusty old swing.

Jolee's old house.

Buzz.

I jumped up and fished my cell phone out of my pocket. "Hello?"

"Kate, are you still downtown? You've been gone a while. Everything okay?" My husband's voice brought me out of the past and back into the present.

How long had I ... did I really fall asleep here?

"Uh, yeah, I'm good. Be back in just a little bit." I swallowed hard, then trudged around the front of the Tisdale's old house back to my rented vehicle.

The dream seemed so real.

It was, the voice said. *You were running away again.*

Resting my head against the seat, I closed my eyes. Memories of the expulsion of my family and the Tyner's from Cross scrambled to the surface, begging me to acknowledge them.

"I see you," I told them as I opened my eyes. The rearview mirror caught my reflection just then.

Isn't it time you saw yourself too?

I stared at myself in the mirror. My eyes looked weary. I was tired of running away from my feelings. Tired of fearing past recollections about Cross. I knew then I'd never truly dealt with all the fear, anger, resentment, helplessness, and overall pain of the reverend's rule within the empire he created for himself.

Twenty years had elapsed since I'd been in this place. Moving far away didn't magically erase life experiences, nor did changing my surroundings give me amnesia. By choosing to ignore or push it away, I'd only succeeded in making myself numb. If I didn't think about it, I didn't have to feel anything.

Avoiding the truth was easier—until the unannounced reminders were triggered. And my walls of resilience found a fracture.

"Where are we going?" I asked later that day.

"Just wait," Pierce said, a small grin playing with the corners of his mouth.

"So, you're kidnapping me."

"Appears so." He laughed. "Kids are going to hang with your mom and dad, so we get to have an evening to ourselves."

"You left three teenagers with my poor parents?"

"It was their idea."

We drove downtown, but instead of stopping at one of the local restaurants, we headed down the hill leading into Ashton, the next city over. A few minutes later, a tall red barn came into view.

"Wait," I exclaimed. "Are we going to An Old Italian Barn?"

"Yes, it's still here." Pierce looked pleased with himself.

An Old Italian Barn—Ashton's treasured gem—was a farmhouse with an attached barn in disrepair purchased by an Italian gentleman who saw its potential. After renovations were complete, he began hosting parties. People around town could not stop talking about his delicious Italian cooking. Once word got out, he opened a unique restaurant that could easily be mistaken for an old barn, except for the sign hanging on his front lawn and the cars parked in the side lot.

"I haven't been here in ages. Oh look, they've added a few buildings."

"Yes. I saw online that they have a wedding and party venue here now, plus they even rent out rooms."

"My mom told you this was an old favorite of mine, didn't she?"

My husband rewarded me with a grin.

Once inside, Pierce gave the hostess our name. She disappeared to look for an open table. As we waited, I glanced around at the décor. Off to one side of the foyer sat a large living room that looked like someone's house. A couch and two armchairs faced one another. In between them sat a coffee table with a few board games in play. Behind the couch stood a large old-fashioned fireplace used for heat during the winter and for lighting cozy candles during the summer. The entire area glowed, begging for one to sit and relax.

Just as I welcomed that idea, the young hostess reappeared and asked us to follow her. We were soon seated at a small table in the corner of the room next to a fifties-style kitchen hutch fully stocked with glasses and pitchers. I began to relax in the rustic, homey setting. The smell of fresh bread and pasta made my stomach rumble. I remembered then that I had not eaten lunch earlier.

"So, what's the occasion?"

"Who says I need an occasion to take my wife out to a nice dinner?" Pierce nodded to our server, who filled our glasses with water. When we were alone again, he placed his hand over mine. "Actually, I did want to discuss something with you."

I felt a twinge of guilt, knowing I had not been enjoying our Christmas vacation. Of course, he had noticed.

"I want to ask if you're okay," he began, "but I know you're not. You haven't been since we got here."

"How so?" I asked, my voice weak.

"You're distant. Quiet. You're going off somewhere to be alone."

Just as my shoulders fell in response, our server came to take our order.

"Am I wrong?" Pierce asked once she left our table.

"No." I fidgeted with my napkin. "I'm sorry."

"I don't want you to be sorry. I want you to talk to me. Let me in."

Time to stop running, the voice said.

"What's on your mind, Kate?"

My mind reeled. For some reason, I was transported back to the first few months at Juilliard. Coming from a small town like Twin Rivers Junction, I was not used to a busy city like Manhattan. I stayed glued to campus as much as possible. The library became one of my favorite places because it provided a relaxed location to study.

Another place I enjoyed was the financial aid department. As part of my work study program, I sorted applications and filed in between classes and practice hours according to my schedule. Maybe I just liked the financial aid office because of my handsome supervisor, Pierce Elliot.

"Do you remember how we met?" I asked my husband. Our server had just placed steaming plates of fettuccine alfredo and lasagna in front of us.

"Oh, you mean when I helped you get scholarship money and kept you around to do all my dirty work in the finance office?" He winked.

"Hey, that hurt. I'm being serious."

"Of course, I remember." He gave me his full attention.

I tried to pick my words. "It was a funny way to meet the man I would fall in love with, but it was meant to be. You've always understood me, no matter what. If things are off, you can tell."

Pierce put his napkin down and looked at me, all joking aside. "You have been strong your whole life, Kate. You've been through some hard circumstances growing up here in this town, and you managed to climb over the rubbish and shake it off. But you're still a human being. And I know there are things that still hurt you. I only ask you share them with me. Maybe I can help. Maybe I can't. But I'm here to listen or offer any suggestions. You don't have to be brave for me or anyone else right now. It's just us."

I stopped twirling my pasta around my fork and closed my eyes. How did I deserve such a caring and loving man? "Thank you, honey. But I really don't know where to begin."

"I think it begins here." Pierce tapped the linen tablecloth. "Twin Rivers Junction."

I had told him about many things over the years. The church. The membership. The rules. The reverend. But I never said much about how it affected me. Maybe because I didn't even realize it myself.

"Coming back to this place has affected you. Can you admit that much?"

I shifted in my seat. "How could I not? It would seem I can't hide it."

"But why try? Why are you trying to hide *from* it?"

"Because." I waved an arm around. "Too many old ghosts here. I wanted to leave a few days ago but knew it would hurt Mom and Dad."

Pierce took a drink from his glass and set it down. Turning the long glass stem around several times, he remained thoughtful. The dead air between deepened the pang of guilt I'd felt earlier. "I think I'm beginning to understand what's going on here," he said in a gentle tone.

I frowned. "What do you mean?"

"You need something." Now his words were blunt. "You're searching for something, and you have yet to find it."

"What?" I said, bewildered.

"Coming back here has been like sliding the cover off a dirty old well, looking down, and seeing nothing but a black abyss. You wish you'd never come and lifted that cover off."

As always, his perceptiveness never failed to surprise me. "But it wasn't like I even wanted to. It just ... happened. All these memories came at me from every side, and there was no way to avoid them."

"So, stop. Stop avoiding them. Face them."

I sucked in a breath. Any words I had in response evaporated. "I don't know how to do that."

"You are searching for something," Pierce repeated. "What do you think it could be?"

I glanced around the restaurant, as if the answer would be right in front of me so I could snatch it up. A flash of red caught my attention just outside the window to my right. A beautiful cardinal appeared to be staring at me through the glass, and if I didn't know better, I would have thought he winked at me. What was he doing there, on that window, at that moment? Was it possible he wanted to show me something?

He is free. You can be too, the voice said.

How could I even begin to achieve the kind of freedom that little bird possessed? What kind of peace did he know that I didn't?

That's it.

"The answer is peace," I found myself saying, my eyes still fixed on the now-empty windowsill.

"Yes," Pierce agreed. "So how can you go about finding that?"

"I don't know," I sighed.

"I do."

I shot him a look of surprise. "How? Tell me."

After a long pause, he said one single word. "Forgiveness."

I was at a complete loss as I let that word sink in. Could it really be that simple? All my life I'd buried my pain and constructed walls to keep from feeling anything. I couldn't change what happened. I'd just escaped it. I tried to make a good life for myself and determined never to live in Twin Rivers again. Wasn't that enough?

Forgiveness. The word burned in my consciousness.

"Why should I forgive them?" I burst out. "Do you know how many lives the reverend ruined? Broken homes? Marriages? Devastated families? My own family included. How about the lives that were lost? The Reverend, his spies, his elders, his blind congregation caused so much suffering and pain to people who depended on him and for what? So they could feel self-righteous for a little while as long as everyone obeyed his commands? So they could pin a gold star to their crown in heaven one day? While the poor sinners in the church, who questioned anything he said, could reap his wrath and discipline? Why should I forgive any of that? I certainly didn't do anything wrong!"

I snapped my mouth shut when I noticed a gentleman a few tables away glancing in my direction. Realizing I might have been a little too loud, my cheeks grew warm.

Pierce seemed unfazed and didn't even blink. "You're right. You did nothing wrong. This has nothing to do with you doing something wrong or right. It also has nothing to do with all the evil things the reverend and his followers did."

"What then?"

He leaned in close. "Forgiveness isn't for *them*. It's for *you*."

"Me?"

He nodded. "Yes, you. But it begs the question, Kate. Are you *willing* to forgive? Forgive all those from that place who hurt you and so many people you cared about? Can you let your hurt and anger go and forgive them?"

"Maybe. I don't know," I mumbled.

"That's something only you can decide. And"—Pierce waited to make sure he had my attention—"remember, Kate, forgiveness is a choice."

We finished the rest of our meal in silence. Our server removed our plates and brought us a dessert menu. I scanned the shiny pages, but my mind was not on tiramisu or cannoli.

Forgiveness is a choice.

A small cup of steamy espresso was placed in front of me. My fingers curled around it, its warmth calming me.

Can you forgive? the voice asked. *After all this time?*

A strange image of myself at a wrestling competition began playing out in my head. Opposition stood on all sides—the harsh sermons, judgmental faces of the congregation, rules, discipline, and devastated families. And in the ring, there I was, fighting with them all. And the upper hand belonged to the reverend.

I am no longer under your authority.

Forgiveness first. Then peace.

"I think I know what I have to do," I said to my husband.

"What's that?" he asked in a kindhearted way.

"I have to go back."

CHAPTER 25

THE HURT

Breathe, Kate.

My heart shrieked in protest and betrayal. I'd sworn I would never return to this place. How could I break an oath I'd kept for over twenty years? Not returning here was the mortar that bonded my walls together. I'd walked away as a teen and never looked back. Time had allowed these walls to harden and thicken. The more years that went by, the easier it became to stay away. Only now—while it stared me in the face—did those walls crack.

I kept gripping the steering wheel in front of me. Gripping so hard, my knuckles ached.

Breathe, Kate. No one is here. You are not a teenager anymore.

The only sound I heard was the soft purr of the car's engine. Forcing myself to open my eyes, I accepted the familiar images in front of me. "You are just three empty buildings," I said out loud. "You are no longer what you once were."

As I sat, it felt like something out of an old movie. Everything was different, like a forsaken and deserted village. The oval sign with its dark green lettering spelling out Cross Independent Baptist Church was no longer there.

In its place stood a smaller sign that showed the property for sale. The crooked sign looked so dirty and faded, I imagined it had been there for years.

"No one has been interested in the property," my dad informed me, shocked to learn of where I was going. "It's been for sale for quite a while."

"Why doesn't anyone want it? It's not far from the state college downtown. Isn't the property worth something?" I asked.

He shook his head. "Too much debt, I think. When Reverend Abbott had his vision to expand the school and build that gymnasium, he called on several families within the church to help with the costs. It just wasn't enough."

"How so? And who are you talking about?"

He rubbed his chin, thinking. "Let's see. I think the Kelley's—"

"Of course." I rolled my eyes.

"The Brayton's. The Hearns. The Holtz family. And I think the bulk of the funds came from Harrison Milton."

I remembered him. Like Floyd and Velma Holtz, Mr. Milton was an elderly gentleman who came to Twin Rivers during the summers before heading south for the winter. Everyone seemed to revere him almost as much as the reverend just because it was a well-known fact he had done very well for himself in his business ventures. And he was generous to a fault. The fault being the church and its *needs*.

"Okay, I get Mr. Milton. But everyone else? Why them? Especially the Hearns. They didn't have extra money sitting around."

My dad frowned. "You don't remember any of this?"

I shook my head.

"The reverend convinced these families it was the Lord's will to take out second mortgages on their homes in order to pay for the gymnasium."

I shook off the disturbing memory and drove further into the empty lot where I could get a better view of the gym.

I remembered how excited the students were at the announcement that Cross Christian Academy would be getting a gymnasium. The construction began my first year in high school and was completed the following year. Since I was not much into sports, I didn't attend many games, often delegating yearbook picture-taking to others.

Once a beautiful structure with shiny wood flooring, bleachers for parents and fans, and even a grand entrance way with double glass doors, the gym now stood vacant and void of life. Ugly sheets of plywood covered the front entryway, and it had not escaped the usual vandal's cans of spray paint with its big bubble lettering.

Turn the car off, Kate, the voice said.

When I did, everything went silent except for my mind.

Get out of the car.

I exited the vehicle and leaned against the door. I was amazed that much had changed, yet much remained the same. The trees were taller. The lot had not been plowed, and there were no tire tracks in the snow other than the fresh ones I had just made. The property stood abandoned. Shrubs around the side of the gym were overgrown with empty branches jutting out.

Walk, the voice said.

I felt the ghosts move in around me.

Leave, my brain screamed.

Forgiveness is a choice. My husband's words echoed in my head.

Zipping up my coat, I placed one booted foot in front of the other. I began the walk down the hill to the school building with small, timid steps as though I were a child.

And just like that, I felt like little Katie again. How many times had I traipsed down this same path to the gym, school, or church? I reached the entrance to the boarded-up school and was greeted by a vision of Brynn and myself as young girls clapping erasers on the landing near the school entrance. White dust flew everywhere. When it cleared, I saw my old friend Randy who I had accidentally helped get expelled. His angry face evaporated as he left, and in his place was my friend Rachel Abbott, whose once pretty eyes now mirrored her father's cold ones. My heart skipped a beat as I saw the image of Jolee appear and fade away.

I squeezed my eyes shut as these memories struggled free from the cavity I'd buried so deep in my soul.

Oh, how this hurt.

Face them, Pierce had said.

A cold gust of wind picked up from the trees behind me. Pulling a knit hat over my head, I allowed the memories to come to me.

I'm ready for you now.

Mrs. Fisher and Mrs. Sullivan came marching toward me. Behind them were the weary faces of Sara and Justin returning from Cobb's camp. Mrs. McKenzie waved goodbye to me as she left for good.

"I see you," I said aloud, unmoving.

Others came closer. I acknowledged every one of them.

One more building. My strong will now in overdrive, I had to put every ounce of effort into getting past the overwhelming urge to race back to my car and fishtail my way out of that parking lot. The sense of foreboding grew with every step I took toward the church building.

I can't do this one.

Choose, the voice said.

I was struck in that moment by another distant memory. My senior year at Twin Rivers High, I was delighted to attend the class trip to visit the Pacific Ocean on the West Coast. One day during our adventure, we embarked on an expedition to the Mojave Desert where we took part in a cattle drive, archery, and rock rappelling. It was the rock rappelling that almost did me in. My brain hit instant replay.

"Katie!" Mrs. Seltan, my homeroom teacher's wife, called from above my head. "You need to lean back and push off the rock with your feet."

"I can't!" I must have sounded like a newborn pig the way I squealed. I could not see her face over the bridge of my safety helmet. Strong ropes and harnesses held my weight, but I was terrified they would snap at any moment. I clung to the rock, frozen.

"Come on, Katie," Mr. Seltan called down. Others from my class came to stand and look down at me. Mortified, I dangled from the forty-foot ledge and stared at one spot on the ugly brownish-gray rocks in front of me.

"Don't look down!" some idiot from my class called out.

After the Seltans hushed the students, they tried again. "Katie, listen. You can't just stay there."

"Pull me back up." I tried not to sound frantic.

"No, hon." Mrs. Seltan shook her head. "You can do this. Don't give up. Take a deep breath. Then place both your feet on the rock in front of you. Can you give that a try?"

"I don't think I can do it. I'm going to fall!" I cried out, astounded to discover I was petrified of heights. Put me on a horse seventeen hands high and I was fine. But a rockface off the side of a small mountain ... Who knew?

"Katie, look up at me," Mrs. Seltan called with an edge of softness.

I did what she asked and saw she had sent the onlookers away. She now lay on her stomach looking over the ridge and down at me ten feet below her. "You can do this. Start with one foot. Then the other and push off, releasing a little more rope each time."

I stared up at her, still paralyzed.

"Katie, you have to choose, or you won't go anywhere."

"I made it." I murmured now, marveling at that day so long ago. Although it had taken a bit longer, I did what she instructed and made it down that rockface. Rope burns and all.

"Katie, you have to choose." Mrs. Seltan's words floated back to me now.

Looking down at the ground, I felt the same as I did up on that mountain that day. Fear held me hostage making it difficult to move. The old church loomed before me, but I stayed rooted to the spot. I found it remarkable the things we recalled from our subconscious in moments of extreme anxiety, fear, or stress. I hadn't thought about my class trip in many years. Yet here I stood, crippled to move just like I had in attempting to repel that rockface.

Start with one foot, then the other...

I can do this.

One foot. There.

Two feet. Good.

I was almost to the front of the church. A few more steps and I would be able to touch the rotted railing. Nausea threatened its way up my esophagus as I envisioned the reverend's hand on that same railing all those years ago as he would greet church members, except for the colder winter days when he'd stay inside the foyer.

I took another step forward and stood in the exact parking spot where Reverend Abbott used to park his luxury car each Sunday. Resisting the urge to spit in the snow, I continued to breathe and look toward the church. Just like the other two buildings, the church doorway had been boarded up and was full of dead leaves that had fallen during autumn. A light gust of wind caused the leaves and debris to swirl disturbing the silence.

Remember why you came, the voice reminded.

"I came to face you," I said aloud to the church, then shuddered.

The pain surrounded me, squeezing hard. I stood in the empty parking lot trembling. I allowed more memories to be unlocked from their vault. My walls were coming down, and each brick hit with a thud on the rooftop of my heart. My eyes blurred with tears as I allowed them to escape my soul and emerge in front of me.

Reverend Abbott's cold, gray face came into focus. He stared hard at me with his steely eyes, but my legs somehow managed to stand their ground.

You! His sinister eyes bored into mine. *You will burn in hell for all eternity for your rebellion!*

And then the heartbreak of the rejection came. My family had been members at Cross for years, and these were people we spent most of our time with. For these same people to allow years of our relationship to evaporate as if they had never taken place made us feel subhuman, like we had never even existed. To be treated this way left us with such an emptiness the only thing remaining for us to feel was numbness.

Even the reverend's own daughter, Rachel, who had been my friend for many years, turned her back on me and refused to speak to me again. Not once did I say anything hurtful or hateful to her after I left. I even tried to give her and her younger sister Jenny a hug when I saw them at the ice rink downtown during Christmas break my senior year at Twin Rivers High. I wanted to show them I was still *me*. Still their friend. But all I received in return was something colder than the ice we stood on that day. Even though their rebuff wounded a piece of my soul, I reminded myself I was doing the right thing—*my family* was doing the right thing in our attempt at moving forward.

I thought then of my mother who used to have a face full of light when I was a child, only to watch the reverend snuff it out over time. My own father felt torn between keeping secrets he wasn't supposed to know about and protecting his own family. Neither parent attended church again due to the damage caused by the reverend. My other siblings couldn't care less about any church or most Christians in general for that matter.

The hurt I felt was not just for myself.

My mind traveled to those outside my family who suffered under the hand of Cross Independent Baptist Church and Reverend Abbott. I thought of how much the Cobb family gave to the church. With little money to speak of, they poured all they had into resurrecting the camp, only to have it fail. This, along with being humiliated for homeschooling their children, broke their spirits, and they had to give up everything and move away. I thought of Dana Terrell's death and pondered what became of her son, Preston. June Britton's beautiful face came to mind, and I wondered if she'd ever touched her autoharp again after her husband passed away from his self-inflicted injuries.

In playing the grandest dramatic role of questioning the reverend, the Tyner family had not escaped unscathed. Even though their hearts were in the right place, they did not heed the many warnings given by the reverend or those he appointed to that task. Desperate to reach the reverend's heart, they were saddened to discover all that was there was an empty organ wrapped in miles of barbed wire. Nevertheless, they bared their own hearts wide open as best they knew how but, in the end, suffered much for it.

Other tragic stories at Cross came to mind, but none affected me more than Jolee's. Looking back at the warning signs she displayed, I wish I'd done more. I never saw my friend again after that night I visited her in Veronica's apartment building.

I cried out, sinking onto the church steps before I fell. The neglected steps creaked in protest from inactivity. A long crack splintered from one end of the sagging wood to the other.

I felt that same crack reach up and split my heart in two.

"Oh, Jolee." I choked back sobs. "I'm sorry I didn't try harder to bring you home."

I will never forget the astonishing news I received a few weeks after I graduated from Juilliard with a degree in music. My excitement at finishing college as well as planning my wedding to Pierce was blown to pieces the day Karina called me, crying.

Just after Jolee turned twenty-two years old, she passed away.

A little part of me died that day too.

I recalled the first day I saw her in kindergarten, in Mrs. Miller's class. Little Jolee wore a green jacket and watched everyone around her with wide eyes. Of course, we were all scared that first day, but we soon found something to giggle about, making us instant friends.

Around sixth grade or so, Jolee's attitude changed. Her inner fuse became short, and it didn't take much for a teacher or fellow student to get her in a bad mood. Over the years, Brynn and I learned to maneuver our way around her temper and do our best to make her laugh, which dissolved any tension between us.

My deepest regret was never learning what made Jolee break, leave us all behind, and succumb to an untimely death. I could only assume she was unable to come to terms with Cross and the reverend's dominion over us, resulting in terrible life choices.

Unsure of how long I sat on that broken church step, I became aware of a new feeling coming over me. I was here, on the property that once belonged to the reverend and his followers, and I was no longer running away. I closed my eyes and allowed the cold air to fill my lungs and release pent-up anguish.

I am stronger than this. I lost my friends, but I am still strong.

My eyes blinked open at the sensation of something fluttering against my nose, prompting my first smile since arriving that afternoon. Huge snowflakes like tiny parachutes fell from the sky and danced around me. I hadn't seen it snow like this in decades.

Did you send them? I whispered, looking up at the sky.

Pride lifted my spirits as I realized I was no longer trembling. I had made it to the church steps and accomplished what I'd set out to do. I looked my demons in the eye and did not run away. Now that my walls were down, I could see again. Watching the quiet snow fall around me, I sat still on the steps and exhaled.

How long had I been here?

Many times I had been asked a similar question by those close to me over the years. *How long did you stay at that place?* they would ask. I would revert to short answers when questioned by acquaintances about where I was from or what school I went to. I often received a curious look whenever I'd pass over their casual questions and respond with one of my own. Why give them a truthful answer when they would gawk in disbelief? I stopped giving details of my experience at Cross when I once received an unempathetic scoff from a coworker.

"Why did you stick around and put up with that?" She looked at me as if I were a complete imbecile. "I wouldn't let some old man talk to me like that."

Or another cringe-worthy favorite. "What kind of psycho religion is that?"

UNDER AUTHORITY

No one could fathom what we went through at that church unless they had also been a part of it. I'd have to walk away and try not to fault them for what they didn't know or envy them a little for being privileged to a different life.

Thinking now about the comment from the coworker made me relive the question all over again. I didn't have an answer for her. Now the question had returned, drifting in and out of the descending snowflakes.

Why did we stay?

Why did we not leave Cross sooner?

And why did we endure so much under the reverend's control?

A long time passed before we uncovered the answers to these haunting questions. But in the end, God heard.

And the answers finally came.

CHAPTER 26

THE WHY

The beauty of the quiet snow descended on the frozen ground, creating a mantle of pure white loveliness, while the three neglected buildings behind me represented darkness in my life and the lives of many others from so long ago.

A darkness I would be hostage to no longer.

With my newfound determination, I stood up from my perch on the lowest step of the old church and walked forward to survey the building. Not only was the church entryway in dire need of repairs, but it was also in much worse condition than I expected. The shingles were shriveled and missing in countless places. Old paint chipped and curled. One of the tall sanctuary windows had broken glass. Below it, a few empty beer bottles lay, while others had shattered near the church foundation.

Reverend Abbott's sudden departure had left everything in ruins.

Emotions raced through me. On one hand, I couldn't help gloating that Cross had failed. Cross Christian Academy had failed as well, permanently closing its doors. Without Reverend Abbott's authoritarian leadership in place, no one was able to pick up where he left off. Without him, they were lost lambs with no shepherd. I had learned bits of information over the years from Brynn. Kevin Brayton, the pastor-in-training, attempted to save the church only to find it difficult to lead the same way Reverend Abbott did. Rumor had it he decided to move west and start over. In the wake of his exit, the church was lost. A significant portion of the membership took this as their green light to make their own getaway. Only a handful of families remained, and Ross Kelley made the executive decision to put the property up for sale.

But no one wanted it.

Too many bad memories for everyone, it would seem.

A smile tugged at the corners of my mouth at how Cross came to its demise in the end. Wasn't it what they deserved?

Heavy snowflakes turned into light flurries. Glancing around, I could see the sky had changed from gray to a lighter fog, one spot brighter than the rest. In that moment, a ray of sunlight managed to break through the clouds.

A light that others can see ... My mother's words from long ago came back to me.

"And grace is free," I mumbled.

Regret settled over me. I sank down on the weathered stone bench and looked over at the church on my right. Any triumph I felt at the collapse of the church vanished. Sadness took its place. I felt ashamed of my shallow satisfaction in the current condition of the church and how it got there.

"There's no coming back now," I whispered. "There won't be any grace for you."

I knew at some point someone would purchase the property. Maybe turn it into a medical facility or office building of sorts. For some reason, I felt certain it would never be a church or school again. No one would shake hands with a future pastor after a Sunday sermon. Students would never walk the halls again. Children would no longer run in the soccer field playing tag.

Pushing away my gleeful guilt, I allowed myself a space to mourn the church's fate when it had potential to be great. As one of only a few churches in the area at the time, it could have been the kind of church that loved its members and community, reached out to others who were hurting, shown people the real love of Jesus, and restored life to families rather than destroy them.

In my heart, I knew God had spoken.

And the reverend was gone.

"They were all so afraid of him," I murmured.

Remember why you came. The voice was back. Reminding me, yet again.

"I came to show my ghosts I am no longer afraid," I whispered. A slight gust of wind took my words and scattered them through the emptiness beyond.

Fear.

Fear was the reason we stayed at Cross so long and why others remained long after we were gone. Fear was just something we lived with, not even knowing it existed.

For most, fear is merely an instinctual reaction to impending danger—an emotional response to a threat. But for me and my family—it went deeper.

What makes one afraid? I pondered. Fear can present itself in many different styles, shapes, and levels. A small child can be afraid of a monster under the bed or blood from a scraped knee. A teenager can be afraid of not scoring at his basketball game or failing a test. An adult can be afraid of veering off the road during a blizzard or failing a project at work. These are normal, everyday fears that humans cannot escape, but we can learn to manage them.

And then I thought about learned fears. A small child will most likely become terrified of all dogs if bitten by one. A teenager will learn the meaning of stage fright if her nervous fingers forget the notes during her piano recital. As adults, our fears are much deeper because life experiences make us more attentive to pain, sorrow, and grief. A sharp word from a so-called friend can make one shy away from future friendships. An abusive relationship can result in deep trust issues. Even an inanimate object can trigger an involuntary fear response from a past tribulation.

Most fears can be alleviated by two main things—support and encouragement from one another. The knowledge that someone—a friend, colleague, or loved one—has our backs no matter what. We have faith then we can push forward through the hard times and be okay on the other side of them.

But for the members of Cross, fear was different. Not only did we have the usual everyday concerns others experienced, but our anxiety doubled under the reverend's reign. Fear became our natural response to the constant threat of discipline, punishment, or expulsion. Our distress became his weapon and the main core of all that we lived by. The apprehension instilled in us was complex. Ugly. Enslaving. Its tendrils dug deep roots within our souls. Our subconscious struggled to remember we were not meant to live in this way. Reverend Abbott used trepidation to control us. We lived in a perpetual state of endangerment while the reverend drilled *fear* into our very beings. We lived in a never-ending state of angst.

"The fear of the Lord," he would boom, "is the beginning of wisdom. Examine your own iniquity. Fear the wrath of God's damnation! Your minister is set in place for the perfecting of saints. Do not respond in an ungodly way to his preaching. Do not gossip. Be sure your sin will find you out. You will be held accountable!"

"No more!" I exclaimed. "You are no longer here dictating our lives. I am no longer afraid!" I kicked the snow for emphasis.

I made my way back to my vehicle. While moving my feet had seemed impossible before, they emerged liberated with each step.

My purpose complete, I was ready to leave, eager to say goodbye to Cross—or what was left of it. I was now equipped to conquer my anxiety, no longer a prisoner of my fears.

I wondered about the others who might still feel captive. Were they haunted? Did they allow the pain of the past to affect how they lived? I thought about a few families who had stayed too long, like my family. And the Tyner's.

And what kept them here so long? The old, persistent question returned.

"They wanted to make a difference but were not permitted to. Why did we continue to try?" I mused, finding my footprints in the snow again.

Ah, yes. The *why*. The other half of the equation. If fear, our normal, was one half, then the *why* was the other half. Wasn't it natural to wonder why someone would stay in a place such as that? Why didn't we just leave?

Most residents of Twin Rivers Junction didn't have much to do with our Independent Baptist world. Anyone who didn't attend a Reverend Abbott-approved church was seen as a heathen. We separated from them, and they ignored us in return. My own dad would often get one such pagan customer in his shop. If the subject of religion came up, and my dad mentioned where he went to church, the conversation quickly became awkward. Now and then, those who got to know us a little better would ask us questions about Cross. Members gave the automatic canned response. "We believe in the inspired word of God" or "We believe we can call upon the Lord Jesus Christ and we will be saved."

Most of the time, this shut down any further questions. But occasionally, the extra curious wanted deeper answers to rumors they may have heard around town.

"Why does your preacher have so many rules?" one would ask.

"Why do you stay in a place where you are discouraged from making your own decisions?" another questioned.

And the most frequent, "Why not just find another church?"

Of course, Reverend Abbott conditioned his congregation for such contingencies. He asserted repeatedly he had been placed directly by God in Twin Rivers Junction for the perfecting of the saints to godliness. That meant there was *no* other godly church anywhere in New England except Cross. They all had false leaders, which meant those churches were full of corruption. Cross congregants accepted it was a true honor and privilege to belong to such a holy place of worship.

With this thought process poured in place, who then would *want* to leave?

In turn, we were led to feel sorry for those who dared ask such questions. They were lost souls headed for the eternal flames in hell. Spiritually dead with no knowledge of what it was like to have a devout man of God leading them into the sacred realm of heaven. How sad for them.

And it worked.

I allowed myself one last look at the church property. His cruel, controlling nature aside, I marveled at the level of intelligence it took for Reverend Abbott to pull it off all those years. How did he do it?

Then, I realized the truth. By cleverly camouflaging the gospel of Christ into every well-planned sermon, Reverend Abbott twisted Scripture to fit his agenda and presented it as God's vision for the church.

Corrupt churches? It's because they have wicked leaders.

Anti-homeschool? It's because Jesus taught in group settings.

Pastor's double honor? (1 Timothy 5:17).

Pastor's credibility? He's a true scholar and highly educated (Titus 1:9, Acts 6).

Submit and follow the pastor of the church? (Hebrews 13:7).

Obey the pastor without question? (Hebrews 13:17).

Church discipline? For the perfecting of saints.

Gossip among brethren? Forbidden (Proverbs 11:9).

Against secular college? One should only seek God's kingdom (Matthew 6:33).

Against seeking wealth? (1 Timothy 6:9).

And the list never ended. Nothing but pure manipulation.

Over time, this brainwashing technique worked. In the same way a farmer plants a seed and expects it to grow, the reverend planted the seed of fear. Over time, he watered his seed with just the right blend of Scripture and hidden agenda to keep our fear growing and standing tall. But every plant that grows needs a little sunshine.

Even Reverend Abbott knew the right time to pull the clouds back and reveal just enough sunlight to have his little plant flourish the way he wanted it to.

"He gave us all something," I said to the wind. "It's what locked us in place."

In response, the wind sent me another memory.

"Hey, Brynn," I said into the receiver as I plopped down on the bed, sending stacks of sheet music sliding to the floor.

"Hey, how's the big city?" I could tell by the sound of her voice that something was up.

"School's great. I love it here," I told her. "But what's up with you? You don't sound so good."

"Yeah." Brynn sighed. "It looks like it's our turn. My family is leaving the church. Remember I told you Leah is getting married?" she asked.

"Oh, that's right. This summer?" I recalled how Brynn and her younger sister Leah were only a year apart in age, and they were attending the same Christian college. Leah had met her future husband in her freshman year, and they were soon planning a wedding.

"Yeah, Travis has a huge family in the Midwest so he really wanted Leah to have their wedding out there. Leah loved the idea, so she started planning. You remember Diana Holtz, right? Wasn't she your friend?"

I grimaced at hearing her name. Closing my eyes, I shook my head and tried to keep the edge out of my voice before responding. "I remember her, and she's not my friend." I didn't feel like going into the details of the letter Diana wrote me when I left Cross.

"Oh." Brynn sounded surprised. "Well, she and Leah became friends when she did a little babysitting for her daughter last summer."

"Let me guess," I interjected. "It didn't end well."

"How'd you know? Anyway, you're right. Leah went home over spring break and told Diana all her wedding plans, thinking she'd be happy for her. You won't believe what she did."

"I think I would," I replied.

"After Leah returned to college, Diana called Reverend Abbott and told him how Leah was planning a secret wedding behind his back in a different church with a different minister to officiate."

"Brynn, you can't tell me you're surprised. You know he has his spies."

"Well, we were anyway. And Leah was crushed. The reverend called a meeting with my parents and demanded an explanation. When they said they were fine with Leah and Travis's wishes, he got furious. He's trying to discipline them for undermining his authority and doing this without permission, saying it was his right as her pastor to officiate at the marriage, not another minister's. He views it as a betrayal."

"Unbelievable," I said, even though I believed it. I knew better than Brynn to what lengths the reverend would go.

"Katie, that's not all. He embarrassed my parents in front of the congregation during last Sunday night's sermon. He brought Diana up front and praised her for doing the right thing, saying how hard it must have been and all that garbage. He even had the whole room give her a round of applause for telling the truth in a difficult situation. She was an example of what a godly woman leading a Christ-filled life looks like or something to that effect."

I couldn't help the loud snort of disgust that escaped my nose. "Brynn, are you for real? He had them clapping for her?"

"Sure did. My mom told me about all the people who gave her hugs and told her how brave she was to bring this deceitfulness to the reverend's attention right away. And you know what?"

"What?" I waited.

"He always does that and usually at someone else's expense." My friend's voice rose. "The reverend pumps them up. He makes them feel good about themselves for their loyalty and obedience to him. Tells them they're storing up treasures in heaven. Don't you remember the times he's done that?"

The long-ago conversation continued in my head as I opened the door to my rental. I slid behind the wheel and turned on the ignition. The leather seat was cold, and I flicked on the seat warmer. I was outside a little longer than I'd planned to be but hadn't noticed the cold much until now. I had a thousand other things on my mind.

"Yes, I remember," I said, as if Brynn were sitting right there beside me. I watched the wipers fling snow from the windshield. "He gave us a spirit of self-righteousness. He had us believing we were far superior to all the other sinners outside of Cross."

The self-righteousness was the warm sunshine we needed, and it made us feel good. Godliness was what we received in return from the reverend for all the honor, duty, allegiance, and everything else we so willingly gave him. The sense of satisfaction that we were spiritual people, obedient to the Lord by following our pastor's counsel and living a better life than other sinners was how the reverend pulled together a body of believers under one roof and got them to do anything he asked. Within the boundaries of fear of punishment, discipline, and shame lay a brilliant self-righteous pathway toward heaven with the reverend leading the way. We expected this man of God to bring us into God's divine kingdom one day.

His control was intertwined into each handcrafted sermon with supporting evidence from the Bible. We had been taught not to question the man of God, so we simply believed. And it continued for many years.

"Until the day it stopped," I said, exiting the parking lot.

I began the drive home, not once looking back.

Yes, God had spoken.

He said, "Enough."

CHAPTER 27

THE HOPE

My blades made a sharp scraping noise as I skidded to a stop just outside the plexiglass door of the ice rink.

"Doing okay?" I asked my mom who was sitting off to the side of the bleachers.

"Of course. And I'm probably a lot warmer than you are." She gestured with her insulated thermos to prove her point.

"I'm fine. I forgot how much fun this is."

"I'm glad. Look at your old dad." She smiled. "He's like a kid out there."

I turned to watch my dad in his ancient black figure skates attempt a spin, nearly losing his balance. Arms flailing, he managed to stay on his feet and in a straight line. How could a man his age keep up with teenage grandkids? I laughed as he and my husband plotted to clothesline the kids with a scarf and clapped as they went toppling down. "Look at him. I can't believe he still skates."

"He doesn't as much as he used to," my mom said. "But he still enjoys it and tries to go at least a few times each winter."

"Impressive."

"How about you?" she asked.

"Me?" My eyebrows wrinkled together. "Well sure, I miss some of the winter sports like this and skiing, sledding—"

"That's not what I meant. You asked how I'm doing. Now it's your turn." She seemed to have a knowing twinkle in her eyes today. "You doing okay?"

"Of course," I said, echoing her own response. "Why do you ask?"

She continued looking over my shoulder as the kids separated from the adults and moved with greater speed. Pierce and my dad glanced over their shoulders as they skated along, making sure the teens weren't trying to retaliate for the scarf prank.

"I know you've been conflicted about coming back here, Katie."

"It's Kate, Mom," I said patiently. "I'm not a little kid anymore."

"I named you. I get to call you Katie once in a while if I want to."

Sighing, I motioned her to continue.

"Anyway, what I was going to say is you seem a lot happier today than you have the entire time you've been here. Is it the fact you get to leave soon? You'll be getting on a plane and traveling back to your own home the day after tomorrow."

"It's not that at all." I flushed. I decided to be honest with her, something I'd always tried to be careful about, especially bringing up old hurts from our years at Cross. I also didn't want to be the cause of her feeling worse, which I was pretty sure she was doing her best to hide.

Seated now on the cold aluminum bleachers next to her, I began to recount all that had been on my mind. I told her how I felt coming back here for the first time and driving down Tanger Mountain Highway. I talked about the old ghosts that seemed to come out of the woodwork all around me. "Everywhere I went, there they were. I knew the time had come for me to acknowledge them and face them. To stop running away from these feelings, I had to go back to the source of where it all began—the church."

Her face turned pale when I told her what I had done. "I didn't know you went there."

"I'm sorry. I didn't want you to be burdened about my returning there. I asked Dad not to mention it. I'm aware your own memories of that place are not pleasant, and I didn't come here to stir things up. It's just ..."

"I know," she said. "It was something you had to come to terms with on your own."

"Yes," I said, relieved she understood.

"I'm not trying to pry, but how did you do it? You seem radiant today. It's a big switch from what I've seen of you."

"It's okay," I said, knowing I owed her an explanation. "Pierce is the one who encouraged me to face these old demons. To stop hiding from them. I've been running from them for a very long time. And then I remembered something you told me once, a long time ago."

"What's that?"

"How we need to be a light that others can see. I was reminded of that yesterday and something else too—"

"Grace is free," she finished.

A moment of silence passed as we reflected.

After we waved at our husbands who were skating by, my mother turned to me again. "It took me a long time to grasp the meaning of grace. I was resentful after everything the reverend put us through."

The reverend or the church was not something my mother mentioned often. I decided to let her talk for at least as long as she didn't start getting upset like she had done in the past.

"What do you mean?" I coaxed.

"Just that it took me years to discover that once I learned what grace is, what it means ... well, only then could I let the past go and forgive the reverend."

"What did you learn about grace?"

"One day, it dawned on me I had become rather bitter. Maybe that's why I've been unable to discuss much all these years without it affecting me negatively. I started exploring grace a little while I was still at Cross, but the bitterness kept getting in the way. Renata and I helped each other, and we began to focus on one thing at a time. For me, it was the part of grace that means *free*."

I unlaced my skates and set them aside. "Right. It's what God gave us when Jesus died for our sins. It was his gift to us. We didn't have to buy it or earn it."

"True, but that's not exactly what I'm speaking of here."

"Oh?"

"Sure, grace is what we received when Jesus died for us, but that's not where it stops. He gave us the gift of grace itself. And now we can give it away for free. Grace can be anything, but it usually means giving or showing others something they don't deserve. For example, a kind word in response to someone who was nasty to us. Did they deserve it? No. They deserved to be treated that way in return. The other half of grace is expecting nothing in return. It costs us nothing, and it's the life God means for us to live."

I nodded as understanding dawned. "And this is the light others see in us."

"And now you understand too. I'm sorry it's taken me so long to be able to talk about things."

"We've all had our own struggles, Mom."

"You know, I think I knew the exact moment when I had to change."

"Really? When was that?"

Without hesitation, she said, "The moment I heard Reverend Abbott died."

I closed my eyes. "I still remember where I was the day I found out." My mind went back to that morning over ten years ago. The reverend's death ignited yet another flashback.

After a chaotic morning trying to get my children ready for school, I was about to reach for a second cup of coffee when the phone rang. Who would call at this time of morning?

"Kate," a familiar voice said as I called out the usual greeting.

"Karina?" I said in surprise. "Is that you?"

Happy to hear my childhood friend's voice, I relished with gratefulness that Brynn, Karina, and I had managed to keep in touch all these years. How ironic we all ended up on the same career path of teaching, with all of us having something different to offer our students.

"Of course it's me," Karina said. "Hey, listen. I need to tell you something. Do you have a minute?"

"I think so," I said, glancing over at the digital clock on the stove. "I need to go soon, though, as I have to get ready to head into the studio. My first voice lesson of the day begins in an hour."

"Okay, this won't take long," she said. "Are you sitting down?"

Concern washed over me. "Karina, what's wrong?"

"I don't know how to tell you this," she began, "so I'm just going to spit it out."

I held my breath and waited.

"Reverend Abbott died." Karina's voice held a measure of shock.

"What?" I shot out of the chair.

"It only happened yesterday afternoon. I'm surprised Brynn hasn't called you yet."

"How? What happened?"

"Well, he went fishing after church service yesterday with his son-in-law—Rachel's husband. From what I understand, he had a massive heart attack and just fell to the ground. Died instantly."

I was speechless.

"I think he was, what ... sixty-two? Sixty-three?" Karina said. "It's so surreal. I don't ever remember there being previous health issues with him. Or, I guess, none that he spoke about. Hey, I hate to cut this short, but I need to get to my first period PE class. Talk soon?"

I hung up, not sure if I said goodbye or not. I tried to rein in my thoughts which were running wild.

The reverend is dead. His life has ended. His regime is finished.

My mother cleared her throat, breaking me out of my trance. "The news of his passing revealed to me there was no glory from it. I thought I'd be glad he was dead. But instead, I felt empty."

"I know. Because now, he'll never get the chance to right his wrongs."

"Maybe. But *we* can."

"Wait." I put my nose in the air. "Why is it *our* responsibility to right the reverend's wrongs?"

"It isn't our *responsibility*. This is a prime example of where grace comes in. We give to others what they don't deserve. And Kate? That includes the reverend."

"How?"

"By giving others what he couldn't."

I was beginning to comprehend what she meant. We were not responsible for all the mistakes the reverend made. We do not bear the blame because he took his authority to such extremes, so blinded by power he didn't seem to notice the hurting people in his own congregation. We had no reason to feel obligated to save the souls he couldn't save.

"Like you, I thought I'd be happy. Glad he got what he deserved." I wondered if I'd given her a jolt with that admission. "Then after the initial shock, I felt relieved because it was over."

"I understand, and I guarantee most of the congregation felt the same way, even if most of them wouldn't want to admit it."

"Karina told me she heard not many came to his funeral."

My mother nodded. "For some reason, Reverend Abbott's family wanted it to be family members only except for the Kelley's. It was a sad time for the church as so many were lost and confused."

"What became of them?"

"You already know we stayed close with the Tyner's for quite some time while they still lived here."

I frowned. "They're no longer here?"

"Burt and Renata decided to sell their old house on the mountain and move closer to their grandkids in the Midwest. We keep in touch."

"But they're good?"

"Oh yes. Renata is the one who first showed me grace."

The kids rushed by us and waved. We waved back. "How so?"

"She's the one who had to take the brunt of my anger and bitterness. And she accepted it with humility and without complaint. Over time, I saw she had something I wanted."

"What was it?" I asked.

"Hope."

I mulled that over, a little surprised.

"Grace begins with us," she said. "But what others receive from that grace is hope."

"Okay, what do you mean by hope?"

"Oh, many things." She leaned forward and extended her hands, palms up. "The realization there is a God who loves us unconditionally and does not seek to hold us under the law or punishment is our biggest hope. This hope liberates us to exercise the free will he gave us. In turn, we want to live the life God designed for us by showing others forgiveness, grace, and hope."

And then out of nowhere, it hit me. As members of Cross, we were all worshipping the reverend. Sure, we sang our sacred hymns, recited John 3:16 a million times, and attended church without fail. But our grave mistake was that our eyes were fixated on Reverend Abbott, following him wherever he told us to go and obeying the stringent rules.

The reverend had us believing there was no way to God except through him. Any feeble hope we ever found was placed in the reverend alone.

And it was wrong.

Knowing and accepting this fact helped me see a clearer picture of what had taken place at Cross. We pursued and worshipped a man, while Jesus desires his children to come to him just as we are and worship only him. He asks us to lay our burdens at his feet and trust that in his own timing, he will give us everything we need.

God wasn't some illusionary being out there in deep space. Neither was he a black cloud hanging over us ready to toss down a lightning bolt to the first offender. He had been right beside us all along, guiding us in the direction that brought us closer to him.

"You know what helps me?" my mother said. "I keep going back to God's promises in his Word. He wrote them for a reason. He wants us to remember he'll never leave us. He loves us and will provide a way no matter what we're going through."

"And he can heal all wounds, no matter how damaged

they may seem to us," I said. A bit of that hope my mother spoke of had become infectious. I was glad to have caught it.

"Yes." My mother closed her eyes, and I swallowed hard at seeing that a little tear had escaped one of them.

"Mom?" I asked. "Is everything okay?"

She opened her eyes. "I've never felt better than I do right now."

"Let's go home."

After calling to our loved ones out on the ice rink, we gathered our things and chattered our way into the parking lot.

And hope led us all home.

CHAPTER 28

CHOOSING FORGIVENESS

I squeezed my husband's hand as I observed the immense snow-covered region in front of me, not quite believing where I was.

To the left of the surrounding area stood the covered bridge that towered over the Patamon River. According to urban myth, Native American Indians who'd settled here had named the river for its fast current and, at times, raging rapids where it joined forces with the larger Tapu River that flowed through the entire state. I remembered swimming in the river as a kid and gasping at its cool temperatures even in the middle of summer. Shivering at the thought of how frigid the water must be now, I took a deep breath and let it out slowly. Here in this place today for a purpose, I turned my attention to my dad.

"This way," he instructed.

This was the last place I'd ever imagined I'd be on my Christmas vacation. I glanced up at the wrought iron sign arched over the two tall stone columns providing the entryway to the grounds. Although I'd been born and raised in Twin Rivers Junction, I'd never been here before.

Twin Rivers Hillside Cemetery.

"Mom," one of my children asked, "why are we here?"

I did not hear Pierce's response to the question. But whatever his answer, it silenced all three siblings. They followed us through the entrance with their grandfather out in front.

"Wait." I frowned at my dad. "You've been here before?"

"Yes," was all he said.

Shifting the bouquet of flowers to the other arm, I made my way down the pathway which had been packed down from prior visitors.

I was amazed how long the walk seemed, as the plot sat at the farthest end of the graveyard. We passed an older couple staring down at a marker below them. A tiny American flag in his hand, the gentleman reached down and placed it in the snow at his feet, causing the gray-haired woman beside him to wipe her eyes.

I wonder if they lost a son who served our country.

"Kate," my dad said. "We're here."

I stopped and looked at him. His face took on a somber look, one I'd not seen in a long time, but one I'd noticed countless times during our years attending Cross. Following his gaze, my eyes fell on a large gravestone in front of him.

I stood rigid, waiting for the old feelings of fear, anger, and resentment to reappear as they had done many times. But instead, I felt none of those things. In their place, a small measure of regret. Maybe because I waited this long to pay my respects, diminished as they were. But I now knew it was the right thing to do.

This was grace.

"You're right," my dad said in a reverent tone. "I have been here. I made my peace with him a few years after he passed away."

I could not tear my eyes away from the oversized headstone in front of us. About the height of a small kitchen table and three feet wide, I was intrigued at its detail. The upper portion of the marker consisted of two praying hands that appeared to be holding a cross between them. On the left of this image read Father, Grandfather. On the right of the praying hands was written Pastor, Leader. And below, in bold printed letters, his name—Reverend Rhuttland Abbott. The dates of his birth and death were listed, followed by a small line at the bottom that read, Gone to be with God.

My dad touched my arm. "I hope you know why your mother couldn't come. She can't walk this far."

"I know, Dad. She reassured me of this earlier today when I told her where we were going. We've been having some good talks the past few days."

Taking a step back, my dad gave me some space to myself as he joined Pierce and the kids, standing to the side.

"We'll be right over here," Pierce whispered in my ear.

Tears stung my eyes as I felt a sudden rush of sorrow for a man for whom I'd stored up so much animosity. No matter what he'd done, and despite all the devastation he'd caused, his death was still an unexpected tragedy. I thanked God for taking down the walls and releasing me from the pain of all our years under this man's authority. Just a week ago, I could not have stood in this place feeling as I did now had I not faced my innermost turmoil over Reverend Abbott and Cross Independent Baptist Church.

I now had a grateful heart that I had made this journey. That I had dealt with and conquered past hurts and was beginning the process of setting them free. Being here at the cemetery today would be my final goodbye.

I noticed no footprints, new or old, anywhere near his grave. In fact, it seemed the weather had damaged a portion of the marker, causing it to chip and crumble in the lower left-hand corner. There were no flags, no flowers, or anything else near Reverend Abbott's grave. It appeared he had been alone and unvisited for some time.

Pulling off a glove and placing my hand on the cold marker, I ignored the chill that ran up my arm and allowed God's peace to travel through my veins instead.

"I didn't come here today to condemn you," I whispered. "I'm not going to say you got what was coming to you or anything along those lines. I'm also not going to say you were only trying to do what you thought was right, or that you did the best you could, because I'm not here to judge. I'm just here to tell you one thing."

I paused and glanced over my shoulder. At the sight of Pierce, my heart received a boost of courage. He lifted his eyebrows and nodded, compelling me to finish my mission.

With a deep breath, I stared down at the reverend's name. "I forgive you," I said, my voice catching.

For all the messages he preached, I recalled none of them in that moment. I focused my thoughts on what my family and the Tyner's had shared together during our weekly prayer circles after we had been cast out of the fellowship.

"But by the grace of God, I am what I am," I murmured, quoting an old favorite verse from 1 Corinthians 15:10. Saying nothing more, I turned away from the grave and rejoined my family.

In forgiving him, I had forgiven myself as well.

"You okay?" Pierce searched my face with a worried expression.

"I am." I gave him a tiny smile.

"Forgetting something, Kate?" My dad pointed to the flowers I still had nestled into the crook of my arm.

"No, these flowers weren't for him."

"Oh?" He looked puzzled.

A moment passed as realization dawned on him. "They're for your friend."

"Yes, my friend."

"I'm sorry," he said. "I forgot she was here too."

"I need to do this alone," I told them. "Do you mind waiting for me back at the car? I won't be long."

After reassuring my husband I was all right, I watched them trudge back down the path between the rows of markers and disappear. Pulling out a small paper from my coat pocket, I found my way to the area of the graveyard where Jolee was buried.

"Row H," I murmured, passing grave after grave as I moved closer to the spot.

There it was. The tiny sign with the letter H indicating I had found the correct row. My heartbeat quickened. Almost there.

Stop, the voice commanded.

As if drawn by her sheer presence, I turned to my right and looked down. My heart lurched at the sight of Jolee's grave. Smaller and simpler than the Reverend's, her headstone was only about a foot from the ground. The top of the marker read In Loving Memory—Jolee L. Tisdale, along with the dates of her birth and death below her name. It was the simple phrase etched in tiny letters below the dates that made me cover my mouth.

GONE TOO SOON.

"Jolee!" I could no longer hold back the tears.

I stepped forward and knelt in the snow, noticing that someone—I assumed her parents—had been looking after her grave and visiting her. The stillness comforted me. No cell phones ringing, no cars honking, no dogs barking, no people talking. I was alone with my friend, and I could finally tell her all the things I'd longed to say for so long.

"Were we really little kids once?" I sniffed. "Did we really go into Mrs. Fisher's desk in third grade when she wasn't looking and steal some of her candies? Remember how we used to tell jokes and play pranks on the boys? Do you recall the time you dropped your ski poles off the ski lift and you never saw them again?"

The tips of the trees fluttered as a slight gust of air passed by.

"I brought your favorites." I set the bouquet of flowers in the snow in front of the grave marker. "I'm sorry I did not come sooner."

I waited for a response I knew would not come, but I still paused as if I'd get one anyway. For a moment, I welcomed the memory of a happier Jolee when she'd receive a special order of pink carnations from her mom and dad every Valentine's Day.

"Man, how come you always get flowers on Valentine's Day?" I'd complain.

"How do you know I didn't send these to myself?" she'd joke.

I sighed deeply, sniffing back more tears. "I know we didn't see this coming, Jo."

I faltered as a memory washed over me.

"Aw, they won't even see it coming." Jolee laughed as we descended the stairs to the cafeteria for lunch.

"You cannot let the guys eat those." I shook my head and attempted to take the tray of chocolate cupcakes away from her.

"Hey!" She scowled. "You know what they said about me. Time for a little retribution."

"Tell me what you put in them first."

"Well ..." Her eyes narrowed in mischief. "Maybe a little *chocolate* substitute."

I gasped. "You did not!"

"Don't worry." She grinned. "A little bathroom troubles for one evening and they should be fine."

Smiling at that memory, I closed my eyes in pain as a new one took its place. Our conversation in her apartment. The last day I saw her.

"How did I not see how bad you were hurting?" Fresh tears burned hot trails down my cold cheeks.

Forgive yourself, the voice said. *You were just a kid.*

"This isn't you, Jolee," I had said, trying to reason as she packed her belongings to move in with her new boyfriend.

"You're right." Her voice sounded bitter. "This is all that's left of her."

I put both my hands over my face as I wept for the loss of my friend.

My mind then went back to the day Karina called me with the news of Jolee's sudden death. Amid my graduation and wedding plans, something unspeakable had befallen Twin Rivers Junction.

Jolee had taken her own life at twenty-two years.

"It could've been accidental, right?" Karina cried on the other end of the phone line. "But Vic says he heard Jolee had been getting into some bad drugs so ..."

"She wanted to die." My voice was empty and hollow. "She found a way."

"But to overdose on ... what was it? Meth? Heroine? Why? Why would she do that?" Karina wailed.

"I don't know." What else was there to say?

I wiped my tears and stood. As I continued looking down at my friend's grave, I reminded myself to be here in the moment. Nothing I could do would change the past. And there was nothing I could have done to save my friend.

Pierce's words came back to me. *Forgiveness is for you.*

"I did something today," I whispered. "It was hard, but I think overall, you would've been proud of me. Even if you didn't say the words."

What was it? I almost heard her asking.

"I forgave the reverend. It's something I needed to do. You know?"

And with that, another memory surfaced.

"I hate her!" Jolee made a rude gesture toward Mrs. Sullivan. "I hate them all!"

"Come on," I chided. "What are you going to do? Why waste your time? You can't hate them forever."

"Oh yes, I can."

"You can't let her ruin your day like this, Jo. It's just not—"

"Shut up!" Jolee screeched. "I will do whatever I want!"

Thinking back on her behavior, I accepted that Jolee had deep and unresolved issues with anger. Instead of helping her, teachers and church leaders would punish her, making the anger plunge deeper and deeper into a gorge that, over the years, had filled to the top with resentment. Those bitter feelings hurt her, and she went looking for comfort and love in the wrong places. It began with a friend, then progressed to a boyfriend—one she fell in love with. But the love was not real, and the mistake cost a human life.

I tried envisioning how agonizing it must have been for Jolee to decide to abort her child. I now realized what she meant the day she told me this was all that was left of her.

The day she lost her tiny baby was the same day she lost her soul.

"You never forgave yourself, did you?" I said, tears flooding my eyes. "In order to cope, you had to become someone else."

The sense of relief at finally understanding her after all this time came at me like a wave so powerful, I staggered. I leaned down and used Jolee's headstone to steady myself. I stared down, my tears splashing on top of the stone.

"I forgive you, Jolee," I cried. "I forgive you for everything, and God forgives you too."

Movement on Tanger Mountain in the distance caught my attention. The wind began to blow, and the multiple windmills that lined the peak of the mountain slowly started to turn their heavy turbines.

The tears stopped and shock registered at what I thought that meant. As the tall towers had been still, they were now moving and gaining speed as the wind picked up.

"She heard," I whispered.

After I finished drying my eyes, I looked down at Jolee's headstone once more. "I can let you go now," I told her.

As I turned to go, my tears that had pooled on the top of the headstone spilled over the side and down the front of her name.

"Goodbye, friend."

My family waited in the car. With each step I took toward them, my sorrow lifted. And peace began to set a new course for me.

Never in all my years did I plan to return here, let alone come home and address all that I'd buried over the years. Although grievous to relive old hurts I'd long tried to forget, I had triumphed over them by acknowledging my burdens and releasing their hold over me.

A long-forgotten verse from 2 Timothy 4:7 came to mind as I neared the car. "I have fought a good fight, I have finished my course, I have kept the faith."

God gave me the victory.

It was a glorious New Year's Day indeed.

CHAPTER 29

REDEMPTION

The sound of baggage compartments snapping shut echoed throughout the cabin of the Boeing 737. Traveler's idle chatter thrummed around us. Children whined about wanting to sit next to a window, while weary parents directed them to sit and hush. A less-than-patient businessman a few aisles up checked his Rolex for the time. Frowning at the noisy kids behind him, he busied himself with the task of straightening his starched business attire.

"Looks like a full flight," Pierce commented as he took the seat next to me.

"Kids good back there?" I asked.

Pierce turned in his seat and peered between the rows. "Headphones in three sets of ears. I think they're pacified at the moment—until they start getting hungry, that is."

I grinned. "Which is in what, ten minutes?"

"Well, maybe I am too—" Pierce pitched forward as an oversized bag assaulted him.

"Sorry," a passenger mumbled over his shoulder.

Pierce rubbed his shoulder. "You'd think people would realize these aisles are narrow and carry their bags in front of them instead of hanging off their shoulder."

"Flight attendants secure the cabin for departure," a masculine voice crackled overhead.

"Doing all right?" Pierce grabbed my hand.

"Better than all right."

"You're different," he said.

"My mom said the same thing."

"Believe it," Pierce said.

The captain announced we were ready for departure. Several minutes later, we were in the air.

We were going home.

"I think I know what's different," I said to Pierce after taking off. "I'm leaving Twin Rivers Junction, but I'm no longer running away. I haven't been able to be honest about that in a long time."

"How does affirming that make you feel?"

"I think I feel ... liberated. I'm not fending off old ghosts. I'm not reburying hurts from the past. I'm not hiding behind my wall anymore. I had no idea how much energy I was spending just *fighting*. Even trying to ignore them was exhausting. I can now release it all."

"No more regrets," he added.

"No more. In fact," I held up a hand, "I got to talk to an old friend yesterday."

"Oh, that's right. Kyle ..."

"Tyner." My head bobbed up and down. "His wife and kids live in the Midwest now and have talked Burt and Renata into joining them there. Kyle's IT company has earned some big contracts, so his dad will help with some of the smaller local contracts part-time. And Burt and Renata get to be closer to their grandkids."

"Sounds like they've really found their own way then, given all they went through."

"They have been resilient throughout everything. From Bryce's health difficulties, homeschooling challenges, church discipline, to Renata's stroke. And through it all, they have kept their eyes on God, vowing to follow only him."

"Wow," Pierce said. "That's inspiring."

An analogy formed in my mind. "Picture two mountains. One side, the side *you're* on, is overloaded with hardships and trials. You see no way out except for a rickety-looking bridge going to some unknown place. But you feel God pushing you closer to that scary bridge and asking you to trust him. Before you know it, you've crossed that bridge with God's assistance. When you make it to the other side, there is a new life waiting for you."

"Deliverance," Pierce said with conviction. "I want to ask you a hard question. You don't have to answer if you don't want to."

"Okay." I waited.

"Do you think that had the reverend lived and changed his life, he would have tried to make amends for his wrongdoings?"

I let that sink in. My gaze shifted to other things such as the backs of passengers' heads bent toward their laps. A flight attendant happened by carrying a small pillow and blanket. She hurried to the first-class section of the plane and slid the dark blue curtain shut behind her.

If given the chance, could someone who shattered lives ever find atonement? I wondered. And just like that, I was transported back to another memory, one from just over a few years ago.

"Hey, Sis, catch you at a bad time?" the voice on the phone asked.

"Hey, look who it is," I said happily. "Nope. I'm good here. What's up?"

"Well ..." Marty cleared his throat. "I wanted to pass on something I learned yesterday. You might not want to hear it, or care, but—"

"Hey, I always have time for you. You know that."

"Right, I know. That's why I called. I wanted to tell you something I found out about a family from Cross. I know you're not crazy about our ... uh ... past life there and all. But I thought this was worth mentioning."

"Okay, shoot."

"It's about Ross Kelley and his family."

I stiffened but said nothing.

"I talked to Mr. Kelley," Marty confessed.

"Really?" I tried not to sound rude.

"Yes. He saw on my social media page that I had a new position within my church, so he wanted to congratulate me. I gave him my number and was surprised when he called."

I bit my tongue and focused on listening.

"Anyway, after a few words of greeting were exchanged, he asked me something strange. He asked me if I would forgive him. He admitted he had blindly followed Reverend Abbott in many things, and at the time he believed he was doing the right thing."

"Interesting."

"I told him it was completely forgiven. And forgotten."

"You're a better man than I am," I grunted.

Marty went on with his story. "I then had a question for him."

"Yeah?"

"I asked him what changed. I mean, he was deep into following the reverend's convictions and practices. I thought he would take over after the reverend died."

"I thought so at first too, but he's more of a businessman than a pastor, so I imagined he was hoping his son-in-law Kevin Brayton would take the helm," I said.

"Which Pastor Brayton did for a time. But it didn't work out, I guess. Back to Mr. Kelley. He told me what changed for him was that after Reverend Abbott passed away, he realized he was no longer being told what to do, when to do it, what to believe, what to say, or how to act. He admitted this left him feeling hollow and empty inside because he had no real values of his own to stand on. He had to start establishing his own convictions, so he began a personal path toward finding out who the real Jesus is."

"And?"

"Right after the church was put up for sale, a work colleague invited him to a life group. The group helped him meet other believers, and you know what? He said the most interesting thing to me."

"Which was?"

"He said it became his saving grace, and his eyes had been opened," Marty said, a touch of awe in his voice. "He realized he had been doing everything wrong. Following the reverend in every way instead of the true Jesus."

"Better late than never, I suppose."

"And it didn't stop there. Mr. Kelley and his whole family dedicated the rest of their lives to living for God and doing his work."

"How's that?"

"They just help people. His businesses were successful, and he was able to retire in comfort. He spends all his time helping people now. Doesn't matter what it is. He gives people rides to places. He buys them a meal if they need it. He pays a medical bill for them. He stacks wood. He hauls trash. He hands out all kinds of random acts of kindness. His wife, too. And his oldest son Jonah. Remember him?"

"Unfortunately."

"Well, I know you didn't get along with the Kelley's—any of them. But Jonah and his wife started an orphanage in South America. In addition to their own children, they've adopted several, plus run this orphanage to help all the homeless kids there."

"That's great to hear," I said, not wanting to admit I was impressed.

"I realize none of this means a whole lot to you now. But I wanted you to know. The Kelley's are not the same people they used to be. They've committed the rest of their lives to making things right."

I sighed. "I do think this is a good thing, Marty. I'm sorry if I'm not as thrilled as you want me to be."

"I'm not looking for you to be anything," Marty said. "I know you don't trust them, and that's okay. I just hope it helped hearing that they turned their lives around. That there was hope for them."

"They found salvation," I found myself saying now.

Pierce nudged me. "What was that?"

"I was remembering something Marty told me a few years ago about one of the prominent families in the church. The Kelley's. All this time, they've devoted themselves to others by helping them through difficult situations. And they even did this before I could."

"You weren't ready yet," Pierce pointed out.

"If you had asked me a week ago if I thought the reverend could change his ways, I'd have laughed and said no way."

"And now?"

"Now I realize the grace God gives us isn't a contest. A winner isn't chosen, nor does it select certain people over others. Grace is for everyone. So, in answer to your question ... yes. Salvation was for the reverend, too."

"You seem to have something else on your mind," Pierce said.

"I've known of others," I admitted. "Some of whom I'd forgotten about and even some that Kyle just told me about yesterday."

"Others? What do you mean?"

"There was a family within the congregation. The Cobbs. They had four children and very little money. They had moved to Twin Rivers hoping to start a Christian camp. But it was too much for the family, and they didn't have any more money to pour into it. They also received a lot of criticism for homeschooling their kids."

"I'm sorry to hear that. Did they stay?"

"No, they moved to be closer to family further up north. I had always wondered what happened to them until Kyle told me they began a camp with a big emphasis on support for families who wanted to homeschool their kids. He said it was thriving, and they even hold annual conventions there as well."

Pierce smiled. "Sounds to me like a successful outcome."

"That's just it," I exclaimed. "The more things I find out about the families who either left Cross or had to leave because the church closed, I learn there are more happy endings than I could have imagined."

"Maybe," Pierce offered, "the reverend was their impossible bridge they had to cross to get to the other side."

I nodded in agreement, then fell silent. The flight crew had finished delivering the beverage service and were now cruising the aisles with garbage bags. I sat still, more so than I had in ages as a sense of well-being settled over me like a long-lost friend.

My mind wandered toward some of these long-lost friends, and I hoped wherever they were, they had joyous and productive lives. I thought of my old teacher, Mrs. McKenzie, leaving Cross to teach at her daughter's Christian college and wondered if she was still a professor there or if she had retired. I knew from Brynn that Rachel Abbott had married and had several children. But we were not in contact with one another and had not been for many years. I never heard from my old friend Del again. Since Sara Kittridge's mother refused to let her contact me, I had heard from Brynn's sister Leah that she had married her forbidden high school sweetheart Justin, and they had both chosen to live in another state to raise their family.

While a part of me would always miss the old friendships I once had, any feelings of regret were replaced with pride that after all these years, I was still close with Brynn and Karina. How many adults get to say they are still good friends with kids from kindergarten? I was also grateful for my own close relationship with my siblings. Marty for becoming a youth pastor in his church. Mark for joining the military. And Kyla's success with running her own environmental engineering company.

A burst of orchestration rang out in front of Pierce at that moment, and I watched the lady seated there scramble around for her headphones. After dropping them on the floor, the music continued to play. The beautiful sound of a tinkling harp levitated above the low blend of the string ensemble. It wasn't long before the harp music was interrupted by the insertion of the headphones and a sigh from their owner.

But the harp continued to play in my head, along with memories of the one woman I remembered who knew how to play such an instrument.

"Oh, she's doing really well," my mom had responded to my inquiry about June Britton. It was the same day we had all gone to the ice rink when we had our talk, the best one in years. "After Glen died, she had to go back to work, and her parents helped her raise the kids. She eventually remarried."

"I'm so glad she went on with her life."

"As did you," she reminded.

As did I. I smiled as my eyes closed.

"I'm glad we did this," Pierce told me a few hours later, after the pilot declared we would be landing in fifteen minutes. Through the muffled speaker, he went on to report that plenty of sunshine was in our forecast and requested we choose the airline again soon.

"I am too," I said, yawning. "But let's wait a while before we do it again. I'm not crazy about flying."

"You promised." Pierce waved a finger at me as a reminder that I had told my parents we would come back for Christmas again.

"It was important for us to do this now. For *me* to do this."

"Not to keep repeating myself, but you are different. *Better* different."

"That's exactly what I want to be," I stated. "I can't change people, and I can't change the past. I can only move forward and learn from mistakes and hardships. I think it's my turn to learn how I can make a difference too."

"So many people aren't able to do what you've done," Pierce responded, his voice low. "You can help a lot of people, Kate."

I paused in the hallway and turned to look through the large glass window of my music studio. The practice room was filled with students. I gazed in awe at the precious scene unfolding before me.

My dream was really happening.

Touched by the overwhelming interest in my new outreach program, I watched with pride as my friend sat at the piano, nodding to the teens to begin singing. Several heads bent toward the sheet music in front of them. It didn't take long for the harmonious blend of the ensemble to reach my ears.

"Hang on." My friend stopped directing and tapped out a rhythm in front of her.

"Tenors, you missed the part of the second stanza where you will be singing with the altos. It's just for the remainder of that section, and it will repeat each time. Ready?" She signaled them to begin, but not before she sent me a quick smile and wave.

Waving back at Brynn, I leaned against the glass and allowed the soft voices to float toward me. I marveled at how much had transpired in the past six months. A simple idea discussed with my old friend hatched into a beautiful project. Our mission was to help others see the light of Christ through the healing power of music. Once I'd learned the school where Brynn had been teaching was not proceeding in a good academic direction, I'd blurted out that she should move here and work with me.

"I'm just not making a difference here," Brynn had said.

"Then partner with me," I urged.

I blinked in surprise as the doors to the practice room opened abruptly. Lost in my thoughts, I hadn't realized the rehearsal was over. Students buzzed by with a quick, "Good night, Ms. Kate." I wished them all an enjoyable weekend.

"How'd it go?" I asked as I entered the room.

"Good. Just a few things off with the tenors today, but they'll get it." Brynn laughed and handed me a ream of music. "Here, make yourself useful."

I'd thrilled to watch her happiness unfold over the past few months. Giving up her teaching position in a school where she'd taught for years was difficult, yet I admired her courage to make a change. Together, we ran the music studio and launched our therapy foundation. Our new group, Singers of the Light, was already reaching many wounded hearts, and Brynn's smile was back.

"Kate," she said, "these kids are blowing me away. They are demonstrating incredible talent, and they want to use it to help people. We are so blessed."

"Beyond blessed," I added. Closing my eyes, I allowed my newfound peace to wash over me as it had been doing ever since my return from Twin Rivers Junction. I thanked God for all his goodness during this time and for showing me that through music, I could reach others who were hurting.

"All right," Brynn announced. "By next week, we will be ready to perform for the seniors at the Bridgeway Nursing Home, followed by Lowry Care Health Center on Jefferson Street, and then ... Kate? You okay?"

I opened my eyes and looked at her. "Yes. I'm just thinking about a rather unusual request I received earlier today."

"Can you tell me about it?"

"We have been asked to go to Flynn Medical Center first. Before we sing at any of the other destinations on our itinerary."

"Oh?"

"The request came from our pastor's wife," I said, as I knew what her next question would be. "She told me our new foundation has been encouraging to people."

"Sounds like she knows someone there at the rehab center," Brynn mused.

"She does. It's her younger sister by ten years. From what I learned, she's been there for over a year now and is still struggling."

As understanding set in, Brynn's mouth fell open. "Flynn is a drug rehabilitation center, isn't it?"

I nodded. We both fell silent in remembrance of our long-lost friend.

Brynn leaned forward. "We knew someone just like that once. We couldn't reach Jolee then, but maybe we can help this young woman."

"With God's grace, anyone can be restored to a full and prosperous life," I said, my voice tight over the lump in my throat.

"Believe in God's promises," Brynn said. "Deliverance is for everyone, no matter their circumstances."

"Since we've begun the therapy foundation, I have found something I didn't know I'd lost."

"What is it?" she asked, her voice hushed.

"Redemption."

"For all of us," Brynn affirmed.

My own path to restitution had come full circle.

My existence under authority was a mere echo of the past.

My life of grace had begun.

THE END

ABOUT THE AUTHOR

Born and raised in New England, Kimalee Finelli attended church with her family just like any other kid. Except—things were different at Cross Independent Baptist Church. After years of noticing troubling incidents, she began to suspect that something was seriously wrong. Reverend Abbott hid his agenda through cleverly crafted sermons and visions. The manipulation and control over his congregation escalated. Over time, his power increased in severity. The oppression Kimalee's family and many others endured left behind a trail of sorrow, pain, and utter destruction.

Based on a true story and written as fiction, Under Authority reveals what took place in this unusual church.

It wasn't until adulthood that Kimalee finally understood why she recognized disturbing events in the church when others didn't—she was meant to recall the situation one day and show those who suffer they are not alone. Under Authority is for victims of abusive church leaders and for all Christians who hurt. They can confront their pain, identify why it happened, discover hope, choose forgiveness, and find redemption.

"Thou Shalt Not Question," published in *Plain Truth Magazine*, was an article Kimalee wrote about her experience. It is a glimpse into the story of *Under Authority*. She has also written articles for *Foster Focus Magazine, Ministry Magazine,* and *ADDitude* magazine. She was a ghost writer for a start-up business as well as a guest blogger. One of her short stories was published in a collection called *The Write Way* produced by author James Hudson (available on Amazon). Kimalee has a website and has been a part of a local writer's group. She is also a member of the writing communities of Facebook, Twitter, and Instagram. Kimalee completed the "Breaking into Print" program with The Long Ridge Writer's Group after receiving a college bachelor's degree in music. She simply had to return to her first love of writing.

When away from her computer, Kimalee is chasing after her two boys, laughing with her husband, and scouring the internet for the newest waterfall to swoon over. She adores pets, quaint towns, coffee, and the feel of a crisp book between her hands. On a humorous note, she will never understand the game of football and has an intense dislike for tomatoes!

Made in the USA
Middletown, DE
30 August 2023